# Renate's Journey

*a novel by*

Nancy Werner Dulin

*the* Peppertree Press
Sarasota, Florida

Copyright © Nancy Werner Dulin, 2008
All rights reserved. Published by *the* Peppertree Press, LLC.
*the* Peppertree Press and associated logos are trademarks of
*the* Peppertree Press, LLC.
No part of this publication may be reproduced, stored in a
retrieval system, transmitted in any form or by any means,
electronic, mechanical, photocopying, recording, or otherwise,
without prior written permission of the publisher
and author/illustrator.

For information regarding permission,
call 941-922-2662 or contact us at our website:
www.peppertreepublishing.com or write to:
*the* Peppertree Press, LLC.
Attention: Publisher
1269 First Street, Suite 7
Sarasota, Florida 34236

ISBN:9781934246-80-1

Library of Congress Number: 2008921280

Printed in the U.S.A.
Printed July 2008

*For my children
            and their children...*

*...with special thanks to my older daughter who was an untiring editor, my younger daughter who even persuaded her book club to read and critique an early version, my older son whose knowledge of the period kept me accurate, and all those who offered encouragement throughout the long process. Special recognition goes to the two readers who knew the story better than I. Two men of my generation who had been German soldiers and, like Renate, walked home when the war was through.*

# Spring 1945

My parents called me Renate, a long awaited daughter after a much beloved son. My father, *Herr Doktor* Otto Weiss, was white-haired when I was a child. Trim in dark custom tailored suits. A monocle from the era of the Kaiser always hung from a black ribbon pinned to his lapel. My mother? Smiling. Dainty. Twenty years younger than the man she married but, as she was in all things, a quiet reflection of his aging. I did well in the most demanding schools. I was sent to music camp each summer. If I glanced into a mirror I saw that I was slim and strong, even beautiful as I grew older, but a greater pride came from the increasing responsibility I was given in the *Bund Deutscher Mädel*, our national girls organization where we sang and danced and hiked in the country and learned to stop thinking at the mention of German honor, German glory. Where we absorbed broad, uncompromising lessons in raw hatred cloaked in utopian visions about our future.

That world ended on a bright spring morning, in a small North German outpost not far from where the river Aland meets the Elbe. Everything I understood, believed in, everything I saw as strength, vanished into rattling gunfire, flying debris, a plea for absolution as life seeped from a colleague's wounded body. "Get low," someone shouted. "Avoid those windows." But at the beginning of my journey I was dedicated to my duties. I ran to our post commander's office, bracing myself when fiery blasts brought plaster from the ceiling. To keep his strategies from the enemy I scattered directives, maps, contingency plans, tearing at them, stomping on them with my feet, until, as the tumult around the building quieted, I realized this pathetic effort made no sense. Not when the officers and men of Aland Nord Battalion were being gathered in a rough formation on our parade field. Their hands were clasped behind their heads.

Boots pounded closer in a stairwell and I escaped back to the women's quarters, grabbed my knapsack from my room, a canteen. Beneath smoldering roof beams across the barracks' kitchen, the miracle of bread that had been baked before the bombing and a round of sooted cheese. I had room for little else. A knife. I wore no hat, no scarf, no heavy jacket. My auxiliary uniform was slight protection from spring's north German weather, but as this thought leaped into my mind I had another. Was I the only non-combatant who hadn't fled? I darted into a courtyard, a disappearing shadow hiding in the patterns of a waning sun, and onto a country road glutted with refugees before the enemy's advances. I found no room to run, no place to hide, no one with answers to my questions as the afternoon receded.

By dusk the old, the injured were passed by. Some with wheels to help them surged ahead. At each convergence with another road a few others turned away, even as I had done, not knowing why this particular road was chosen, only knowing I must keep moving away from defeat at Aland Nord and toward some preparation for the last resistance. When full night fell I was alone in the darkness, whimpering softly, a small shape curled into a hollow before a padlocked shed. Exhaustion was my narcotic and I slept.

New day was a thin bright line across the eastern sky when I awoke, instantly alert to the sound of another person waking just beyond the shed. The chill of morning held me, a stiffness from waking on the ground. I was groping for the knife I'd taken from the kitchen when a woman peered around the weathered wall between us, her pale hair disheveled. With one hand she smoothed it back and waited as her eyes grew wide with recognition before they blinked and lowered to the ground. I almost blurted out 'the laughing girl', a name I'd given to a stranger, and felt a quick burst of curiosity as I had a month before at my desk outside the colonel's office, reading the personnel papers everyone carried in the world we'd known. She came from Mannheim, a city near my home, but because of my position I'd not shared the comfort of that information. Only marveled at her insolent confident manner as she made friends with her fellow telephone operators, stood silently amazed at how soon her arms looped playfully around the soldiers. Now, as she began to back away, I almost shouted, "Wait, Anna Wehrhahn. Please." I can only guess at my expression because a flash of interest changed her face.

"*Jawohl, Gruppenleiterin Weiss.*"

Group Leader Weiss? Here on a road fleeing from the rout of what had been our lives? I wasn't anyone's group leader any longer but I did have bread. I fumbled for my pack, twisting the ties until they opened, and held out a piece from one of the loaves I'd seized before I fled. I think she thanked me. I do remember she said she'd taken nothing, she was so afraid. I mumbled something about who wouldn't be afraid and bent to brush my skirt, to push away the pain of my remembering. My glance fixed on a lumpy knapsack dangling against her knee.

"I do have apples." She flipped the knapsack back behind her. "They were in my room."

My back stiffened. My fingers twitched. What sense of duty to the *Reich* had been denied her that she'd hoarded apples in those last weeks of deprivation? But my outrage disappeared in resignation. I took a deep calming breath and put my fingers through my own dark hair. I said her apples were a stroke of luck. Perfect with my bread and cheese. Almost as if we were meant to go on together. I needed someone. Anyone. Anna. And I suspected her need was greater than my own. I sometimes felt alone in the company of others but I'd seen her come alive in the center of a crowd. She adjusted her cache of apples while I watched, for the first time really looked at her. Her clear blue eyes, her soft curled hair, the way she smoothed her uniform and waited. I remembered her age was twenty-one, a scant year less than me. Average height, perhaps a little taller. She seemed strong. I asked what she'd brought besides her apples.

"A picture of my sister."

The faces of my parents and my brother had been in heavy frames but beside them on my dresser was a pair of small glass dancers, fragile figures caught in an intricate step. My mother sent them from a holiday in Venice and I'd found magic in the way their glass embrace caught light in fractured rainbows. I could've taken those. Forcing back a sudden panic, I stared out over a field we'd crossed in darkness. "Did you bring a coat? A scarf?" I asked.

"It wasn't raining."

I knew I was capable, clever. I'd had an advantage of education and position, but I was as ill-equipped as Anna, and I knew our problem was more than clothes. We had no map, no compass, no certainty of highways, rivers, cities, or a great area of dark trees to the south and west of Aland Nord that had been a training ground for armies. I turned east, away from that direction.

We followed country roads when we were able, feeling safer in a sun-splayed pattern beneath a canopy of trees, crossed narrow, arched brick bridges spanning channeled streams that drained the land. Anna trailed silently behind me until I heard her wonder why there were no others. Yesterday the roads were full. I turned to each direction. In the flat bare fields around us were a few isolated cows on water-bordered islands. A glint of sun across a windshield?

Anna said, "That's not a car from any army."

A sleek limousine rushed toward us, lifting on the humps of bridges, squealing around a curve. I thought: a physician. My father was one, too. He'd been allowed to keep his private transportation when most civilians gave theirs to the war. The limousine screeched to a stop just inches from us and a man's thick shoulder filled the door as he forced it open. His knuckles on the frame were white. "What are you two doing here?"

"I … We …"

In the overloaded car a woman reached across to catch his sleeve. He shook her free. "Get off these roads," he shouted. "You have no time."

The woman smoothed blond hair beneath the contour of her hat before she left the car. "Hans, be civilized," she said as she approached us.

I backed away from the effort with which the man sought calm while still shouting that these roads led only to the Elbe. We couldn't mean to go in that direction. I tried to explain our homes were south, in Schwetzingen and Mannheim, but we'd brought nothing when we escaped the fighting. We needed help, safety, a German command where our skills might be of use. His next words chill me to this day. "There is no help. No safety. No way to be of any use to anyone near here."

The woman said, "Hans, tell them so they understand."

"I've just come from the American army in Magdeburg."

"You? The American army?"

"He wasn't in the American army," the woman said.

"I'm a surgeon. In the days leading to our capitulation, I helped with casualties, ours and theirs. In return they filled my car with petrol, let me go free to find my wife who stayed near here in what we'd thought was safety."

My fingernails dug into my palms. My heart pounded. Had he no fear of the testimony I could give to others?

He said, "The Americans and the British have stopped their armies. They have orders not to cross the Elbe. When I left Magdeburg I was warned I had four days before the Russians reach us. I've used two already."

"Do you know about the Russians?" the woman said.

In our isolated outpost, pincered between advancing armies, even official information hadn't always been believed. Spreading derogatory rumors had become a crime and messages often differed by who sent them. I'd not listened to reports about the Russians until vague rumors of reversals changed to General Zhukov on his way, the Mongol hordes behind him. Then I'd found fear's antidote in duty.

"The Russian commanders let their troops take retribution," the woman said.

"German husbands, fathers, sons are forced to hold lamps while whole squads of soldiers violate their women."

"Hans, stop. They're only children."

"If the men protest, they're shot, or castrated. Women who resist are disemboweled."

The woman started toward their car, unsteady on stiletto heels. "We learned from those who escaped the east."

The man followed. "We're little more than fifty kilometers from Berlin. With the *Autobahn*, the Russians may not need four days."

"Berlin is a furnace," the woman said. "A sea of fire. Zoo animals are loose and roam the city."

"But our armies?" I reached for Anna's hand, finding her sleeve, clutching for her fingers.

"Our armies have gathered on the Oder, with orders just to stand and fight. They're holding off the Russians. Fighting only to hold them off. You understand? They're forfeiting their lives so the rest of us may flee."

At their car, the woman glanced back at Anna and me. "With your homes in the south, we can't help. We're going north. To Bremen. To my husband's brother. Only luck will let us reach there."

"You must get west," the man said.

I fought back a flurry of indecision. The *Führer* must be plotting strategies to turn the tide of battle. "But the forested moors," I said. "Which army has the *Heide*?"

"Two women aren't safe with any army. Go home. Go home."

"Hans, that's enough."

The man lifted his wife's rich coat away from the door before he slammed it. He only nodded in our direction before the motor scraped to life and the car was gone. Anna started crying. "No. Please. Oh, Anna." I struggled to keep my voice even, to hide the fear in my confusion, my desperate need for certainty when I had none. "We'll just do as he said. We'll just go home." And suddenly home was all I wanted. But home was hundreds of kilometers away.

"Will the Russians get us?" Anna asked.

I grasped her hand and started walking. South. Fast. Across flat fields, the roads behind us, filling my flask from streams we splashed across, resting only when we ate, but long before twilight dulled the sky, rain fell in a blinding, drenching burst of water. Frightened, discouraged, bewildered, ill, we climbed into an isolated windmill. The place reeked of damp and rotting.

Rain was now an enemy as well, and cold, and dirt as it settled in scraped knees, torn fingernails, the uniforms that never left our bodies. In woods grown thick with red-trunked pine we circled Stendal, sharing little but each other's presence. We did agree not to trust others but near Tangermünde our desperation for survival overwhelmed our fears. When streets were empty, houses still, we crept into barns, stole eggs where we could find them and grain and dried cobs of corn to chew on. One night we filled our packs with sprouted soft potatoes set aside for seed. Eventually, we joined other fleeing strangers. "Is the war through?" I asked a woman who pushed a baby carriage. A man leaned heavily against her.

"Can it go on?" the woman answered.

The man's face was waxen, his head wrapped above dried, caked cords of blood. "Get west," he said. "Cossacks cut off arms lifted in surrender."

"But the roads south?"

"Get west," the man repeated.

Anna held her sides in monthly cramping, catching the flow in rags, and we hid in a church with blue-white windows. Through the day the church was empty, just the two of us with Anna groaning, but when night came others entered. Women shrouded in black shawls, old men, their wheelbarrows and low wagons with them. They opened suitcases, loosed quilts from frayed belongings, fashioned beds in quiet corners for children who fell forward uncomplaining. One man found a candle in a room beside the chancel, another produced a match. A soft glow drew others to them and I left Anna to listen, silently, near their circle.

"My daughter first saw heavy boots between low branches." An old man's gnarled hand covered the hand of a woman who sat beside him. "An officer was hanging from a tree."

"He wore a sign," the daughter said. "It had one word: traitor."

"We saw a group hanging," another said. "All common soldiers. They had signs as well."

A younger man lurched toward our light on primitive crutches, his foot a fold in shortened trousers. "Perhaps their arms were leaden. Perhaps they no longer lifted in the holy salute."

"I've heard military courts pronounce such justice."

"A look, a word, exhaustion can be mistaken for defeatism."

"I met someone from the south who saw civilians hanging from the trees. Like ripe fruit," he said. "The *Wehrmacht* had retreated but when the *SS* saw civilians draping white sheets from their windows, they took the people out and hanged them."

"From trees?"
"On public roads?"
"And left there after they were dead?"
"Who would touch them?"
"I'd chop down any tree used for such abomination."

My mind whirled like my glass dancers and I pushed up from the worn stone where I was sitting. "Would they really hang civilians?" Anna asked as I approached her.

We fled toward the isolation of the forest Heide but the flat gray skies absorbed direction, each black stone road appeared as every other. Where a half-tracked vehicle had left the paving and plunged into a shallow river, decomposing corpses with bloated stomachs, bluish faces sent us racing toward an orchard with the beginning of white blossoms until a woman's high-pitched screeching wail and a man's gruff demanding answer sent us splashing back across the river. Anna tripped on a booted leg that had no torso. She started screaming. Everywhere an acrid stench of spent brass casings from small arms fire.

We came upon a highway, four lanes divided by a fence. "It's the Autobahn to Berlin," I said.

"Are you sure?"

"Look at it."

With the Autobahn we were past the Heide but if we were above Halberstadt, I wasn't sure I should take us there. Halberstadt had been bombed in early April. A colleague, whose home was Hamburg, once tried to explain why children had been sent away from cities: hundreds of planes darkening the sky in massed formation, dropping incendiary devices that exploded first in attics before crashing through to lower floors. His face had paled, his voice broke as he described families seeking shelter in their basement who'd been cooked in water gushing from burst boilers. If only part of what my colleague said was true, Halberstadt's fires could still be burning. Recovery gangs in their striped clothing could still be slipping down stairwells thick with maggots where the heat was less intense.

Anna touched my arm. "Do you hear motors?"

I grabbed her hand and started running. Across a dividing sweep of grass turned green by April's weather, the fence, an opposing strip of highway. Clinging to each other, we ran deep into the night.

Undifferentiated days turned into weeks as a growing undulation of the land made each turn longer, each rise higher. The horizon changed, veiled in blue hazes. Late in what was surely May, as a setting sun absorbed our light in its yellow glow, planes flying on some unknown mission, filled the sky. Anna slumped to the ground beside her pack. I stooped for a jagged leaf of dandelion, chewing the tangy flavor, offering another leaf to her, but when a long keening animal sound was my answer, I spat the bitter aftertaste. My home in Schwetzingen was strategically unimportant but Anna's Mannheim had been a secondary destination, where enemy planes dropped undelivered bombs if they couldn't reach a target. I helped her stand, brushing the dross that clung to her, looking for a fallen log where we could rest, but the rotten stench of wild pig spread upward from a freshly deserted wallow. The night took on grunting, threatening shapes.

I was the first to see a ladder caught in the branches of a tree below skinned saplings lashed together to form a sagging platform. Steadying the cross-steps for each other, we climbed to safety above the ground. Below us was a hole of empty darkness but above soon filled with life. Leaves muffled a screech and released a cry, branches parted for dark shapes winging out into a darker night. When Anna's quiet sobbing started I put my arms around her. "It's all right. We'll be all right." Like a frightened child, she backed into my embrace. "Have I told you I had a brother?" I said at last. "He had a friend, Paul. Paul's mother is my second mother, my confidant and my friend." With *Frau* Schuler's gesture, I lifted Anna's fine light hair, straightened snarls between my fingers, rubbed gently where her shoulder blades were sharp beneath my touch. "Tomorrow we'll climb higher. We'll be all right hidden in the mountains. Hush, hush now. We'll be all right."

Anna's sobbing quieted, changed to deeper breathing, and eventually she slept. But sleep continued to elude me. Each time I closed my eyes the faces of my father, mother, or Frau Schuler shimmered just beyond my reach. I saw a shadow of Anna's sister rising from a leveled Mannheim. My eyes stung with tears I would not let fall and I held the warmth of Anna closer.

Light penetrated late through clouds that gathered while we slept but full morning found us on our way again, following a stream into a steep-sided valley. The distant baying of a dog sent us struggling upward, sliding on layers of curled brown leaves. We were deep within a forest, far from any path, when a first bright splash of lightning leaped across the sky. My words were lost in roiling thunder but Anna had seen me pointing, and we ran, stumbling around logs a forrester had stacked to be disposed of later, until we reached his shelter where we stood caught in rigid panic between the hut's storm-filled darkness and a sheeting rain behind us. Inside was the shadow of a man whose upright carriage confirmed he was a soldier. We didn't move, not even breathing, until a match scratched across rough paper and in a round glow of illumination we saw wide-set eyes below straight brows, straight nose, a smile that curved across a ragged growth of beard. "Welcome. Come in. My name is Günther Lange." His voice was incongruously refined and free of accent. "I saw you coming as I forced the door." He struck another match and held it high between us.

I took a short step closer, assessing the breadth of his shoulders, the tightness of his waist, his dark hair curling long above a Wehrmacht infantryman's gray collar. "What's a soldier doing here?"

"Seeking shelter. The same as you." The second match burned to his fingers. When he didn't reach to strike another, I stumbled backward into Anna who was clinging to the reassurance of my back.

"Please don't be frightened." He edged around until he was more visible in a rain-soaked shaft of light coming from the doorway. "We'll need all my matches for my American cigarettes. And I have American chocolate, if you're hungry." He groped through the pockets of his heavy coat.

"Are you an American?" Anna pushed around me.

"An American? Here?" His laugh was a wonderful soaring sound and filled with joy but when I demanded to know about his unit, a strange ferocity crossed his face. "I'm not a deserter. You can't think that." He'd been in a hospital in the vicinity of Rostock when the wards were cleared of anyone who could walk and hold a weapon. He thought a battle had been planned, perhaps along the Aller, but before their convoy reached a destination, a pair of fighter-bombers found them. Anna's fingers curled through mine as he described wood-burning trucks running on anything their drivers put their hands to, diesels blown to the heavens because they ran out of fuel. Tanks, horse carts, a baggage-filled Mercedes with high officers from God knew where, honking through civilians on the road. He stepped back into the shadows. The commander of their makeshift unit had been severely wounded and the men no longer walking were assembled and stayed with him. The rest were told their best choice was to stay on course and be taken by the British, but to be wary, a segment of any army could be anywhere. If they stumbled on an American patrol, they'd likely be given over to the Russians because they were from the eastern front. His cap hit once against his leg before he jammed it in his pocket. A group of them who'd been together east of Rostock decided they'd be better off to scatter and try to make it home. "We'd not thought of surrendering while we fought the Russian Second Army across the width of Poland, why should we think about it now?" He pointed to his weapon, still wet from the rain, leaning beside the open door behind us. He'd used the last of his ammunition against a British tank just days before he'd used the last of his money to bribe a man with a boat to get him across the Elbe.

"Yes, but the chocolate?" I insisted. Outside the rain was unrelenting.

He was smiling when he stepped back to the light. That had happened near a village close to Halberstadt. He'd been asking directions from a farmwife when American trucks rounded a curve in a cloud of road dust, a shimmer of fuel. A lead jeep towed long, low artillery. In a line of lumbering vehicles, rolled canvas sides exposed two rows of soldiers sitting shoulder to shoulder, their faces shadowed by their headgear, their weapons upright between their knees. He'd plunged beneath her wagon but the farmwife shouted "welcome army" and the Americans threw chocolate and cigarettes toward them. He pressed a white-wrapped bar into Anna's reaching hand.

I thought the two of them had lost their reason. "You didn't think it could be poisoned?"

"It didn't seem to matter at the time. I was hungry. I needed a smoke."

"But …"

Almost imperceptibly, the soldier straightened. The Americans hadn't seen him slide beneath the farmwife's wagon. That made him very grateful. And cowering there in the dirt with his empty rifle, he'd realized he was beyond wanting to start anything with them. "I wanted only to reach home, to study, to sing, one day to stand on the stage of the National Theater in Mannheim …"

Anna stopped tearing at her bar's slick wrapper. "You are from Mannheim?"

"Very close. Across the Rhine in Ludwigshafen."

"I am from Mannheim!" She snatched his outstretched hand, pulling his other arm around her as she danced, excited, in the circle of his arms.

I backed against the shelter door, my palms chafed by the roughness of the thick wood planks, the colder roughness of heavy rusted nails. "Schwetzingen," I said when he turned back.

"Also a neighbor." He extended his hand.

I smelled of sour armpits, groins. A blister on my heel had bled where it rubbed gritty stockings. He smiled in shared amusement. The winds of change have blown harshly through the years but nothing can erase the intimacy of that moment. In his calloused grip I sensed an experienced soldier, but in his half bow, the way he lifted my fingers in an old-fashioned gesture, was a home whose daily life was ordered. Parents who cared about their children's manners. I accepted the chocolate bar he offered, peeled the wrapper, bit hard, chewed firmly. The melting sweetness filled my mouth.

In no time we were friends, laughing, joking that in our torn and filthy clothing we'd even begun to look like one another. While the storm whirled around our primitive shelter, we listened to each other's stories about our homes and families, our holidays in distant places. No one spoke about a future and the past was just too painful. We dwelt on soccer games and swimming and smells from a well-remembered kitchen until that world was so real in reconstruction, I knew I'd have it again when I reached home.

Night obscured the mountain before Günther spread his coat across the flooring and with Anna on one shoulder, I on the other, he told us how brave he thought we were, how proud he was of our survival. Sleep was long in coming, but it was deep and dreamless.

The storm that brought us together left no trace of clouds, no sound but our footsteps in the dampness of a forest grown taller, denser. Ferns closed in across our path. At a first clear view of layer upon high blue layer of mountain, Günther shrugged from his coat and slung it across his shoulder. I stood awed by the unfolding distance. Anna's face was to the sun.

From a meadow we plunged downward through a tangle, grasping at each other, bracing our feet on mossy stones. Before we leaned into another climb, we rested by a stream of bright, clear water, splashing wet across our arms and faces.

We followed roads of deep brown silt, crossed carpets of yellow buttercups, dropped again over roots exposed by weather on pathways rain had washed to make a gully. We slept in the open and watched the stars, woke to fogs soon swallowed by the morning. When storm clouds gathered we hid from rain and Günther spread his coat around us. Anna, as she had with the men at Aland Nord, soon took her place beside our new companion. I found it disconcerting to watch her reach for his help when the climb was steep, the lighthearted way that he responded. I wanted more than quiet smiles to match her laughter when he remembered another antic of his six small brothers. I wanted her words of extravagant praise when he sang in the deep base voice he said would one day be heard from celebrated stages. In meadows soft with hazy sunshine, blue forget-me-nots, white butterflies, while Anna and he dug roots to assuage our hunger, I stooped to cup blue petals in my hand.

Looking back with the detachment of age, it's hard to explain how we let time pass. We didn't intentionally go slower but weeks slipped away before Günther brought his last match from his pocket and passed it before our faces.

"Tonight we have food for our souls in place of supper," he said.

"What kind of food is that?" asked Anna, but I understood. Günther had grown to manhood in a world where men provided and we'd passed beyond ordinary hunger. A slow-moving pool was no longer meant for swimming. We'd gaze into its watery depths, smoothing our hands across the surface, whispering that we'd eat fish raw if we could catch one. The day a rainbow arced across the sky, we stretched out in a golden meadow and fantasized rabbits, squirrels, and other rodents caught in snares we'd built from grasses. That was the night Günther brought his match from his pocket.

Tall flames were holding off the darkness when Anna unfolded her lithe body and, like a lineal descendant of the witches from Brocken, began to sway. "*Walpurgisnacht*," she said. But she soon tired of her solo performance. Complaining that no mere fire could satisfy her hunger, she dragged Günther's coat a distance from where he and I were sitting. I'm ashamed to admit I can still smile when I remember her disgruntled stare when he didn't follow. His attention returned to the fire. Leaning back, out of his vision, I chided myself for thinking the grass did grow greener in his presence, the early wild strawberries really did bloom more delicately white. He moved so easily in his body, with such agility and grace, I was imagining the two of us as my glass dancers gliding across a polished floor in a sensual embrace when he startled me by saying, "How many times in these past years have I wondered why I lived while better men were dying all around me? I'm convinced my singing is the reason. Music is my soul. It's who I am."

My answer blurted out from my confusion. Defining myself had never occurred to me. I just was. Of course, when Anna snorted, I felt completely bereft of social graces.

"Don't you dare laugh," I said to Günther.

"I'm not laughing."

I stumbled on about being my parents', no, not my parents', my father's daughter, my brother's little sister, the colonel's secretary. There I was sinking into murky water. In Aland Nord, Anna always had an admirer or two hovering around her. I glared in her direction. "I hope you think I'm more than Anna's friend."

"I think I was lucky to find two such beautiful women."

My pale complexion was weathered, my thick hair coarse with dirt and needing combing. I grabbed it back with grubby fingers and sought refuge in describing how I'd fussed to look my best the day I left for my last assignment. My parents had insisted I risked missing my train at the Heidelberg station. A log slipped, and Günther kicked it back among the others scattering sparks in a brilliant fall. His father had taken him to the station after his last leave but his mother wasn't with them. Only Karl-Heinz, his next brother down. He said Karl-Heinz had seemed such a boy, more suited to kicking a ball in a field near their home, but Günther had tried to treat him as an equal because it was the day before his brother reported for military duty.

I'd been to the station in Ludwigshafen. I'd marveled at the vastness of the building, the churning energy around me. Ludwigshafen was a railway center. Its chemical plants were world renowned.

Günther said his father was an educated man, with a dream his sons be educated too, but he'd let Günther leave his formal schooling to study music before his *Abitur* exam was taken. His mother cried when she told him it was because there'd been so much talk of war. His father knew his son would be a soldier.

I told Günther my father studied music, too. The violin. But his parents were pragmatic. He'd stayed in school and eventually became a physician. "He is respected, even admired, but I've often wondered what he might have been if he had chosen."

"Happier maybe?" Günther said.

"Maybe that."

A large animal crashed through the brush, leaving us the rise and fall of resettling to fill our silence until the logs in our fire turned to ash. Günther pushed to his feet and stomped coals beneath his boots until the final orange faded before he reached out to me. I stood and he brought my fingers to his lips. Long after the other two were breathing deeply, I was still awake. Sleepless, staring, I could still feel the gentle kiss that had brushed across my fingers.

In the morning we began our search for habitation. The Harz mountains are a vacation land. Goethe came there. Schiller. But we'd wandered into the highest ranges and happened on no trails, no roads that we could follow. We passed no streams. The more we circled back on ways we'd passed before, the more our desperation included talk of a small black box Hitler had made available so families could hear his speeches and announcements. We needed to know what had happened in a war that was not yet over when we left it.

Beyond a stand of towering pine whose lower branches shriveled from no sun, we happened on a cluster of small wood houses with steep-pitched roofs and shutters to close against the winter. Excited children ran to meet us, touched Günther's weapon, shook Anna's hand, pulled me forward while calling to their mothers, but these villagers were as eager for news as we. A grizzled man, through missing teeth, told us their post had always been erratic, telephone lines were in a distant city, and radio reception had never reached them. He thought that made them lucky. From an earlier visitor, they'd learned that on radios in the valley, Goebbels had demanded destruction of anything left from the air raids. Factories. Rail lines. Bridges. Speer compounded the confusion when he warned people not to harm the land. He said if they did, no food could reach the cities. Starvation would kill anyone who'd survived the bombs. The old man said he wasn't sure whose advice was followed. A subsequent visitor had told them stores were closed with nothing to replace what had been sold or stolen.

We slept in a hovel that reeked of sweat and muck and animals that'd been kept there in the winter but when we emerged our packs had been filled with dried wild meat and blood-thickened sausage. Bread. This food was carefully allotted. Used to stave off hunger as our pace grew faster, our pauses shorter until one day we realized the mountains had given way to rounded hills. We were looking out on gentle valleys rife with green in patchwork patterns. Green headless fields of wheat, the silver-green of clover. Yellow-green hay for mowing in the fall, and green, thick-stalked, knee-high corn whose ears would feed a farmer's pigs through winter.

Günther looked back on the patternless way we'd left behind us and straightened his cap across his forehead. To me, the gesture was an exclamation, a trap door closing. I heard the smashing of my dancers.

"Well?" Anna said.

"Even if the fighting's finished, we still have enemies," Günther said.

"Me? I'm not an enemy." Anna flipped an imaginary scarf across her shoulder and took the first step forward.

A footpath took us onto paving where we stepped around dried clumps of dung, straddled dusty crossings where a farmer led his cows. In the glare of a noontime sun we entered a redbrick village, Günther first, alert to all directions. With no sign of any soldier, enemy or ours, he bent over a low stone trough and pumped hard with a wooden handle. Anna put her face to his. I listened to a chicken's cackle. One soft crow. Static?

Beside a house some distance from the others, a diminutive man in an overlarge coat leaned on a long handled hoe in a neat rowed garden. Behind him, in an open window, was

Hitler's black box. The device was not built to accept a foreign broadcast but when the static cleared, it was to English. The farmer asked if we needed help in understanding. He said his brother lived in Manitoba, he'd spent a year with him when he was young. Because he could speak the enemy's language, he'd manipulated the box to receive their broadcasts. Before we could do more than wonder at his skill, a woman, her broad smile in blunt contrast to what she was saying, emerged from a shadowed courtyard where tobacco leaves were hung for drying. One look at our obvious exhaustion had convinced her we'd been crossing the mountains and she asked if we knew the Führer was dead. I slipped on the pitted, hard packed dirt of the driveway, my face hot, then cold, then burning as my thoughts exploded on a fiery river I'd witnessed as a ten-year-old during a family visit to Berlin, a river flowing under the Brandenburg Gate and past the Reich's chancellery building where Hitler smiled down in triumph on thousands of blazing torches in the hands of his jack-booted followers marching through the night. I hadn't understood the politics of the time, the bitter battle for president in which Hitler was defeated, but I'd felt a childish participation in the outburst of joy that came from the people when the distinguished old man who'd won the election accepted Hitler as Reich's Chancellor, relinquishing to him unheard of power. Now, twelve years later, the Führer who'd promised us a reign of a thousand years was dead.

"The Allies say he killed himself," the farmwife said.

"A suicide?" Everyone turned at Günther's exclamation.

The farmer was quick with another explanation. Near the end of April, when we were already in the isolation of our journey, Radio Hamburg played music for an hour before Grand Admiral Karl Dönitz announced from Flensburg that he was now the Führer. Dönitz said Hitler had died that afternoon fighting with his soldiers.

"He had to say that," Günther said. "A suicide betrays the men he'd forbidden surrender."

"Oh there was surrender all right." The farmwife linked her arm through Anna's, urging us toward her kitchen. "Eisenhower called it unconditional even with Himmler offering to help him fight the Russians."

"Eisenhower wouldn't go to any signing," the farmer said. "Because of what he saw at Ohrdruf."

"What's Ohrdruf?" Anna asked.

"Some kind of camp, near Gotha."

"Eisenhower said Washington and London should send leaders to see and newspaper editors to make records."

Günther's arm was tightening around my shoulder.

The window from which the radio drew us was small, uncurtained. Embroidered pillows were on each chair. As we settled at her table, the farmwife ladled soup from a simmering pot on a cast-iron stove that filled a corner. She said she'd give Günther clothes that had fit their boy but the farmer instantly objected. The radio had reported soldiers, found out of uniform, were shot. Günther should find a garrison and surrender. The radio had said that too.

Günther shook his head. We'd head for the nearest city.

The farmwife warned us not to go to Kassel. She'd heard Kassel was a heap of rubble, with nothing moving except rats. "Go to Frankfurt," she said. In Frankfurt, *Trümmerfrauen*, women using nothing more than their hands and wheelbarrows, had done some clearing. She said train tracks had been repaired where the Americans needed them.

"Do we have money for a train?" Anna reached for the rough country cheese the farmwife hurried to the table.

While we ate, steam rose in a wispy cloud above a large tin tub that had been placed on the stove. Anna was the first to use the water. She laughed hugely over billowing suds of fresh lye soap from behind a cloth that screened her. When she emerged in a borrowed gown, even the farmer clapped as she pirouetted.

At the farmwife's suggestion, I used scissors brought from a drawer and clipped insignia from my uniform before I held the scissors out to Günther but he didn't clip as I had done. His fingers drifted up to cover a wound badge hanging from his pocket. "A few pulled threads won't change a single thing that happened," he said.

We carried blankets to a great dark barn and fashioned beds in a loft above the restless lowing of the farmer's cows, the grunts of a nursing sow. Staring into cobwebbed rafters, I struggled to understand why, when he emerged from his bath clean-shaven and in pants and shirt that almost fit him, Günther had been so unsmiling despite our admiring exclamations. Anna had tried to pat his face but he'd caught her hand in one of his and reached for mine with the other. His touch had been hard with a strength that somehow disturbed me. In the dark of the barn, trying to sleep, he was as restless as the livestock until he reached out to me, not soft but stiff and watchful. With his lips against my ear, he whispered that war had taught him a simple lesson, just one above the others. We trust in man's compassion for his fellow beings at our own peril.

We woke to the cooing of doves in a cote we hadn't noticed, the sounds and smells of someone milking. Günther wrapped his rifle in oil-coated paper and with the hovering farmer, buried it in the farthest reaches of the garden. The farmer gave him crumbled tobacco and strips of newspaper to contain it for smoking. The three of us devoured all the eggs and bread and yoghurt the smiling farmwife placed before us and listened to what, in morning's light, I dismissed as enemy propaganda. The farmer's eager translation about a conference planned for Potsdam, where he expected Germany's borders to be established, seemed unbelievable. How could Germany be split into zones, each governed by a different Allied power, each with a different document of occupation?

We walked more long weeks across broad valleys filled with rain, to rolling hills spread bright beneath the sun with yellow rapeseed. We climbed through another high forest and followed rivers we couldn't name. Enemy convoys owned the highways but refugees filled our back roads. Fleeing west were Germans from the Sudetenland, the Volga regions of Russia, from the Memel lands and Silesia. In the opposite direction, Lithuanians, Latvians, Poles who'd been held in camps near Frankfurt. Young women, ignoring repeated warnings and returning to their homes in the fir and white birch forests of Prussia. Released Russian prisoners looting as they moved east.

Each day became a race against our need to hurry. Each night, around fires lit with other people's matches, a litany of change. In the American south, where we'd be living, all traces of the old regime had been burned or buried or hidden away in attics. Courts and schools had been closed without notice but bureaucrats had been kept at their posts while being cleared for regular employment. One terrifying rumor concerned a *Fragebogen*, a questionnaire that was required in our zone but not the others. Penalties for not answering questions correctly and completely were said to be prison or even death, but the form must be completed before ration coupons would be issued. Everything was rationed. Bread. Potatoes. We'd be allowed some meat. No fat. Everything was weighed and measured down to the number of grams of salt or sugar before being totaled into a caloric allotment bought with *Reichsmark*. Günther questioned the use of money whose value had been eroding under Hitler and a man who'd walked from Bad Reichenhall, limping, told us there'd been an effort to issue a new exchange as soon as hostilities had ended. He thought it an ironic joke that the Americans had shared the printing plates with other Allies, including the Soviet Union. "What did they expect?" he asked. "That Stalin would stop printing money when it was backed by the US dollar?"

One day we passed three men with the silent downcast look of prisoners. Their clothes were ill-fitting pieces of American uniforms. Günther turned to watch. "Are you all right?" I asked him.

"Yes."

"No," he said later.

That night as Anna tossed and groaned beside us, Günther pulled me fiercely to him. He didn't speak but his hands explored my body until his tensed strength slipped away. "We must prepare ourselves. We must be ready," he whispered.

"For what?" I asked.

"For all the world discovers. The things we have done to one another." I didn't question. I didn't care. Even with Anna watching. The roughness of his beard was a welcome irritant on my face, his sweat an aphrodisiac, but when our mouths eventually parted he said, "All of us are guilty."

# Summer 1945

*D*awn light streaked red across a clouded sky as we made our way into the outskirts of Frankfurt. Singly, one behind the other, hushed by the city that lay around us. Our silence only deepened as a pale sun climbed high. No horns, no traffic, no wakening bustle of a population setting out to meet the day. Frankfurt had crumbled in upon itself. Dead tongues of rubble flowed from mouths of hollowed buildings. Fire-blackened walls supported gaping windows. No life, no movement, a waking bird's call was a startling intrusion.

Nearer the center of the city, where parallel bands of steel defined a street, we picked our way through hanging ropes of streetcar cable, tangled electric wires, knotted telephone lines from tilted poles. Charred cars. Trucks. Armored vehicles. A broken rifle. A child's shoe. Everywhere the smell of seeping gas, the stench of broken sewers. With our backs to the river Main, we stumbled into an old part of the city and found the cathedral buried in its ashes. Medieval burgher's homes were roofless blackened timbers. Where Goethe wrote, a crater.

A pink-cheeked old man braced himself against a doorway. His pale eyes were bloodshot, his meticulously tailored suit infused with dust from bricks and plaster. Around him, the front wall of a multi-storied building had dropped in a broad obeisance, exposing shadowy figures crawling across high floors. Anna pointed.

"They're foraging for food in abandoned apartments." The old man's voice broke but strengthened with defiance when Anna turned away. "They're not frenzied looters," he said. "They have to feed their families." Above him sagging pictures hung on tilted walls.

Günther caught my arm, and Anna's, to guide us further down the street. A woman with a bucket at her side polished a lone unbroken window. Another swept a patch of sidewalk. "I know Frankfurt well," he kept insisting, but he was wrong in the way he'd chosen and we circled back across another field of rubble.

When we reached the arched entry to the central station, I honestly expected the usual orderly confusion, maybe some posted information or at least an official with answers to our questions, but there was only the vast hollow of that room. Chipping paint, iron heat vents dead from lack of fuel, a little pile of filth where someone, careless in defeat, had paused to relieve himself.

Günther tapped a stranger on his arm. "Sir, we must get to Mannheim."

The stranger shrugged him off.

"Sir?" he asked another who hurried on his way.

Finally he confronted an older man whose empty sleeve was tucked into his pocket. The man studied Günther's stained uniform, pausing on the wound badge. "Mannheim?" he repeated as his gaze met Günther's. "Who knows? Few trains move, and those at the discretion of the Americans. Just get in any coach where you can manage. If the train goes north, get off. If it goes south, hold your place as long as you are able. Maybe you'll get to Mannheim." Seeing my disbelief, the man added, "But be aware we Germans ride in common coaches. Soft compartments are for the victors."

He was lost in the crowd before we turned into a cavern where a soaring dome of sun-gleamed glass once protected all who entered. Now, beneath the shattered panes, where steaming trains had stood between the rows of concrete, people were shielding themselves from a summer drizzle. People on the walkways. People on the tracks. People packed into compartments of stalled trains, seating seven on wooden benches meant for four. Clutching outside doors, clinging between the cars on couplings, looking down from tenuous places on top, their eyes watery and red-rimmed from a journey that had brought them into Frankfurt.

"Is all Germany trying to be somewhere else?" Anna was almost breathless with confusion.

I recovered enough to read a startlingly bright, newly painted sign. "Railway Transportation Office." Red arrows brought our attention to a flight of metal stairs.

"Is that where we need to go?" asked Anna.

"It's for the soldiers," Günther said just as a group of uniformed Americans crowded the platform with bulging duffle bags they carried on their shoulders. I clutched Günther's arm. "Surrender changes everything," he said. But it hadn't. Not for me.

The last soldier in the line glanced back and I saw Anna smile.

Before a wooden coach, low to the walk and narrow, Günther opened a door and, ignoring the protests of those already packed inside, forced our way past knees and leather suitcases and bundles made from what seemed rags. In a narrow corridor, thrust close by those already claiming spaces, we waited, not speaking, not looking at each other until the train began to move. We were beyond the devastation of the city before we knew we were traveling south.

Hour after hour, we stood while the train braked to a halt at every station or waited motionless on empty sidings for another train that never passed. A baby cried. An old man vomited onto his shirtfront, and still we stood. Only glancing at the others, I pried my way into a place at an open window. My eyes, my mouth, my nostrils soon rimmed with soot. Günther stepped over the legs of a man who'd collapsed across the aisle and pushed his way into a space beside me. His hand brushed across my forehead. I hurt inside from all I longed for but in that crush of unwashed bodies, I could only sigh, desire, reach for the hand that touched my face. An unexpected sway as the train crawled into another station brought Anna up against us. "Will we go to Mannheim?" she asked.

Günther forced his head and shoulders out the window. "I think not. We're in Weinheim. The train will go to Heidelberg from here." When he didn't draw back, I leaned out beside him to see the crowd on the station platform part for two American soldiers striding forward, their side arms accessible below their jackets, their white-striped helmets almost tea-colored in a rush of evening sun. A glowing cigarette was caught between the lips of the taller of the two. Below our window he blinked long tendrils of smoke away from his eyes and, with his head tilting, spat his cigarette back across his shoulder.

Three men lunged forward but a ragged boy was quicker. He squeezed between the reaching arms to snatch the burning butt and, while all watched, snuffed the cigarette between his fingers before depositing a crumble of tobacco into a small tin box he carried.

The tall policeman drew a crushed pack from his jacket pocket and put another cigarette between his lips. My smattering of schoolgirl English was enough to guess his colleague's question and I pulled Günther's arm around me as slowly, deliberately, perhaps with the idea that some of us had understood, the tall soldier answered, "This is the master race that tried to kill me. I like to see them scramble." Then his shout cut through the air as though a shot were fired. "Fucking bastards!" Spittle hung in a long, slick line across his face. Günther shoved me away from the window, shielding me with his body, but instead of reaching for his pistol the soldier drew his khaki-covered arm across his face. Never glancing away from those staring down from the roof, the whites of their eyes stark in their soot-blackened faces, he took the fresh cigarette from his mouth and, with a swinging motion, jabbed it upward only once before he split the fragile paper and scattered tobacco in the wind. "Goddamned *Krauts*," he muttered as he put another cigarette between his lips. He produced a folded book of matches and cupped his hand around a flame. The two of them resumed their pacing. The crowd closed in behind.

Anna wanted to know why the cigarette was so important, and a small man pulled himself back from leaning out the window. His carefully tailored uniform of an *SS Einsatzgruppenkommando* was covered by a coat that could have been a woman's. He straightened the coat, adjusted the collar, saying to no one in particular that if Anna didn't know already, she'd find out.

Anna's lips formed a tight line of disapproval when he made an obscene gesture by twisting his index finger against his head. She asked Günther why the boy was collecting useless ends but Günther had turned away. A vein bulged across his forehead. The muscles in his neck were taut. A woman with a cranky baby touched Anna's arm. "It's the money," she said kindly. "No one is certain about the money."

"The boy was trying to get the soldiers' money?"

The woman nodded although she said, "Well, not exactly. Cigarettes are money."

Günther fumbled for our hands, a wordless anger in his roughness as he began to shoulder a way through the press, the activity, the questioning confusion along the corridor. "We'll get to Mannheim quicker if we walk," he said.

As we left the train, I glanced back. The small man was leaning out the window.

We stumbled through a gutted orchard. Günther first, Anna stolidly behind him until she flung her pack against a tree and slumped to her knees beside it. The setting sun was a brilliant ball across the wide Rhine plain. Günther wandered back to sit beside her. Anna said she'd been to Weinheim with her sister. Günther asked if they'd eaten apple cake in a café, he said his brothers would have insisted. I'd been here with my family. My brother had insisted, too.

Surrounded by the detritus of battle, we ate the last of what we carried, each of us with thoughts we didn't share. Günther spread his coat and, like our first night, drew the three of us together. With Anna on one shoulder, I on the other, he began to anticipate the meetings with our families. Anna's sister. My parents. His many little brothers. I was besieged by loss, by a loneliness from deep within my core, where a friend had never been, no lover, but gazing through a labyrinth of branches to the first bright points of stars, my last thought before I fell asleep was of the stranger on the train who'd caused Günther's silent anger.

We woke by morning's light, stretched, did our toilet. From an unbroken branch on a nearby tree, dark burnished drops of fruit hung fully ripened. Günther gathered high handfuls and we ate breakfast, spitting pits, as we inched our way across a trestle above an empty Autobahn. On the other side, rough pavement curved out toward Ladenburg's red stone spires. A man approached on a wavering bicycle, a dark felt hat pulled low to shade his features. Before we reached each other, the man glanced back, down, and stopped by putting both feet on the pavement. Loosening a pump tied to the bicycle's rusted frame with knotted string, he began working over a flattening thick rear tire.

"Good morning, sir," Günther said.

The man did not look up.

"The day is warm for repairing a tire," Günther added.

The man tapped the bicycle pump against his palm before he stood and pushed at his hat, revealing piercing eyes and a pointed nose. He seemed not to see the hand Günther extended toward him. He said he expected that like others he'd met along this way, we wanted to know how life was on ahead.

"In Ludwigshafen," Günther said.

"And Schwetzingen."

The man turned to my direction, his sharp eyes narrowed at the corners as he told me I'd find Schwetzingen almost as I'd left it. My relief was so great I found it hard to look at Günther, or at Anna waiting. "Few bombs fell on Schwetzingen," the man continued. "Or Heidelberg, except the zoo. Even with red crosses painted on the roofs of all the hospitals for wounded soldiers, dozens of planes dropped thousands of kilos of bombs on Heidelberg at the end of March but only hit the zoo." He laughed.

Anna stepped forward, stopping the man in mid-chortle. Her accent in a mumbled question was enough for him to know she could be from Mannheim. Slowly drawing a round-faced watch from his pocket, he squinted at the sun. "In another hour, maybe two, when the sun is high you'll recognize the odor." Dropping the watch back in his pocket, he turned to Günther and me. He'd lived in Mannheim through the war. "Because of this." A gesture of impatience displayed two solitary fingers on his right hand. After an early bombing, his family was assigned living space in an apartment where a merchant had an extra bedroom. That was bombed and they'd had another only this time not so good. After that he went home to live with a neighbor. "I return every day to dig for my wife, my daughter. I haven't found them in the ruin of that bad apartment but my nose tells me they are there." A breeze drifted across the plain bringing a sweet smell from the Rhine. The freshness of the morning was unsalvageable. "Once a week I pedal out into the country on this borrowed bicycle to bargain with the farmers for food. I part with what my neighbor gives me and maybe I return with a round head of cabbage or a few soft apples. On lucky days I find spring fruit across the trestle." He nodded toward the way we'd come. "When people ask about their homes, sometimes I can tell them and sometimes I cannot. Sometimes

I don't stop or look at them at all. Sometimes I tell them to lift their noses in the air. Now. It's almost time."

Günther grasped the deformed hand. "Thank you, sir," he said. The man nodded. "Thank you," Günther said again.

Ignoring the hand Günther settled on his shoulder, the man returned to his flattened tire, pumping again, looking away as the three of us passed, our footsteps ringing loud against the pavement.

"My sister moved to Mannheim when she married." Anna's face was bloodless. Her eyes were stark round holes. "She had two babies of her own but when our mother died she took me, too."

Günther stopped walking. He reached back to bring the three of us together, our fingers probing for flesh, for bone, for reality beneath our worn familiar clothing. He said all of us should go to Schwetzingen first. He said Anna and he would see me to my parents before he went with Anna to find her sister.

"You won't leave me, Günther?" Anna asked.

"I won't leave either of you before I know you have someone waiting."

We walked in exhausted silence those last kilometers we had together, circling widely when we passed a wagon with a gutted horse still in the rigging. Green iridescent flies with their incessant buzzing were an echoing reminder of all we'd seen until we reached Schwetzingen where we found no fire-blackened walls, no glassless staring windows. But wide walks had not been swept or splashed with water. No flowers bloomed in oblong gardens. Where a broad avenue spread out before the city's castle were rows of closed shop doors, dirty windows where once was freshly shining backlit glass. On a corner was a butcher shop from my childhood. A skinned head of a calf had often been displayed there. Circles of red and green had adorned its eyes with tiny waves of blue beneath its ears. Fat sausage hung above it and thick smoked haunches of ham. On the broad streets were little Renaults from France and Fiats from Italy, German Opels and Daimler-Benz. A policeman stood among them, making them obey each smart twist of his pointing white-gloved fingers.

Günther's gentle touch brought me to the present. A woman with layers of rough peasant's skirts thickening her figure pulled a cart with wooden wheels around a corner.

In an area of overarching trees, where tall houses secluded families behind decorative fences, I caught a glimpse of my father. His slight figure was just visible through high arched windows. Tears of childlike relief filled my eyes as I explained to Günther and Anna that he was in a small salon where my family read or listened to the radio. "The interior is dim," I said. "The room is always lit."

"If that's your father, we'll say good-bye," Günther said.

My tears were gone, replaced by panic.

All the concern and understanding of our journey, all the tenderness of our last weeks together were in the way Günther put his arms around me, telling me I couldn't complicate my parents' greeting by introducing strangers. "My little brothers will be all over me," he said. "That's our way. I'm aching for our kind of greeting, but I'm not sure I'd have it with two strangers standing by."

Anna was already turning away.

Clinging to our decorative fence, I watched the two dirty, loved, familiar backs hurry toward the broad avenue leading to the castle. When they looked back for one last wave, Günther's rich deep voice called my name. Anna's good-bye was lost as she turned the corner.

Beyond the fence. Along a drive. Up three broad steps. Quickly. I leaned into a massive door, my fingers curled around its handle. The door would be unlocked. The house was always open, always properly prepared, like the persons whom it sheltered. I pushed. The light from behind leaped forward to meet a light from a window partway up a gently curving flight of stairs. I stepped into the pale illumination and my mind peopled the hall. My father. My mother. My brother, Hartmut. His memory rushed to greet me, running, laughing, pulling at my long braid. Gerda, round face resolute above her starched collar, would be in the kitchen lightly rolling sweet-tasting dough or wiping her hands across her apron in a cloud of flour, bustling between the kitchen and a formal dining room to serve our meals. Across from the dining room was the music room where I'd grown tall to the beat of my father's metronome, where, as I grew older, I'd listened to him play the violin he'd purchased with honors money he'd been awarded from his research. In that room I'd struggled through duets with Hartmut, hiding giggles until his clarinet squealed and our father frowned, saying nothing but beating our rhythm firmly with his bow.

Upstairs, high-ceilinged bedrooms squared off on each side of another hall.

"Who's there?" My father's voice was startlingly firm despite his age. I dropped my worn pack beside a stand for umbrellas and coats, anxious that he see me well before he heard my voice.

My parents, illumined by the electric glow apparent from the street, sat in broad straight chairs, their arms resting on an empty table. Joy swept my mother's face, surprise crossed my father's but neither cried out in greeting. In this house no one made loud acclaim. Only Hartmut, me, when we were children. Hartmut would have shouted if he were here. I would shout for him. I smiled at my parents. My father struggled from his chair to grasp my outstretched hands. I kissed his cheek, my lips lingering on the wrinkled familiarity of his soft skin. His hands trembled and he returned to his chair, his face ashen as he sat upright with his arms at rest again upon the table. My mother touched my face, her fine head erect. In my arms, she felt so frail, so sunk within herself. She sat down opposite my father and I took my place between, covering a hand of each. This is what I remembered, this gentle touch, this quiet voicing. This was the dignified core of my home. But having seen my parents safe, I wanted Günther. Anna, too. I wanted to be with them in their searching, to share their joy, their grief if they should have it. I stroked my mother's delicate hand, only half understanding all they were saying until I realized my father was recounting the black hours of five years before when Hartmut had been killed in a plane crash early in his military training. My mother's eyes grew red-rimmed as she listened. Hartmut had been dead so suddenly, without the preparation of worry as he moved toward the fighting. My father had refused to let my mother view the body.

As gently as I could, I asked the questions that brought them forward, let me learn what they endured while I was absent. The cold winters. The increasing shortages of food. My thoughts fled to Anna in Mannheim, to Günther in Ludwigshafen when my parents both looked toward the ceiling as my father described the nights they'd huddled in the cellar, their arms around each other, listening to an unrelenting drone of bombers making their long returns to the cities on the Rhine. To my increasing distress, they seemed alternately lucid then confused. They slipped between the past and present. An explanation of what happened to the Nazi official assigned to the Steynor house next door to Frau Schuler was followed by a flurry of indecision until they agreed that American officers lived there for a time before it became home to an ever-expanding group of refugees. Ordinary American soldiers kept mostly to the castle. They'd built a kitchen in the garden and lived in tents before they moved into the circular buildings.

"We were told they just looked tired," my father said.

"And why shouldn't they?" my mother said. "We were tired, too. Tired of war. Tired of worry."

The soldiers were gone now, to barracks built in the days of Hitler.

I lifted my father's hand, freckled and heavy-veined with age, remembering how his touch had soothed my childhood aches. My own hands seemed profaned with grime. Each moon was rimmed with black, tipped with black beneath the nails. My mother asked if I was hungry. She told me to go upstairs and care for myself while she fixed something we could eat.

Upstairs I stood in the doorway of my room, not really seeing, feeling a past I couldn't keep in focus. Across the hall I leaned over a high-backed tub, each of its clawed feet clutching a ball, and let water rush across my fingers until I was convinced it would not flow warm. My stained uniform was discarded in a corner before I stepped into an inch of icy water.

Bathed and dressed in familiar clothes found folded in a drawer, I returned to my parents. In the kitchen my mother was pressing a wooden spoon through a scattering of packed browned flour. She lifted her cheek for my kiss when I came to stand beside her and added milk. Just milk. When the mixture was slightly thickened, she ladled it into porcelain bowls and carried the bowls through the hall to a formally set table.

"We nap in the afternoon," my father said when the milk-meal was finished.

"We sleep downstairs since Gerda left to find her family."

I wouldn't expect my parents to complain, but that they made no comment disturbed me.

Alone upstairs I couldn't sleep in spite of my exhaustion. Frau Schuler must have been the one who moved them to the warmth of the small back room beside the kitchen, who saw they had at least fresh milk. I needed to go to her and find my answers but if my parents awoke and found me gone, they might be frightened. I went downstairs. Working around the kitchen, I realized why my mother heated milk and called it soup. Among the heavy utensils once used for making extravagant meals, I found sprouted soft potatoes.

After they awoke my mother hovered, my father followed us from room to room. In the music room he cradled a black wood case that held his violin. "We retire early," he said when we'd finished the potatoes I'd boiled for our evening meal.

"You don't mind," my mother said.

"I'll find Frau Schuler," I said.

They were quiet under thick down on their narrow bed before I darted into the street and around a corner to a vast old-fashioned house with pointed turrets. A garden bloomed in colored splashes. Snapdragons. Roses. Geraniums at each window, pink and red. Purple lilacs made thick hedges separating Frau Schuler's from the Steynor home where American officers had lived after our local *Gauleiter* had been arrested. I closed my eyes to the obscenity of laundry spread across the bushes Herr Steynor had tended with such devotion and tried to remember the hours I'd spent playing among the sweet familiar scents. Eva Steynor had been my friend. A best friend who shared my secrets. I ran to ring Frau Schuler's bell.

Frau Schuler cried when she saw me on her doorstep and clasped me to her breast. "What has taken you so long," she kept repeating. Frau Schuler was tall for a woman of her generation, with a smooth face and patrician nose. I'd loved her since, as a toddling child, I'd followed my brother to this house to claim warm cakes and kisses. Later, my knobby knees covered by my thick stockings, I'd been indulged no differently than Hartmut or her son, Paul. As I followed to her kitchen and settled into the familiarity of an armed oak chair at a thick oak table, I remembered how Frau Schuler ruled this place, intimidating a hulking cook who fretted and sputtered when she added salt to a simmering stew or cinnamon to a strudel. My mother wrote how they both had wept and clung to each other when the cook was taken for the army. But my thoughts wouldn't stay in those days of polished houses, servants in both kitchens, flowers on the table when our families shared a meal. What was Frau Schuler saying? That they were safe enough in Schwetzingen but they shook from the bombing in Ludwigshafen and Mannheim? That at night a terrible light was in the sky?

"Gas lines were destroyed but electricity was back within days of the occupation." Frau Schuler rinsed her teapot in a trace of heated water. She spooned used tea leaves into a metal ball and added a modicum of freshness. "American soldiers were in our homes before the fighting ended, telling us we owned nothing. Anything could be requisitioned without notice or appeal. Now it's Germans. Living space is to be assigned by meter." I struggled to make sense of what she was saying. "I hadn't seen my sister since she evacuated Kassel for the safety of her mother-in-law's summer cottage across from Neckargemuend, but Good Friday had such beautiful weather." She was talking too fast, her voice too high. She paced restlessly behind me, her fingers clutching at my chair each time she passed. "I was caught in a crowd trying to keep our soldiers from setting explosives on the *Alte Brücke*. Clearly they needed to stop the enemy's advances, but that bridge was already blocked by tank traps at both ends." By the time she'd decided she couldn't go to Kleingemuend with no way to get back if all the bridges were destroyed, she'd learned patients from Heidelberg's hospitals for wounded soldiers were being moved into railroad tunnels to save them from the region's inevitable destruction. No one knew a group of physicians had already defied the Führer's orders by telephoning the Americans who occupied Mannheim. A single line remained undamaged and a single woman was at her post to relay the doctors' surrender information.

"A miracle," I said.

"Not the only one that night. Heidelberg was more than a dot on the map to the Americans' commanding general. He'd translated THE STUDENT PRINCE in high school."

I tried to imagine, tried to understand, tried to reconcile this Frau Schuler with the woman I'd always thought was regal. I'd been curious about Heidelberg's survival but must I know, at just that moment, that the Neckar was high from rain and a full moon made everyone a target. "Ten minutes after the bridges were destroyed, the doctors, who'd been ordered to appear in Mannheim, returned with word that only with absolutely no resistance could our region escape destruction. A child, a girl of just sixteen, rowed them across when grown men faltered." Frau Schuler supported herself on the back of my chair. "Scattered firing did come from above the castle, and a canon was stuck on Bismarck Platz with no *Benzin* for a vehicle large enough to tow it." The once mighty German army had waited for a team of oxen. "Now we're expected to obey, immediately and without question, any instruction the Americans give us but how are we to know? We've had no post since March, no telephone. Blackouts kept us in our homes before and now a curfew."

I mentioned a newspaper I'd found on my father's desk.

"The *Süddeutsche Mitteilungen*. It's published by the Americans. They broadcast from Radio Stuttgart as well but what we learn from those official sources rarely agrees with rumors returnees bring us from the east." Tiny beads of moisture gathered on her lip when I mentioned the Fragebogen, the questionnaire required in our zone. She'd wiped them with her finger as she assured me my father's records were in order. A colleague who understood his incapacitation had taken him through the formalities after the Nazi Workers' Fund was seized. My family had its ration coupons and my father's pension would continue, but the American denazification process had singled out teachers and professors for particular attention.

Professor Schuler had always been a presence in my life. I can still see him standing before a portrait of the Führer in the Schulers' upstairs library. A stern man with a heavy mustache, comfortable in his life of privilege while he took pride in Hitler's humble beginnings. Professor Schuler never wore a uniform, just a little Golden Party Badge on his lapel, but Frau Schuler had been warned the Americans would know he'd given lectures at a few small meetings and been honored at a party conference or two. I wouldn't have paid attention when the Nürnberg laws were enacted, except Professor Schuler had a sister. A woman I knew as Auntie. Auntie's face was round and smooth, her eyes had little color. Hitler had said the mentally and physically disabled were living lives without purpose, worse, their care exploited those whose skills were needed elsewhere. I was terrified by

Frau Schuler's vehement objections when Auntie disappeared. Frau Schuler's demands to be responsible for Auntie's care. But Professor Schuler's response in those days of shouted slogans is gone. He must have said or done something I should remember. The university in Heidelberg was a center of radical thinking.

I told Frau Schuler not to worry. I'd take care of her. I'd find work.

"There is no work in Schwetzingen," she said.

On our long walk home we'd learned about bans on gathering in groups of more than five, but with the roads and forest pathways crowded in both directions, I wasn't prepared for travel restrictions. Frau Schuler must have realized Heidelberg was within the ten kilometers Germans were allowed to travel without official permission because when I said I'd go there to find work, her answer was only that Heidelberg was filled to overflowing with three times its wartime population. I wouldn't be discouraged. I had youth and strength and vigor, even curiosity about the city saved by doctors. I was thinking I'd find my pleated skirt. It flattered my slim figure, and somewhere I must still have the pale yellow blouse made by Frau Schuler's tailor. I wanted to look my best. I expected to find a job commensurate with my successes in the German army. I didn't know that as the only city of any size not destroyed by the war, Heidelberg had become a magnet for some of the 400,000 ethnic Germans who fled west as soon as peace had been established, with another explosion of population from the seven or eight million who followed from East Prussia after the Potsdam Agreement ratified the Russian's borders. I returned to my home through night-blackened streets and pushed our always open door. I climbed our curving stairs. Ignoring my old room at the end of the hall, I turned into a larger room with three tall windows, two marble-topped chests, and an ornately inlaid wardrobe. Undressing quickly, I slipped into a massive bed that, when I was growing up, had been my parents'. Finally able to close my eyes, I tried to imagine what Günther and Anna must be finding. Certainly the antithesis of Heidelberg where a plethora of homes larger and grander than the Steynor house next door to Frau Schuler must be absorbing the increasing population. But as thought of the Steynors flashed across my mind, from out of the dark came a discordant bleating, a remembered siren from long ago that had stopped at their home while neighbors peaked from curtained windows. Eva and her mother had already gone to England. The siren had come for Eva's father.

# Autumn
## 1945

*I* knew Heidelberg well. In the years my father had his practice there, I'd wandered its quiet streets, its shadowed alleys. Together with my brother and Paul, I'd climbed hills on both sides of the Neckar River or spent long languid afternoons exploring a red-walled sweep of castle above the old part of the city. The morning I left Schwetzingen to walk my allotted ten kilometers, I had few reservations. I'd found my pale blouse and pleated skirt. I wore sturdy shoes. From other walkers, I learned tactical units of the American army filled all of Hitler's barracks with a regional headquarters in *Grossdeutschland Kaserne*, the largest in the area. I wasn't halfway to the city before I knew the occupation had seized office space in random buildings, our swimming pool, the city hall. A hospital. A church. Hotels that once served an international clientele were clubs and dining rooms and residences for their workers. The imposing homes I'd imagined as absorbing Heidelberg's burgeoning population were occupied by ranking officers, with lesser houses and apartment complexes emptied and being refurbished for families that were expected to arrive in Germany before spring. I suppose I'd expected ordinary soldiers to be confined by duty but they were on every corner, shuttled about in three-quarter-ton trucks converted to military buses.

The switchboard skills I'd been exposed to in the German army seemed the most saleable of my skills, and I went immediately to the *Arbeitsamt*, the city employment office. An American jeep was parked outside. American police restrained a man they were leading from the building. I moved into a line alive with whispers.

"The Americans can take anyone."

"They can even shoot to kill."

"Some say they seek revenge."

"You know, the camps."

But my needs were too immediate, my concerns too focused on my family. I shuffled forward, concentrating on what I'd say when I reached a man behind a counter who had the upright carriage of a former officer and a steel hook hand. He didn't listen. He snarled back that it was July. *Deutsche Post* rosters had been filled since May. With telephone lines providing service only to the city, opportunities were limited. When I tried to explain my secretarial experience, he laughed. In a voice certainly harsh, but equally dismissing, he told me to try an employment office the Americans had established near the Schriederhof Hotel, but I should be aware, thousands stood in line the day that office opened. Thousands for a few jobs offered.

At that office, a woman with translucent skin smoothed hennaed hair with orange-tipped fingers. Not German, I thought, or American, but little doubt in her demeanor as she explained the American's Community Commander decided how many hires were needed for each day's duty. Where work was for the occupation, priority was given to applicants from countries the Allies considered liberated and not vanquished. If I were a man, perhaps a Labor Service Unit, the military's auxiliary guards. "But no, that's not a job a former enemy can fill."

I wouldn't be discouraged. In a city of Heidelberg's size, there would be work and I would find it. But Heidelberg had closed down upon itself. Along Hauptstrasse, the crowded cobblestone heart of the old part of the city, I passed just two open doors. The first was to what had been a popular department store. At the entry, a Labor Service guard was checking passes. Beyond him, I glimpsed counters filled with British woolens, French perfumes, and what looked like an entire wall of cigarettes in cardboard cartons. A woman no older than myself, blundered into me as I stood gaping. She steadied me from falling while managing to tell me that everything inside was brought to Germany by and for the occupation. It could be purchased only with their private money, their military script. Guiding me away from the entrance, she also advised me to be careful of the crowding. With just one bar of soap allotted with our ration, few touched each other for fear of skin diseases. She'd hurried on before I'd gathered my wits enough to ask if she were working.

The second door was to Perkeo's restaurant. Beyond the familiar open windows, white-coated waiters brought heaping platters to tables filled with American soldiers. I'd eaten little since our potatoes my first night home and the sight of thick slabs of meat, the odors from the grilling brought me up against the building. A man whose tongue was thick with Slavic accents leaned close enough to whisper, "No hope from this soldier's mess hall, *Mädchen*. Here leftover food is soaked in gasoline before a hungry man can get close enough to steal it."

In Hercules Square, between Holy Ghost Church and city hall, I almost tripped over a legless man maneuvering along on a low crude cart. I'd heard of catastrophic wounded from the Great War but such men weren't abandoned to the streets by Hitler. Desperate for some other focus, my gaze caught on a scrap of paper hanging from a nail on the wood-covered Hercules fountain. Before it, a hunched and elderly woman studied the note from under the brim of her crushed felt hat. Her explanation that such lists of each day's black-market rate for various brands of American cigarettes were posted throughout the city immediately recalled the wall of cigarettes I'd seen in the store that only the victorious could enter. According to the list, a single pack of Lucky Strike cigarettes was worth 135 *Reichsmark*. With her finger smudging down the paper, the woman complained that was the cost of a three-pound loaf of bread on the illegal market. With a ration coupon, in an official store, it was only forty *Pfennig* if it could be found. Her high-pitched, incongruous giggle made clear that such a find went only to the lucky.

Near *Karlstor*, a massive archway at the eastern entrance to the city, leftovers from the noontime meal at a gun emplacement on the hill were thrown onto the street. Scavengers appeared from everywhere to fight each other over the slippery garbage. A man whose heavily knuckled hands spread quickly across the pavement, smiled at me through a broken tooth. "This morning, I scraped together enough grounds to make a cup of coffee," he said.

I started running, back through the teeming desolation of Hauptstrasse toward the Kornmarktplatz. "Hey, good lookin', what's yer hurry?" A cluster of soldiers lounged around the narrow entry to a former interrogation station. "Will you look at the tits on that one," another soldier said.

No such coarseness assaulted my life when Hartmut and Paul were with me. We'd often lingered over coffee and cake in a café around the corner. I shuddered at the café's boarded entry and escaped down an alley, to a brick path along the river. Concrete slabs of the bridge the doctors seeking to surrender had hoped to cross on their return from Mannheim were collapsed into the water. The arches of the Alte Brücke were a sunken heap of ancient bricks and mortar. My heart pounding, I stopped where haphazardly aligned boards served as a landing for a shallow boat. Another line, more patient than that at the Arbeitsamt, waited to be rowed across even though an empty pontoon bridge was only a slight way up the river. A woman whose each hand clutched a toddling child said, "That bridge is for the army." Women clustered at each end, looking up when soldiers passed. "Men who go with such women break the law," the mother added. "No American can speak to any German, except to give an order."

Where the river walk widened for quiet strolling I sank onto a bench, promising myself I'd never speak to any soldier. Closing my eyes, I tried to recapture the contentment I'd often found while waiting there for my father, for a ride home to Schwetzingen in his long black car. Hartmut was often with me, or Paul. We'd thrown bits of crusty rolls to swans upon the river.

By Bismarck Platz, a *Gymnasium* had been converted to a military barracks. Children on the steep front steps munched sandwiches whose soft white bread could only have come from an American kitchen. A soldier in heavy boots and crumpled fatigues adjusted a boy's hands along a bat while another soldier waited to pitch them a ball. Still another, nearer soldier offered chewing gum to a small shy girl. He looked up to see me watching and held a slim foil-wrapped stick toward me. His hair was blond like Hartmut's, like Hartmut he pushed it back across his forehead, but I wasn't a child to transfer my acceptance to the occupation.

Glued to a wall around a corner was a notice frayed from summer rain:

# OFFICE OF MILITARY GOVERNMENT FOR WÜRTTEMBERG-BADEN
## We came not as liberators but as victors
## 1700 is curfew
## After that you will be shot
Posted by Order of the Director

I'd seen and heard all I could manage for that first day. My need to secure my family's future was overwhelmed by a more immediate need to protect my senses. I fled back to Schwetzingen, back past fields left fallow. When I'd made sure my parents were safe behind closed doors, I retreated to the modicum of comfort I'd found in Frau Schuler's kitchen. She seemed different from the night before, less fearful, but now I saw in her the withdrawal into routine I'd seen in Frankfurt, the acceptance of degradation I'd seen along the crowded streets in Heidelberg. Gathering last night's tea she'd spread again for drying, she told me the curfew had been changed to later but I should be home anyway. For a young woman, home was safer.

I tried to explain my day, starting with the man who'd been taken from the Arbeitsamt. She guessed he'd been more than an ordinary soldier. Former soldiers weren't arrested in the American zone. Only in the French.

I struggled up from my exhaustion. Somewhere in that confusing day I'd learned Ludwigshafen, Günther's home, was in the zone that belonged to the French. But he must be safe, or I would know it. Anna would've come to tell me. I kept my voice even as I told Frau Schuler refugees were being sent to live where there was room. Someone would be sent to us.

"Did you hear if the state pays compensation?" she asked.

Despite the desperation in that question, I could only think: With what? Our inflated Reichsmark? The Americans' military script? Their green dollars? I'd learned that a continuing threat of counterfeiting made their greenbacks illegal, even for their soldiers. I shuddered as I remembered the woman on the train who'd said cigarettes were money and in my imagination saw again the towering wall in the store where guards checked military passes.

Frau Schuler spread the last of her seed-filled jam on bread turned hard and dry as she asked if I'd heard anything about a tailor near the students' prison in Heidelberg who was known to still have cloth. People brought food or shoes for his children, and traded. A printer would have paper. She said our neighbors insisted we had things that could be exchanged for food with a farmer who grew or killed it, but she'd looked throughout the house and couldn't find a single thing that such a man might see as useful. I accepted her bread and tea tinted water determined to find our answers. Instead, I altered clothes I'd worn as a child for the niece of a neighbor whose family had evacuated Stuttgart. The neighbor, in return, brought fresh fall apples from a sanctioned trip along the Neckar. In exchange for the contents of my father's office, a refugee physician, setting up practice, repaired our roof above the dormers. Over tea made from strawberry leaves I'd tried drying, he told me he'd escaped to the west after the British Royal Air Force, festering with thoughts of retribution since our bombs ravaged Coventry, obliterated Dresden. His teacup rattled in his hands as he described firestorms that, with the sound of a mighty organ, sucked oxygen from the air with such force hurricane winds were created. People, cars, animals of all sizes, were dragged into whirling centers. Clearing my father's office took two days because he had no transportation. He finished on the second day because he'd borrowed a wooden cart.

A family of German Catholics who'd been expelled from Poland was assigned to our home. Herr Ziegler's squat, square body, his sturdy legs, the directness of his gaze beneath his bushy eyebrows all marked him as a man who'd set off across the Warthegau with his wife and two young children, bringing little more than what they wore and an ancient Bible. Frau Ziegler seemed too frail to have made the journey. She was tiny, somewhat absent-minded, with questioning eyes and a prominent nose. The children were Tomas and Inge.

As the bleak days of July became a discouraging August, I finally gave in to an ache that never left me. I couldn't live another day remembering only enough of Günther to cause me pain.

Defying both French and American occupations, I arranged for a trip to Ludwigshafen. The man who agreed to help me cross the Rhine, at first refused. He said such a trip was both dangerous and futile. I should leave to the French that fetid ruin. Only Berlin had more air raids. But I offered him coal from my parents' cellar if he got me safely there and back. With winter almost on us, such a bribe was beyond refusing. On a morning when fog obscured the river, we made the crossing. The neighborhood Günther described as having such beauty was scored with craters, strewn with debris. Our troops had cut down every tree as they retreated. In the future, we'd mark the passing of years by the length of vines, the height of new trees that somehow flourished in the blackened rubble, but now I saw no one. Heard nothing. I decided no one could have survived and be living in those ruins and fled back to the Rhine. Beneath the cables of a bridge that no longer reached beyond the water's edge, I lost myself in the rhythm of the river waiting for the man who'd rowed me across. Dark wouldn't come for hours.

September passed in a repetitive blur.

During October, I worked in a formerly titled household helping an uncle bring order to his accounts, but he paid in increasingly worthless Reichsmark. Finally, he couldn't pay at all. After my last day with the baron, I walked beyond Frau Schuler's to the refugee-crowded home that had belonged to the Steynors. I stood quietly, grasping the fence, seeing in the twilight shadows the child I'd been with Eva. The summer I'd been sent to a Bavarian village to learn if I had my father's talent for the violin was the summer Eva had been sent to England with her mother. Herr Steynor had stayed behind to arrange for the sale of his home and the pharmacy that had been his father's. When the sirens came and he was taken to an area others explained to me as more fitting, another name appeared on a porcelain plaque above his door, but before our local Gauleiter moved into his house, the wide entry had been left open, like a public building, and the public entered. A distraught Frau Schuler had come to find my father. I remember her telling him that on a table near the kitchen was a plate of small apple-topped cakes she'd baked and given to our neighbor.

"For his journey?" I had asked. I don't remember if I had an answer.

In the shortening days that brought us to the edge of winter, bakeries closed for lack of fuel, while hungry children died from eating mushrooms they'd picked in the woods while their parents gathered berries, a rumor spread throughout the city that an insect in the potato fields had killed the harvest, and Anna came to Schwetzingen. Anna, looking fed and beautiful in fresh foreign clothes. I shouted when I saw my friend and demanded to know why she hadn't told me she was coming. Anna hadn't changed. "And how should I have told you? You have a special postal service? A secret telephone?"

Anna had recovered the laughing person I remembered from Aland Nord, her arms around new soldiers, but even as we embraced, I searched along the walk for Günther waiting to surprise me. I stepped outside. Anna brought me back and thrust a cardboard box into my hands. From the dark printed label, the way the contents slid and rattled, I knew American chocolate candy bars covered the bottom of the box, enough for trading. Anna had wanted me to be pleased.

"Günther isn't with you?" I asked as I led the way across the hall to a room heavy with furniture, dim from leaded glass. My father's library filled shelves to the ceiling. "I've heard the French ..."

"Oh, he's all right." Anna's eyes widened as we entered the formal room. Her fingers smoothed the finely woven fabric that covered every chair. "He convinced the Americans he belongs in their zone and he's registered in Mannheim." She sat where I pointed, carefully, on a horsehair sofa.

I steadied myself against a table. My delight at being with her vanished into red-faced humiliation that Günther hadn't come to share that news with me. In a stammering attempt to recover my composure, I asked about his family and Anna said they'd disappeared when Ludwigshafen's chemical plants were burning.

The doctor who'd repaired our dormer described finding bodies roasted brown or purple as the fires in Dresden had abated, bodies doubled over into pools of their own melted fat.

"All of his family? In the fires?"

"Well, apparently not Karl-Heinz, the next brother younger

than Günther. He was killed in Italy, and Otfried died in the bombing. Konrad volunteered for an anti-aircraft unit. Günther hadn't even known he was in the army. He said Konrad was so young when the military took him, he was issued a ration for sweets instead of tobacco." Anna licked a finger and touched a snag in the silk that smoothed her leg. Her lips kept moving but I barely heard. I just watched the slash of unfamiliar red as she was speaking, the prim way she sat stroking her new stockings. While Günther tried to find if any of his family had escaped and was living someplace other than their home, he'd stayed with Anna's sister but he was like a stranger. She said he hardly ate. He was gone each day by dawn. He was crazy for his family's safety and for fear they worried about him. Anna's sister had traded one of her iron pots for a shirt and trousers that fit him when his uniform became illegal. "Imagine the risk she was taking," Anna said. "The French believe surviving the war is a crime against them. They jail anyone who helps a former soldier."

I fought an image of Günther as immaculately fresh as Anna although I'd heard water wasn't wasted on washing clothes in Mannheim. Finally I managed to ask why he'd never come to me. Anna said she thought her sister said he'd come here twice but perhaps she was mistaken. She repeated he was different. He wasn't the man we knew along the trail. Her fingers slid across a table's polished wood and lifted a heavy ashtray turning it in her hand to read the etched signature of an artist whose name meant nothing on the utilitarian piece. Günther had finally found a message scrawled in chalk across a building. The message was for someone else but it led him to a woman who'd been in Ludwigshafen through the war and knew someone who'd been a member of a church where he'd sung in a choir. Anna said she and her sister guessed even before he told them. "We knew when we saw him there was no more hope."

That night she'd heard him crying. They were all in bed, but she'd heard. "Honestly, Renate, I wasn't prying, I wanted to help. He pretended to be sleeping but I knew he wasn't so I said his name." He was furious. He told her to go away and let him weep for the pain his family suffered. The hollow sound of metal against wood echoed in the silence as the ashtray settled back upon the table. "Now he does odd jobs for the Americans. It puts food in his stomach. And he's found a place to live close by my sister." She described a street in Mannheim where he lived.

I needed to be out in the open. I needed to suck into my lungs great gulping breaths of cold fresh air and let an exhalation drain away my hurt and anger.

"At least Schwetzingen is undamaged," Anna said as we stepped into the garden. "My sister said that between Mannheim and Ludwigshafen there was bombing night and day. I won't listen to her stories. Maybe the terror is in her bones. Maybe it will stay with her forever but don't tell me about it." Anna laughed. When she first got home, she said she couldn't look at her beautiful city but her sister had insisted she go out. She said Anna couldn't spend her life in a darkened room. "Can you imagine the time she was having with me and Günther?" Anna asked.

We walked along the street where the two of them had left me, where Günther had turned to call my name.

"Then one day, I did go out. I met a soldier," Anna said.

I mumbled something about the fraternization ban.

"Oh, that. What can the authorities do?"

Beyond the confines of the city where fertile soil once covered rows of coveted white asparagus, Anna chattered on about her niece as tall as she, her nephew returned from the army and not yet seventeen. She told me she hadn't stayed in her sister's small apartment, not even as long as Günther. She liked the soldiers in Mannheim. They were generous and full of fun, but different. Mannheim had the dark ones. Her neighbors had seen the color of their skin and started acting like old Nazis so she'd found a room in Heidelberg. She felt more than lucky because the room was near the Stardust Club, the only mess hall in the city where her new friends could take a German.

The Stardust Club. I knew the building. An imposing structure of pale stone along the river where an elegantly attired population had spent festive evenings before the war.

Dusk was close around us when we walked back into town, back through the castle's gate of iron curls and figures, to stand where arm-like buildings embraced a terrace. We pressed our faces against long windows, searching an interior where elector princes from the hill above Heidelberg had made their summer home before the soldiers. We saw nothing beyond the dirty glass. Finally we rested on a low smooth wall enclosing a silent fountain where angels played on swans and Orion rode a dolphin. Around us, in carefully even rows, cabbages were planted where once bloomed flowers of every season and carefully tended ornamental trees. Anna wondered, as she had so many times that afternoon, how I'd survive without the American soldiers. "It's not just that they feed me," she said. "We talk. They teach me English. They give me things."

I watched Anna pointing her new shoes, remembering other shoes worn beyond repairing by the time they were patched together in a hidden village in the mountains. Anna was the embodiment of survival. I looked out over the garden of cabbages someone had planted, also to survive. And Günther? Was he surviving? I pulled at my sweater until the sleeves stretched over my wrists and covered both my hands. In the night air I could feel the coming of winter.

The day after Anna's visit, I began roaming the countryside around Heidelberg, probing into farm villages, seeking out grizzled farmers, learning to be as inflexible as they. I didn't understand why they would want a Sevres vase or a Wedgwood platter, I just began trading my family's valuables for food, even as the man on the road to Mannheim had done.

*Berchtesgaden, 14. November 1945*

Dear Renate,

Isn't it fun to have letters again? And did you see the postmark? Where Hitler had his holidays. Roger and three of his friends asked me along on their leave and now I'm here, too.

The first night we stayed in a military Kaserne near Ulm. I hid on the floor of the car before we reached the guard gate and no one saw me, not the whole time I was there. Of course I never went near the barracks with the others. They stole blankets so I could sleep in the car. You'll laugh when I tell you I pee'd right there in the parking lot. It was like the mountains.

It's easier to get around in Berchtesgaden. The hotels are all taken for the soldiers but ours is nearly empty because the skiers are in Garmisch. The Americans own that city, too.

Each morning one of the guys brings breakfast to our room with as much real coffee as we can drink. They go to dinner without me, like in Ulm, but what they bring back! Chunks of steak! Tiny mushrooms cooked in butter! The kitchen packed a knapsack with more food than we could eat and, in spite of the cold, we climbed toward the Berghof. Today we'll walk around a lake.

Renate, you must meet Roger. He's so funny. I told him I'd like to see him out of uniform, and he put his shirt on backward. That wasn't what I meant at all but we laughed and laughed.

Oops, they're back.

My best to you and your family.

*Anna*

# Winter
## 1945-1946

The day of Anna's letter my mother didn't leave her bed. She didn't complain. She asked nothing that wasn't given to the others, but she stayed in bed in the tiny room she shared with my father. A sympathetic neighbor told me about a farmer near Seckenheim who planned to kill a cow that was long past breeding. The flesh would be more than I had for trading, but I was certain my mother's watch would buy meaty bones to make a warming soup. Warmth was an obsession since I'd sacrificed our coal for the wasted trip across the Rhine. Each time I left our house I searched for any kind of fuel. The smallest neglected piece went immediately in my pocket. I even burned some furniture which left my mother crying.

Dawn was only a suggestion the morning I left Schwetzingen. As I wrapped my winter coat around me, I told myself I'd share the soup with my kindly neighbor but I knew that wouldn't happen. Reciprocation had long since been abandoned. At the city limits I began to run, anxious to be in the farmer's small village before others' desperation made him drive a harder bargain. I'd dealt with the man before, I was sure the watch would please him, but this time he demanded cigarettes or coffee from the American soldiers' store. I thrust the watch toward him and he pushed my hand away. I shouted that short weeks before he'd taken my father's car in exchange for little more than potatoes and turnips, but he shouted back that a car is useless without Benzin and slammed his door.

I turned toward Heidelberg as the first hard snow of winter started. My face, my hands lost feeling. I had to find work. I found boarded storefronts, clogged courtyards, a few pedestrians clutching wraps against the cold. Each glint of light drew me to it. I pounded on each closed door. I found frowns if a door were opened. Shrugs. And then a soldier. Across from the Holy Ghost Church, near the Haus zum Ritter, he was suddenly before me, straddling the sidewalk to block my way. "I'll give you nylons," he'd said in crudest German and I had run from him.

Above the sunken arches of the Alte Brücke I stared into the wind-whipped river, taking in great painful gulps of freezing air. One gloved hand stretched the collar of my coat across my mouth, the other brought my mother's watch from my pocket. For one brief angry moment I wanted to dash it into the river, watch it splash through the surface of the water and disappear with the need it represented. Instead, I dropped it back in my pocket. Around me, the silenced darkened city was wrapped in its struggle to survive.

The memory of another river crowded in. An unnamed river at the base of a bluff on the long walk home. That time, too, I'd been gasping from exertion. Great laughing gulps of fresh spring air with Günther big beside me, and Anna, our bodies damp from the heat and from a steep climb up a hill. We'd been hungry, but the hunger was different. We'd laughed and caught at flying elbows as we raced each other down the slope, abandoning our packs, our heavy outer clothing, throwing ourselves forward into a sun-warmed pool. In the freshness of deep water, I dove beneath the surface to send Günther sprawling, roaring with him when he stumbled upright sputtering and wiping at his eyes. He caught my hands and held them. "You feel like playing?" he'd said and I felt his strength, the slickness of his body. "You have to catch me first," I'd said, twisting away and throwing myself across the surface of the water. Later, the two of us sat quietly in shallow water, our shoulders touching, waiting while Anna stroked toward us across the pool. When we turned back up the incline to find our clothes, I remember watching as Günther stood in the protection of a tree pulling the remnants of his uniform over his wet body.

Above the wind-swept river, a freezing gust caught at my coat. Out there, where this river met the Rhine, was Günther. Anger had kept me from him since Anna's visit. Anger and guilt and disappointment and the way hunger filled my time, but sometimes in the hidden corners of my mind where my thoughts were always private, I'd imagined finding his room. I whispered his name, and in that moment, my desire for him was greater than any need to help my parents.

Half stumbling in the darkness, I retraced my steps around a medieval archway, turning down from the bridge on time-worn stairs to a brick walk at the level of the river. No light penetrated to this darkness. I was alone. A solitary figure hunched against the cold, hurrying along an ice-slicked lower pathway shielded from the street. I heard the motor of a single car and looked up to see its headlights pierce the darkness but nothing more until the Stardust Club where my gloved hands clutched my ears against the lashing of women's voices calling out in English to the American men.

At the frail lacework of an emergency bridge built to carry a streetcar on a single track to Handschuhsheim, I scrambled away from the river, crossed a wide street to Bismarck Platz. Another. By the Bayrischerhof Hotel, two laughing American women, wrapped in the brightness of their heavy coats, hurried from their heated rooms over slippery tracks to an American restaurant in the Reichspost Hotel. There, I'd been told, black-coated waiters served steaming fragrant meals to the military's workers on linen-covered tables. I pulled my worn dark coat around me. At the corner a dull glow from inside a brown urban train illuminated the word MANNHEIM printed on a soiled board. I had to run to catch the supports on either side of an open doorway before the car crept forward. I thought I probably had enough Reichsmark to buy a ticket but with no permission to travel the twenty kilometers to Mannheim, I could only hope no authority would find me packed into this crush of strangers trying to reach a destination before curfew. My eyes closed against the stench of damp clothes on close-packed bodies, the swaying motion of the train. What was dignity? What was decorum? What did it matter that Günther hadn't come to me? I wanted the hardness of his body. It was no use asking again at the Arbeitsamt or the American employment office. I had just one way to feed my parents and Frau Schuler but I wanted Günther's love before I met the soldiers. I forced my hand into my pocket where my gloved fingers tightened on the rejected watch.

The broad front of the Rosengarten brought me bolting from the train. I hadn't known Mannheim well before the war and a terrible urgency lifted my heels as I raced into a sunken garden, stopping to breathe only when I reached the remnants of a fountain fringed by ice-taut grass. The district was as Anna described it. Across that broad street, beyond the stark skeletons of those circular buildings was a church with a single steeple. Two other buildings would stand nearby, whole among a block of burnt-out shells. Günther's room was created by a wall that blocked one end of an attic at the top of the taller of the two. I pushed away from the fountain, slipping on old and dirty snow. The blackened spire of a church was visible when I glanced up. Near here. Look. The finality of curfew with its military patrols brought me close to panic because only dark cavities of buildings loomed around me. Then, in another block of the architecturally laid-out city, I saw his building. Caryatids supported an iron balcony above the door. Anna told me it'd been an elegant hotel but I could smell the stopped-up toilets when I stepped into the lobby.

Through the noisy ride to Mannheim, in the frozen walk along the river, before that on the bridge, my only thought had been of the man whom I remembered. I knew the months had changed him but when I stood before the ill-fitting door to his makeshift room, I clenched my fist and pounded boldly. A soft lisping rasp of slippered feet moving closer sent me back into the shadows. The door opened. Günther lifted a candle that lit my face. "My God. Renate. Come in. Come in." He reached out to bring me forward, urging me to forgive his appearance. He'd been in bed. For warmth. His army coat was pulled over a thick sweater that covered worn pajamas.

I wanted to surprise myself, to behave in ways I couldn't yet imagine. There'd been times I thought him dead and here he was beside me. His arms closed around me and I opened my mouth to let it press against the coat so well remembered, imagining a lingering hint of wood smoke while my face was chafed by the cold and by the roughness of the fabric. "I heard about your family," I said. He scraped his only chair back from its place beside his table and gestured for me to take it. Only the slightest hesitation let me know he'd heard my comment. His answer was to ask about my family. "It's hard," was all I said, and then, "Anna told me how to find you." A narrow bench was pushed in close to the opposite end of his table. He lifted its cache of books and music to the floor before he brought it to the long side of the table and sat down close beside me. My gaze darted past him to a rough nightstand with a broken leg supported by more music, beyond that to his bed. It was low to the floor. Linen sheets worn soft with age were covered by a thin blanket. I turned from where the pressure of his body had recently left what warmth he may have found there. "Anna went to Berchtesgaden. Did you know?" I said.

"Her sister told me."

I didn't want to speak of Anna. Why had I mentioned Anna and her trip? Yes, she must have known it was illegal for a German staying in one of those grand hotels the Americans have taken for their soldiers. Yes, she told me what they ate. In my laughter I heard a note of falseness. From the question in his eyes I guessed Günther heard it, too. I pushed away from the table and paced the space his furniture permitted, pausing only to stare into the darkness beyond his lone, high window where illumination from a brittle moon reflected across an undulating sea of rubble. Wanting his love before I met the soldiers seemed so irrational in his presence, only the inevitability of blundering into an American patrol in this strange and hostile city kept me from bolting back into the stairwell, down the stairs, and out into the open to let the dark absorb my need to have his body.

Günther came to stand beside me. I must have flinched when his arm fell across my shoulder because the arm became a needed support. I let myself relax against him and he whispered that through all the ugliness of these last months, he'd been sustained by thoughts of when we were together in the beauty of the mountains. Our shared remembering became like painted dreams, blunting the reality beyond his window. But then he went too far. He laughed and said this mural of our mountain travels could only have been conceived by innocent children. "Innocent" cut through my relief as though a knife had slashed it. Nothing about me could be called innocent. I'd already lied. I'd already stolen. I was making plans to prostitute myself with those who brought about the devastation in which my innocence lay buried.

I know he felt me shudder. We turned away from the window and I was alert again to the bitterness of cold beyond his building, seeping through the walls, hovering in the corners. Conscious, too, of the dark circles under both my eyes, the pallor of my skin. I backed against his table, dizzy from a dozen dilemmas like a swirl of colors from a mature artist's brush. He removed his coat and wrapped its warmth around me.

From the storage in an incongruously ornate wardrobe filling a wall opposite the slope of his ceiling, he brought a box sealed in waxy paper and two heavy glasses. With a bottle of wine caught by his elbow, he fumbled through a drawer in his broken nightstand until his fingers closed around a corkscrew. My gaze caught on the bottle's garish label. I told him life had little meaning when it was nothing but a struggle for the next slice of bread, the next lump of coal. I despaired about the future and hating the present, turned for comfort to the past. He motioned me to his table and sat beside me, smoothing the leather on my gloved hands, telling me it was pointless to look back. Whatever was before me, I shouldn't be afraid. "We must live in the world as we find it. We have no other choice." He removed my gloves and chafed my icy fingers.

In a burst that left room for neither pause nor reflection, I began to detail my day, backward from the encounter with the soldier, through the futile hours seeking work, to the hopelessness of walking for hours to have the farmer reject as trinkets what I'd brought him. I asked Günther in what world he'd have me live. The one whose farmers demanded cigarettes and coffee from the soldiers' store? I recounted every humiliating detail about another day when I'd gone to an American barracks, stopping soldiers at the gate, willing to wash clothes, shine shoes, run errands. His eyes turned blank as unused paper when I told him how the soldiers laughed. They weren't shy about describing what they wanted from me.

Releasing my hands, Günther opened the box he'd placed between us and withdrew a waxed sheath of white foreign-looking crackers. He shook a few onto the table. I'd had nothing to eat since early morning but I couldn't stop or even touch them. I told him about the struggling family who'd been assigned to our rooms upstairs. About Hartmut. About Paul. About my need to help Frau Schuler whose pension was no longer paid because her husband was a Nazi. I told him my mother had forsaken hope and that would kill her. I didn't want to take my father's violin, but perhaps the farmer wouldn't want that either. He didn't want my mother's watch. I found the fragile timepiece in my pocket and threw it on the table. It spun around and, for a moment before it was still, ticked softly from the motion.

I began demanding answers, for Günther to tell me what to do, but he was arguing that not too many years ago, Germany had produced a Martin Luther, a man who defied the greatest power in the then known world. Yet in the years where I tried to see such glory, we'd become a nation of marionettes, leaping about while a madman pulled the strings.

I had no answer.

He crushed some of the crackers and swept the crumbs into his palm before he released them to an ashtray. "Doesn't that business in Nürnberg tell you something?" he asked. "Smaller tribunals are happening all over Germany, ferreting out little Nazis, judging defendants by degree. Doesn't that tell you we must be responsible for our own decisions?"

He was cluttering my mind. I couldn't think about our country. My mother was already curling down into her bed, eating only when I urged her. My father no longer played his violin, only wrapped his arms around it, drifting in a place where none of us could reach him. Günther said an acquaintance, another singer, had told him of work in American offices. I accused him of not listening when I'd told him I'd been to every kind of office, that I'd asked, no, I'd pleaded everywhere for any kind of work. "My mother won't survive the winter if I don't …"

"If you don't what?" His bench clattered back as he pushed around it. I had to fill his silence. I said I knew the Americans could be kind. Our household ate for a week from a sack of potatoes an American soldier gave to Tomas, the Zieglers' boy. Had I mentioned the Zieglers? It didn't matter. I told him Frau Ziegler made house shoes from yarn inside a broken ball another soldier gave to Inge. He said it didn't take incarceration for him to recognize them as a source of his survival. He'd cleaned American boots, he'd hefted American luggage, he'd sung at their gatherings if they asked, and sometimes he didn't even remember that not too long ago, his mission was to kill them before they killed him.

Through all the years that have now followed, I've wondered how I missed the word incarceration. Perhaps my attention had been diverted by his stepping behind me, by my wondering if he'd put his arms around me. His hands settled on my shoulders. He said there were ways to get what the farmer wanted and I pushed his hands away. Standing, face to face, I demanded to know if he was telling me to be a whore.

Our breath hung in little puffs before our faces as he searched every angle of my face, finally reaching around me for the bottle of wine, tipping it over each of our glasses. "*Liebfrauenmilch*," he said. "The Americans like it. Some months ago I gave this bottle to Anna's sister but yesterday when she saw me again, she gave it back." I still remember a nick in the rim of one of the glasses.

In a voice lowered almost to a whisper, he asked why I'd come to Mannheim at this hour. We both knew I couldn't leave because of curfew. My voice must have been beseeching when I said I needed his help. His eyes came alive with puzzled anguish. "Help you? Me? No. Not in this."

He'd forgotten Paul's name but I knew what he was saying when he asked if I and "that neighbor's son" had ever climbed into bed together. I shook my head and his expression changed. "You've not heard from him in years and the Russian winters are cold so on this cold night you come to me. What kind of game are you playing?"

"Günther, I ..."

"Günther, I what? Be careful, Renate. Pride is a German strength but also a German weakness."

Only then he tried to hold me but I stood stiff and silent in his embrace. He stumbled away. At his makeshift door, his head sunk between his shoulders. His clenched fists hit the wall. "Did you really think I could tell you to be a whore?" He stopped. When he turned, I was looking at a void, a void who suddenly wrenched his sweater over his head, saying we had the night before us. Maybe I needed someone to blame for my decision. Or maybe I needed someone to hate because I was too self-righteous to hate myself. He was groping at my coat, fumbling with the buttons, splitting a seam where the sleeve met the body of the garment.

I felt a chill as my shoulder bared, warmth where his lips followed.

"It's all right," he said. "Go ahead, hate me."

How many times since those first days in early summer had I tried to imagine what it would be like to know his body? How many times in the hungry months that followed had I sought relief in imagining the two of us, our arms around each other. Now here was everything I'd hoped for. With my fingers digging in his hair, I rose to his hands in breathless sobbing, heard cries from my own throat and from his. Eventually, we fell back in mutual exhaustion.

A pallid dawn filled every corner of his shabby room before I opened my eyes to find he was awake before me, lying quietly so I could continue sleeping. I reached out, finding the back of his head where his hair was curling, bringing his face toward mine, and he was kissing me again, gently now, caressing every curve, finding every hollow, but in this gray world so close to sleep, I could taste the hunger on his lips, feel it in the sharpness of his hipbones. As we slowly moved toward orgasm, I had to fight to obliterate an image of the soldiers.

"Breakfast?" he asked at last. "I have crackers."

"Not yet. I need a toilet." The toilet was down the stairs and along a hall with a dirty carpet. He told me to wear his coat.

Back in his room, back in his arms, I asked why he'd never come to Schwetzingen. As Anna had suggested, he'd been there twice. The first time, he'd tried to explain to my uncomprehending father why he couldn't stay. He hadn't found his family. The second time, when my father closed the door, he'd roamed the streets of Schwetzingen asking strangers if they knew me. If they could tell him how to find me. My teeth clenched on remembered grit from fallen houses as I described my day in Ludwigshafen. The light changed. The sun moved into shadow. I told him of my weeping as I hid beneath the bridge, praying he'd miraculously appear from all that devastation and find me. In the hall below his room, footsteps stopped and then retreated. He said he couldn't have found me. Shortly after his second visit to Schwetzingen, he'd been confined in an American stockade. Last night when he opened his door, he thought Anna had told me of his release and I'd come to find him. I twisted free, hugging his thin blanket around my shoulders as my ears filled with that discordant bleating. I saw him struggling among protesting refugees Americans were still forcing into trains heading east and that became confused with an earlier train that had carried Eva's father in that direction. I began bursting with excuses. Maybe some answer on his Fragebogen aroused suspicion. Maybe the fires that swept Ludwigshafen had spared a file. His assurance that he'd been cleared for now or the Americans wouldn't have released him was only partially convincing. He had no discharge papers. He couldn't even get a tobacco ration without them. I was consumed by the same hollowness of loss, the same futility of hoping for a future as the afternoon I'd stared into the muddy waters of the Rhine. I rushed into another incoherent explanation. If a Nazi neighbor had been jealous of this room ...

He caught my face in both his hands telling me no war is cleanly finished. There are always actions no one talks about or thinks about if they are lucky. He said even honorable men are capable of dishonorable actions.

I shuddered and he brought the blanket back around us.

He said, "The Czechs, the Russians, the Poles, they took their revenge on individuals, leaving German sympathizers flopping in the street with hacked Achilles tendons, nailing collaborators to barn doors. Men stripped women bare in public places and shaved their heads for loving German soldiers." He said, "Americans need their vengeance, too. An American government official named Morgenthau demands the quarantine of Germany from the rest of Europe. Their document of occupation actually prohibits economic rehabilitation."

The crowding, of course, the cold, the dirt that clung to everything in a nation once obsessed by hygiene. We both knew there wasn't enough work for all who needed it and now he was telling me the Americans had made certain there was little hope for any in the future. I clutched my ears against the voices of the women by the river, wanting to forget my parents and Frau Schuler, the American plenty that was so close I could smell it through an open window, see it in discarded wrappers.

"Renate, stop. I'm free now. I'll help. If I don't resume my lessons I'll have more time. I'll work harder."

"And divide what you earn to support four more?"

"American families are expected by spring. They'll bring opportunities."

"By spring?" I brought my arms above his covers to sweep around his room. Crackers on his table, that was now. Ice not melting on his window, that was now. "You don't have enough for two and I have three more." If I had three children, I'd be all right. Children were on the street. They're very appealing. My old people kept to their rooms while I worried about what uncontrolled inflation was doing to my father's pension. "Americans feed old people and refugees at *Schloss* Langenzell. Do you think I should send my parents and Frau Schuler there?"

"Frau Schuler must have a family."

"A sister living with nine others in a summer cottage across from the ruins of Neckargemuend."

His mouth crushed down to stop my speaking and for a moment I responded to his desperation, until my fists began to flail against his shoulders. Cold was an explosion when he bolted from the bed, the heel of both his palms pressed hard against his temples. He told me nothing in his life had prepared him for the way he loved me. The only thing that kept him sane during those months in that military prison were his dreams of a future with me beside him as his wife, the mother of his children. How could I expect him to accept my impossible decision? He reached for the heavy coat that I'd discarded.

I was dressed and sitting at his table across from the window blurred with ice when he returned. We didn't speak. We didn't look at one another. We drank cups of hot, black, bitter ersatz coffee Günther made from water heated on a camping stove and picked at the crackers he'd spread across his table. He asked if I wanted him to walk with me to the streetcar. I told him that wasn't necessary, but he followed me down the long flights of stairs to the entrance of his building where he reached around me to push the door. A chill blast sucked at my good-bye as I stepped into the open. By the time I passed the fountain where I'd rested the night before, clouds had slid across the city creating a strange world without shadow.

The last of my Reichsmark bought a ticket on the next urban train, and with my face pressed against a frost-covered window, I stared back across a broken field of rubble, back toward Günther's building, back toward his room beneath the eaves. I saw nothing through the blurring.

I covered my eyes with clenched fists and wondered if the farmer's wife made soap.

Mannheim, 8. December 1945

Dear Renate,

What can I say? Can all men be as stubborn as Germans?

I'll be truthful as we must always be together. I was thrilled. We can have such fun. I even know of a room in Heidelberg that will be vacant soon. You can't legally live there, of course, but I know a man who'll take care of that. You'll be surprised how little you'll have to pay him.

Don't misunderstand me. I'm sorry for the way Günther is reacting. I can even imagine it's wonderful to be so loved but terribly restricting. What does it matter how we frolic?

For now, my warmest greetings to you and your family for the coming Christmas season. I'll write when the room is free.

Anna

I crumpled Anna's letter to keep from reading and shoved it into a pocket of my coat. Outside a wall of cold was relieving in its stillness but I nourished an unreasoning jealous anger. Günther had gone to Anna. With fists pushing into both pockets, I headed for the woods behind the castle but clawing for roots, even with frozen fingers, was reminiscent of the mountains. Tears froze on my cheeks. At Anna's sister's he'd have shaken her nephew's hand, put a friendly arm around her niece. A laughing, teasing Anna would have taken him to the kitchen where she'd made real American coffee in a tall stained pot.

My dirty fingers spread her letter and I read it one more time.

Cutting back through the castle gardens I crossed behind its Moorish Pavilion, a full-sized ornamental building made for royalty at play. In the first days of occupation a group of American officers had ignored their orders banning fraternization and created a private nightclub there. Beds and tables had been seized from closed hotels and restaurants. Musicians, bartenders, cooks were bought with cigarettes and coffee. I took a closer look around the pavilion's daytime silence drawn by the reflection from a pale winter sun on a scattering of bottles. Some of the bottles weren't quite empty. Prepared to run if someone saw me, I gathered every one. What alcohol I could glean together I would trade for eggs or bacon drippings. Even the glass could be of value. I hated the Americans for what had been discarded. I hated them for everything I needed. At home, I took the bottles to the basement to hide them from my mother's questions before I uncrumpled Anna's letter to look for answers I knew from my first reading were not there.

Anna's next letter arrived one cold morning as the year crept toward its ending. This time I walked with it, unopened, to stare at a small side garden through a window in our hallway door. A tree branch I'd swung from as a child had dropped in last month's storm. It lay covered by more recent snow. I read this letter slowly. The room in Heidelberg would be vacant in a fortnight. Anna had already contacted the man who'd take care of the documentation. Before that afternoon was over, I'd made excuses to my parents about work that required a move to Heidelberg. My father held his violin. "He'll miss the music," my mother said.

I worried through several days and anxious nights about the way to tell Frau Schuler. She'd understand as my parents hadn't but she'd ask no questions if I told her with them present. I needed that silence. I needed time. I needed for both of us to absorb the absolute inevitability of my decision. The curfew had been lifted for Christmas Eve but the difficulties of travel would keep Frau Schuler from her sister. The Zieglers would spend the holiday with another Catholic family. I'd tell her Christmas day. I made a cake from an egg that I'd been saving, stirring the yolk with malt coffee and milled flour I'd traded for my bread ration. Whipped egg white mixed with apple juice was a decorative cream. Our family dinner was salt herring the Americans had added to our ration and potatoes I'd traded for my mother's watch. We spoke of Hartmut and of Paul, of festive dinners when Professor Schuler was alive. Frau Schuler's voice was high with false merriment for the season as she told us Paul would have been eager for next month's elections. He'd always been interested in political advancement. She said that he'd once confessed that when he'd achieved high office, he expected the two of us to marry. He'd told her that with my natural dignity and beauty I'd make a perfect politician's wife.

I bent for a linen napkin my father had let slide unheeded to the floor.

When we finished our meal, we left the dishes on the table as though we still had Gerda and sat in the faded grandeur of the main salon with blankets stretched across our shoulders. I leaned toward Frau Schuler. She was beaming. "I've taken a room in Heidelberg," I said. "I'll leave Schwetzingen by the time of the elections."

A cold grew in her eyes. An Arctic cold. A clear blue cold of deep crevasses. She wrapped her blanket across her head, clutching her fingers around the fabric. "It is God punishing us," she said at last.

The sun shone for the first time in weeks the day I met Anna by the wood-covered Hercules fountain in the Rathaus square. Every roof ledge sparkled. With her arms spread wing-like behind her, she came skating across slick cobblestones, whooping joyously about our new adventure as our embrace became unsteady grasping. A lumpy bag swung between us. I'd determined not to mention Günther but Anna was bursting with details about the day they'd been together. There wasn't coffee. He'd asked that they seek privacy and they'd left the shabby comfort of her sister's small apartment to walk in semi-darkness though it was day. Anna's voice roughened to imitate Günther's when she told me how he'd pleaded for her to stop what I was planning. She exploded into laughter when she said she'd demanded to know if he'd come to her to cast a stone.

We turned into Untere Strasse, where cobblestones sloped to the center, then Pfannengasse, an alley curving toward the river. Ignoring the birthplace of Friedrich Ebert, president of Germany's long ago failed Weimar Republic, Anna chattered on about how she'd defended the American soldiers, telling Günther they liked to talk, they liked to dance. She said his voice was as dark, as bitter as the day, when, walking faster, stumbling on a crack in the sidewalk, he'd said they both knew there'd be more than talk and dancing. Covering his face with his hands, he'd said every time he closed his eyes, he saw a stranger whose arms were filled with an abundance he couldn't offer. His empty hands spread out to embrace the freezing air before he jammed them in his pocket. When she'd reminded him he was the one who insisted we must live in this world as we found it, he'd said, "My God, don't blame me!"

At the walled expanse before Mannheim's palace, Günther strode ahead. Without looking back to see if Anna followed, he turned through an archway into a tangled park behind the building. Anna said she ran to catch him, calling him an obstinate fool. "Life is meant to be enjoyed," she'd said. "How can you enjoy life the way you're acting?" A harsh wind off the Rhine threw her words back against their faces.

He'd asked how I could even consider what I was planning.

She'd asked what else I should consider.

"You didn't answer my question," he'd said. They'd almost reached the river. "When I think of her on her back for any soldier, I can't breathe."

"Then stop breathing," she said she'd told him. "What good will that do? If it bothers you so much, don't think about the other."

He'd turned in one convulsive movement. "Anna, I can't. I love her."

Anna seemed surprised those words had stopped me and reached back to grasp my hand. "Who are we to put conditions and call it love?" she asked. "Don't we all have things that need to be forgiven?"

Near the end of Pfannengasse she paused before a curving building with two separated entries. Above one was a faded plaster horse's head. Before the other she dug into her lumpy bag and brought out a leather strap binding two long keys together. As she shook and twisted one key in the rusted lock she said she and Günther had walked along the Rhine where thick, uneven platforms of ice reached out from the river's edge. From there they could have seen the broken bridge where I'd waited the day I went to Ludwigshafen. I wanted Günther to have looked for the bridge and thought of what I'd told him, but Anna said he'd turned to stare back at the city, at the blackened, burned-out shells of buildings whitened by a cover of snow.

The door's lock snapped open to Anna's forcing and she gave a cry of triumph as we stepped inside to a space not quite deep enough for two. It was dark and reeked of dampness, above us an empty light socket hung on a long black wire. As we climbed a steep flight of stairs, angry voices reached us, but this was not a house where others paid attention. Anna used the second key at a narrow door and pushed before me into a room caught in pale sunlight filtering through the mottled glass of a single window. A scarred nightstand was pushed against a table across from a low chair with dirty orange cushions and wooden arms. I hovered on the threshold watching Anna smoothing sheets on a narrow bed, telling me she knew a cook from the American hospital in Kirchheim. She said a cook was a real advantage. He'd bring me things I couldn't yet imagine. She said she'd send him over if I wanted, but I couldn't meet with Anna's friend. I had no acceptance of myself as Günther once said of her, only revulsion, a suspension of belief. I clenched my fists against a shrillness I heard rising in my voice.

"Wouldn't it be easier if you only went with men I sent you?" Anna said.

I didn't want it to be easy. I needed to punish myself for what I was planning. I reached out to close the wardrobe doors which were hanging open but instead stood staring at a newspaper-lined interior where Anna had placed a folded towel and an extra khaki-colored blanket.

"Renate, do you have condoms?" She took a packet from her pocket and forced it into my hand. She said I must insist each soldier wear one. They had their own. Condoms were issued at the company level, but I must keep some handy. I must think of the problems I'd have if I got pregnant. She told me I must always insist on eating first, then if anyone made demands I was resisting, I could threaten him with their police because I'd already eaten. He'd know I'd do it because their police kept good order, at least here in the city. She lifted the lumpy bag she'd left by the table and withdrew three newspaper-wrapped pieces of coal. "I'm not sure you realize how much you have to learn," she said and opened the front of a low, squat stove, placing the coal on its crumpled paper into the dark interior. "Do you know enough to walk away from anyone who may be brutal? Not to stay with anyone who gets drunk. Are you listening to what I tell you?" Clearly frustrated by my silence, she rose, saying a friend was expected at her room in about an hour. It was special he was off this early and they had plans. She brought a half-used book of matches from her pocket and threw it on my table. "Renate, do you know how to use your fingernails? Not scratching. Gently." She laughed at what must have been my expression and patted my cheek before she kissed it. "I'll check on you tomorrow."

Closing the door drained the last of my strength and I leaned against it with my forehead on the panel. I could hear Anna whistling as she stepped into the street. It was no use longing to drag the door open, no use longing to escape down the stairs and out into the open. Across the river, among the trees on Heiligenberg I could fall to earth, clawing at its darkness, but what was in the dark but more dark and more dark to follow after? I flung my fraying knapsack onto the bed, my hat after, and draped my coat over the wardrobe's only hanger. A small bright key turned easily in the lock but even as it clicked shut, the door swung open.

Kneeling before the stove, I adjusted Anna's coal and struck one of her matches. In the brief flame before the paper blackened, I thought of Günther triumphantly lighting twigs and grasses in the mountains and a wail tightened my throat. What strength I had left was barely enough to quell my howling as my fingers dug into the rusted heating grill. Later I could try to cook there.

Water from a single tap above a basin in the corner filled a bowl I found beneath it. I placed the small bath on the table not quite square against the wall and, stripping naked, scrubbed myself with a corner of the rough towel Anna had provided. I had no soap.

I was early at the temporary bridge. The last light of day still reached across the Rhineland plain, sparkling in snow-packed corners. A few women gathered in clusters of two or three. The snow corners turned steel blue and disappeared in darkness as more soldiers crossed from Bismarck Platz, and more women, until a thin receptive line stretched all the way to the Stardust Club. Only a rusted guardrail separated me from the wind-whipped river, but I couldn't bring myself forward, not if I had to stand frozen to the rail until morning came with its pale light to warm me into mobility again. Hard night closed around me and there were as few women as earlier in the evening.

"Ya wanna dance, Schatzie?"

The soldier had the darting movements of a chicken, an enormous chicken with flat yellow eyes filling the hollows and a half-smoked cigarette dangling beneath his heavy-nostriled, pecking nose.

"Ya wanna dance, Schatzie?"

I turned away.

"Okay."

I clutched his heavy khaki sleeve. "I like to dance. I'm a good dancer."

His thick-soled government-issued shoes moved out across the pavement and he motioned me to follow. He didn't speak. When we reached the Stardust Club, he walked before me up broad stairs and across a lobby into a columned ballroom. A small band played from an elevated stage. At one of the tables, he ordered drinks instead of food. With each drink, he became more clumsy, leaning heavily as we danced. His growth of beard from morning scratched my face and his strong odor mixed with smoke and drink to assail my nostrils. I'd thought my last scrap of pride had vanished into my family's hunger but I couldn't bring myself to scoop up the cigarette butts he was crushing in an ashtray even though I'd seen a woman buy a fist-sized lump of pork fat with fewer than he discarded. At a break in the dancing I took my coat and excused myself to find a toilet but went beyond it through a heavy side door where all my determination left me and I shrank against the stone facing on the building.

"Are you ill, Fräulein?"

I looked up into the face of another soldier. I saw that he was small and clean and pressed, but I saw more than that. I saw my parents waiting, and I saw Frau Schuler. My eyes closed and I saw a child's drawing of a golden sun suddenly tempered with black coal and white lard, purple cabbage, and yellow cheese. "I'm hungry," I said.

He bought me food before he took me to my room. Toward morning, he left me cigarettes to be traded with the farmer.

From the distance of time I've managed to look back on those uncertain days with some dispassion although I've never been able to accept a reason for not returning to Schwetzingen as soon as I'd acquired enough to ease my family's hunger. My reality was so vague, with so few absolutes, nothing was really true or false. I don't remember when I began to leave my crowded room and go out in the daylight looking for men who were looking for me, but I do remember believing such daytime meetings were needed to pay my bribe to Anna's contact who'd insisted on more than she'd suggested. I also deluded myself by thinking I needed to accumulate enough to prove what I was doing was not only necessary but productive. Of course, the irrefutable truth was that I couldn't face my parents and Frau Schuler. I was so repulsed by my own body I found it hard to touch myself or look in any mirror. Each man added another layer to my loathing and I punished myself by seeking out another man. Still, through it all, I was so haunted by my family's desperation I couldn't endlessly delay. One day I just pushed what I had into two string bags and started out toward Schwetzingen. Cold seeped through my shoes but I trudged on, trying to concentrate on what I carried. The cigarettes, tinned meat, soap, and chocolate came from the soldiers' store. A fat package of powdered potatoes I'd been told would make a meal if I added boiling water could only have been stolen from some mess hall's kitchen. I spent several kilometers wondering what exchange had bought the fraying Reichsmark I'd stuffed into my pocket, but after Waldorf I had no thought beyond forcing one frozen foot in front of the other. I wasn't even aware I'd entered Schwetzingen until I looked up and realized trees that had lined the avenue since I could remember were gone. I began to hurry. At the corner of my street an aura of quiet made me break into a run. "What is it?" I demanded of Frau Schuler as my bags burst open on the hallway floor.

"Your mother, Renate. The Zieglers helped me move her to your upstairs room. It's where the light stays longest."

In the high-ceilinged bedroom, my eyes went first to the slight figure of my father who stood silhouetted against a window and then to an outline just visible beneath the blankets on the oversized bed. My mother's face was ashen against the pillow. Her shallow breathing barely moved the cover across her breast. I fell to my knees, leaning forward. Her lips formed words but no sound followed.

"Why didn't you send for me?" I cried. But of course no one knew where to find my wretched room except Anna.

Little of what followed remains with me. Frau Schuler preparing bits and pieces from my sacks. All of us around a table. Frau Ziegler had taken on the duty of stealing branches from the castle garden while her husband made the long, discouraging forays into the country with whatever Frau Schuler thought might please a farmer, often returning with only enough to feed the children. Tomas and Inge were unnaturally subdued. My father uncomprehending. In the darkest hours of the night, it was Frau Schuler who touched my mother's eyes, straightened her arms close by her body, and guided my father into the hall so Frau Ziegler could clean the body.

She led me to the small salon where we sat on an ornately carved dark wood chest brought from China by an uncle in the early days of Hitler. There she held me while I wept. For my mother. For my father lost in his confusion. For the Zieglers who couldn't feed their children. I wept for shame. Mine. My country's. Choked on tears for our survival. I wept for Herr Steynor who loved his garden where laundry now profaned his bushes. And I wept for Günther and all that kept him from me as he struggled for expiation from a past he couldn't integrate into his life.

In Gerda's small back room, Frau Schuler helped me find a black skirt and a black blouse that covered my arms and my throat. I pulled black stockings over my legs and changed my own for black-laced shoes. The mourning clothes my mother wore when her only son had died I put on for my mother before I went back upstairs to sit in a chair beside my father.

When morning returned, Frau Schuler with it, I announced I was going to Mannheim. I'd thought I was beyond confronting Günther but through the night he'd kept intruding on my thoughts. It was as if he had to hear before I could accept my loss. Frau Schuler dug into her pocket for a few of the Reichsmark I'd brought from Heidelberg. Enough for a ticket on one of the rare buses and then the urban train.

The outline of the Rosengarten was starkly familiar, as was the church with the single steeple. I remember walking calmly along the desolate streets but by the time I'd pushed through the door below the caryatids, my heart was racing. I took the stairs by twos. At the top, Günther's door was padlocked. I slid to the floor, my back against his wall, plagued by a memory of how unambiguous he'd been at our last meeting but I never thought of leaving. I spent the time trying to devise a dignified way to approach our meeting until I heard the heavy entry door fall shut below me and Günther's familiar footsteps scraping on each stair. We met on a lower landing by a stranger's door. I forgot everything except finding solace in his arms. "It's mother," I said.

"Come," he said when I was still. "I've things in my room that we'll be needing." To the newspaper-wrapped apples he pushed into his pockets, he added cigarettes he'd been saving for his lessons and cocoa in a commissary bag. He returned with me to the darkened house in Schwetzingen to greet Frau Schuler, to formally meet my father, to stand with us at the family plot when my mother was buried close by the grave of Friedrich Ebert.

In the days he spent with us, Günther took over the care of my father, calming his confusion. While my father napped he sat with Tomas and Inge and answered endless questions. As a natural part of our extended family he lingered with the rest of us greeting those who'd come to our home after the funeral, but as the last of our guests was leaving, he said he was expected back in Mannheim.

My mother's death didn't change the cold, the empty cupboards, the need to provide for those of us still living and I prepared to return to Heidelberg, spending my last hours in the music room with my father where I could try to keep Heidelberg at a forgettable distance by remembering the hours my family spent with music. With Hartmut. With my mother humming softly. While Günther had been with us, Heidelberg was mentioned only once, and that time only named, but his haunted look had hardened. He didn't move but something in him pulled away. I was beyond trying to imagine what battles could still be raging in his mind.

From my place at the piano, I heard the front door open.

"Do you want to take a walk?" Günther asked. His eyes were dull with pain but he was smiling. "We haven't done one for a while."

I didn't answer. Not right away. I just stood there staring and then I laughed out loud. I grabbed my hat, my coat, my muffler. When we stepped outside, I put my hand in his.

# Spring 1946

*A*pale light from behind the hills above the castle seeped into my consciousness. A red-tinged dawn light promising March would offer little change from February's frigid weather. My arms reached out into the cold and a throb of wakefulness stretched full into my body. In my half-dozing dreams, I'd been sleeping in the mountains, comforted by Günther's coat across our bodies. Often, in my wretched room, I went back in time to find him and was freed by those innocent weeks together. The kaleidoscopic brilliance of our night in Mannheim was too painful to remember compared to the profanity of my life now. Curling back down, I pulled the covers over my head, but under their protection was the scent of another soldier. It flipped me to my back, my elbows tight against my body. That one had eyes of faded blue whose expression held both scorn and laughter. Before him, squinting eyes and short fat probing fingers. I tossed aside my blankets, dressing quickly, trying to forget my struggles not to shrink away while the soldiers stripped my clothes with harsh caresses, contorted my body to their wishes, groped, and labored until cigarettes were thrown across my table, sometimes tattered Reichsmark, or the soap.

On our January walk through the frozen fields behind the castle, Günther and I shared frantic kisses, but he'd said he wouldn't return to Schwetzingen. He said he couldn't stand before my father and Frau Schuler until he was able to protect me. I was left to wonder if our vulnerabilities would ever be anywhere but on the surface.

When we met in Mannheim we were too careful with each other, too courteous. Alone together, we were too hesitantly responsive. It was as if he thought, we thought, our desperate need to be together would be at risk if he touched me in any way that was reminiscent of the unacknowledged life I traded to the soldiers.

On my last visit to Schwetzingen, I'd found a scribbled postcard telling me Günther had been allowed to sing in a concert. This was the day we'd look for a review of his performance in the Mannheimer Zeitung, that city's only newspaper which would be spread out in a long display across the front of the newspaper's office. I tugged an extra sweater over my head against dark clouds already dulling the red sunrise, moving quickly because increasingly reliable schedules would allow him to be waiting when my urban train ground to a stop near the Rosengarten.

He grasped my hand as I descended, telling me Horst Wegner had been in the audience the night of his concert. Minor critics had called Günther a man with exceptional gifts, a man with a larger purpose, but praise from Horst Wegner, a wizened man but Mannheim's foremost critic, could make a difference in his future. Any thought of any soldier was lost in our excitement as we splashed through puddled streets toward the newspaper's office, until a group of enlisted men from the segregated companies in Mannheim's Transportation Motor Pool appeared around a corner. I clutched Günther's arm. He looked back after the passing soldiers. America's system of segregation kept dark men away from Heidelberg, or Schwetzingen, and their difference frightened me. "Don't draw away when you have no reason," he'd said and another memory crowded in. The first time I'd seen Herr Steynor with a star sewn on his jacket, the day was rainy, like that day. I'd passed him near Frau Schuler's. He'd smiled, but his eyes were clouded and his fingers drifted up to touch the yellow emblem. How is Eva? I wanted to ask. By this time, Eva had gone to England, but a withdrawal from the difference made me turn away from the father of my friend. I started running as soon as I was out of sight around a corner.

At the Mannheimer Zeitung office, where we'd often been the only readers, a crowd obscured our access. Günther laughed. "Surely they can't all be curious about how I sang." We pressed forward to the smudged glass where the usual black headlines reported news from the trial going on in Nürnberg. Beside them was a display of glossy pictures. People lying naked, stacked like cords of wood. Bulldozers shifting rigid corpses into trenches. I'd deliberately avoided looking at such pictures when they'd been circulated early in the occupation. I'd dismissed them as American propaganda. But here they were in a newspaper office, substantiating survivors' testimony given in an open court. My startled gaze darted from a sagging breast, a flaccid penis, to skin stretched thin across a knobby hipbone. I clung to Günther's arm unable to look away from a group of naked women cowering to shield the exposure of their bodies on a snow-dotted expanse of parade field while black-overcoated SS officers examined them with obvious contempt.

The crowd parted for a man whose slim patrician features were partially hidden between his blocked felt hat and a soft furred collar. His leather-gloved hands splayed across the window as he shouted that the exhibit was a hoax. An exaggeration by the Allies. I whispered to Günther that I'd read of such displays in a newspaper wrapped around a cabbage I'd traded from a farmer. I'd saved the paper for Frau Schuler. He demanded to know if she was another who would deny it. Frau Schuler had said when families on each street were taken, she hadn't put all of the families from everywhere together. She'd only begun to suspect when she heard about so many. I'd wanted Frau Schuler to tell me there were no guards who reassured their victims before the disinfecting showers, that no factory owner worked a hungry man to death. I didn't want to wonder if my father knew about hospitals where diseases were induced and left untreated. My genteel mother, did she know about such places? The medical community was among Hitler's earliest supporters. They'd ostracized their Jewish colleagues before such action was made law. Frau Schuler had said Herr Steynor petitioned Professor Schuler for help in his last attempt to leave the country. I didn't want to know if our neighbor's desperation brought him to my father. I edged away, pulling Günther with me. I couldn't think about the Steynors in relation to those naked bodies.

Needing to walk where paths had been and children playing, we fled to Luisen Park.

"You heard no rumors?" Günther asked.

In Aland Nord our rumors had been about high officers who carried poison in their pockets so they'd not be taken by the Russians.

"The killing camps were a human invention. Human administered. Human maintained. How dare we call ourselves human when we've done that?" I told him I couldn't think about it, and he said, "Can't, or won't?"

"It doesn't matter. I didn't know."

"You mean you didn't pay attention. Renate, think."

The transports left from so many stations in the center of our cities, in broad daylight. The trains had guards. Secretaries must have typed reports. Accountants must have done the math.

"The murder of so many millions took the complicity of what? Tens of thousands?"

Ruts in the path were dark puddles from the rain, the trees a barren starkness. From the shattered city all around the park came dark and haunted shadows: Jewish doctors, dentists, lawyers unable to offer their skills to an Aryan population, submitting passports stamped with the letter J. I'd been twelve the summer of 1938, when Jewish real estate was transferred to Aryan owners. I remembered no outraged protest from my parents or Frau Schuler. Twelve was old enough to know Jewish athletes couldn't compete in our sports arenas or attend our movies, but I never asked a question.

Günther said, "People disappeared. Did you wonder where they were taken?"

"To someplace for reorientation." A child's answer. A child's explanation. Frau Schuler said it was easy to think the detainees could survive by working hard and obeying orders.

A wind from across a lake cut through our clothing and Günther opened his coat to shield me. A stranger's coat he'd brought home from a trader's market. I wondered if the stranger was a Jew who'd left it behind when he was taken. I shivered in its protection, not yet realizing such thoughts would cling to my memory forever as the prisoners clung to the wire fencing in the photos at the newspaper office.

An earlier day's wind had caught black swastikas in the scarlet folds of banners lining the Odeonsplatz in Munich, from the Feldherrnhalle to the triumphal arch at the northern end. With friends from the Bund Deutscher Mädel, I'd screamed my adulation and thrown white and yellow flowers at Hitler waving from an open car. Günther must have shouted the Hitler Jugend motto: Blood and Honor. Did he think he was obeying orders from officials who'd been elected by the people when he raised his arm and marched forward in formation, prepared both mentally and physically to fight and die for the Fatherland on foreign soil? But German soldiers didn't swear allegiance to the Fatherland. They swore allegiance to Hitler. Günther had defended with his blood what Hitler ordered for the Jews, the dissidents, the homosexuals and gypsies, anyone considered an enemy of the state.

I looked up. Sweat caught light on Günther's forehead. He said that when he'd been arrested by the Americans, they weren't interested in where he lived or had his schooling. They wanted to know where he fought while he was in the army. "They were looking for illegal actions and it couldn't have been easy. The Fifth fought across the width of Poland and we shot everyone. Partisans. Commissars. Jews. Or anyone we thought belonged to any of those groups. Gender didn't matter. Old. Young."

My fists dug at my eyes, pressing in the sockets, trying to obliterate an image of him sighting down the rifle we'd given to the farmer.

"We were conscious of just two things on that long retreat from Leningrad: A Russian army was right behind us, and we were far outnumbered." He was standing rigid, almost at attention. "One mosquito-ridden summer, I fought beside men from the SS Einsatzgruppen. How can every German not feel naked before the world when he thinks of those other human beings, stripped, looking down into pits of layered, even writhing bodies as German soldiers shot them one by one?" He took my arm and we left the park, walking briskly. "Come," he said. "I'll take you to your train."

April passed.
May.
Anna bounded into my room on Pfannengasse shortly after the sun had warmed the morning. She came whirling across my

crowded space, her pale hair whipping ringlets against her face. "Renate, it's for a weekend. We'll go to one of their illegal clubs. Aren't you even a little curious?" She stopped to open my window and breathe deeply of the day's new freshness.

After my last meeting with Günther, as the unimaginable became real, I'd rarely left my room. "We're the nation of Beethoven. We're the nation of Brahms," he'd said before we reached my train. "We're the nation of Goethe, and it happened while we watched." His clenched fists had pounded the air between us. "I'll never let myself forget the rotting corpses we left there in the forest."

Now here was Anna, offering a weekend in the country where I'd earn more than I would in a month with the soldiers. Two months maybe. She wouldn't let me say no, her friend was a major. I knotted a thread I'd been weaving into a scrap of stocking and removed a wooden oval from a toe that had needed reinforcing.

On the appointed day, I let Anna roll my hair away from my face in the newest fashion and gave only a small protest when she added a suggestion of lipstick to my lips. I have to admit, I felt elegant for the first time in years as I smoothed across my hips the dress that Anna lent me. We were watching from her window when a drab-painted car from the Headquarters Motor Pool parked across the street. The driver was Anna's major. He waved toward her window, looking very much like the kind of man who always loved Anna. Handsome in a pretty way. Sure of himself and what he was doing. He'd known we were behind the curtains although he couldn't see us.

The officer who emerged from the passenger's door and slammed it solidly behind him was straight and tall and smiling, and I knew he was a Jew as surely as I knew I wasn't.

"Renate, this is Major Brad McClellen," Anna said as she opened her door.

"Roy Siegel," the other man said.

Hitler had said the Jews were freaks. He called them vermin. He charged them with global conspiracies that could destroy civilization. As my eyes met those of this man whose eyes were meeting mine directly, I couldn't help but wonder how many men who'd spread my legs for their intrusion were just like him and I'd been too cold, too hungry to think or even notice.

Captain Siegel repeated my name when he shook my hand, telling us he'd managed to be included because Brad and he had known each other back in Indiana. They'd started university the same year and, until Brad left to join a fraternity, they'd shared a dormitory room. In Mannheim I'd seen where students from that city's newly reopened university had moved deep into excavated bomb shelters, living in tiers of wooden bunks. And there they were again. Those gaunt Jewish faces staring out at me from primitive bunks in the Mannheimer Zeitung's display of photos.

Anna sat in the front seat of the government car, her arm stretched out to find the major's shoulder. Periodically, her fingers wandered up his neck and into his hair but her attention, her smile, her ringing laughter were for the captain who sat in the back seat beside me. Captain Siegel was funny and friendly and with his flair for imitating accents, he eventually made me laugh.

We crossed the fragile temporary bridge to Handschuhsheim, turning right along the river toward where Frau Schuler's mother-in-law had her crowded summer cottage but before we reached the village of Kleingemund, Major McClellen turned left into the forested hills of the Odenwald. Anna laughed when he announced our destination. Captain Siegel's look was a question for me but I couldn't be the one to tell him officers from the *Waffen SS* had once sponsored the same secluded country inn.

The wine with our dinner was French, as were the cheeses. The Chateaubriand was carved at the table. Before we parted to separate rooms on an upper floor, we drank brandy in front of a large log fire in an already heated lounge.

Although our car was the only traffic on the narrow road along the river, Major McClellen drove slowly on our return to Heidelberg. I tried not to think of Günther. He'd have enjoyed our walks through the woods bursting with new green, but he'd have called obscene the extravagance of heat in the quiet lounges, the plates sent back to the kitchen with enough uneaten food to feed a family. He'd have reminded me of the black-uniformed men in that other army who ate their ragout of wild mushrooms in pastry cups that defied cutting while Jews like Captain Siegel were selected for prison labor.

On my next visit to Schwetzingen, I found three postcards waiting. Günther's first card was noncommittal, just telling me of Mannheim's plan to offer opera in a building the Americans had relinquished. Not the National Theater, that was still a ruin, but a new and larger venue. The second said he'd added duties as an unofficial city guide to his other work in the burgeoning community of American families. The third that he'd been granted permission for another concert. With the extravagance of the two cartons of cigarettes I'd been given for my weekend, I had the luxury of time and an abiding hunger for a meeting. I wrote immediately.

When we met, Günther held me with such need, denial, and a loneliness that matched my own, but with all I was trying to assimilate into my life, our chaste clinging to each other in the sun-shadowed remnants of Mannheim seemed an artificial closeness. Günther said that because we had time before his concert, he wanted to show me a store that he'd discovered. Germany still had no economic structure, no new money as we approached the second summer since surrender but the day before, he'd happened on a tattered tarpaulin shading dirt-fresh vegetables on a wooden stall. Beyond them in a narrow room cleared from a damaged building, brown eggs flecked with straw were in a basket on a counter.

The store's owner had the gaunt look of a man who'd once been larger. His graying hair was brushed across his forehead. Preceding us into the unlit room, he informed us that the freshness growing in every tillable space since last summer was to be denied the Americans. The military order was not written but clearly understood.

Günther drew his coat around him. "That makes sense after last winter."

The man's thin face changed color. "You mean when we were forced to live like political prisoners."

I backed against the store's primitive counter waiting for Günther's reaction but it was as if he hadn't heard. The harsh words he might have spoken were lost in a shout of surprise and discovery as he picked up a wrinkled, thin-skinned orange. He rubbed his thumb across the texture before bringing it to his nose, asking the proprietor how he'd come by such a treasure. He was told the proprietor's wife did sewing for the army men. A soldier gave her that.

"It's the first I've seen in years," Günther said. "Will you sell it?"

In the rustic elegance of our room, Captain Siegel had juggled for my amusement three plump oranges that had been brought there from some army kitchen. He'd laughed as he grabbed for a fourth from a polished bowl and his circle of fruit plummeted to the carpet. The scattering fruit had been kicked under the bed before I engaged in sex with him above them.

After giving up all he'd earned to barter, Günther presented his small pale orange to me. Resting lightly in my hand, it had a weight of unbearable proportion and I sought solace in wondering if Tomas Ziegler or his sister Inge had ever seen an orange. I imagined them holding it, feeling the texture, bringing it to their noses as Günther had done. Tomas would surely have some questions and I'd tell him about places that were warm and fragrant.

On my next trip to Schwetzingen, Frau Ziegler greeted me with the news her husband had been accepted into a Labor Service unit of Polish guards. I had nothing to offer by way of congratulation until I realized I'd been too absorbed in introspection to see I shouldn't have kept possession of the largest bedroom on the upper floor. When I was home, I was with my father. The music room and the small sitting room at the front of the house were where we spent our time. Now with Herr Ziegler's new position and irregular hours, I was convinced my heavy bedroom furniture should be moved to the room beside the kitchen, the dining chairs and table to the little used grand salon. Günther could help. After the triumph of his concert, he'd agreed to come to Schwetzingen for a visit.

The move was accomplished on a cloudless morning. Tomas and Inge were constantly underfoot until the heavy lifting was completed and the dining room furniture crowded the grand salon.

Günther rolled a finely knotted carpet while I studied a stack of pictures newly cleared from the upper floor. The top one was my brother. My fingers lingered on the frame. How

Hartmut had fussed the day the picture was taken, insisting he wanted to look a proper pilot. The shutter had caught his familiar gesture of brushing his hair across his forehead. I lifted the print. Beneath it was a picture of a team of boys. On the left was Hartmut, in the center Paul, their faces flushed with triumph. Paul was taller than the rest. A thin-faced boy with a way of standing that set him apart from the others. Chin up, arms crossed, a glimpse of the superiority he felt in the way he challenged the camera. I held Hartmut's picture out toward Günther. His glance dropped to the other and he asked if Frau Schuler's refugee family had a son. He knew Frau Schuler's family had grown daughters. Taking the rolled carpet, shoving it behind the sofa, I warned him if such thoughts as I knew he was thinking crossed his mind again, I'd see the housing authorities before the week was over and ask if a son could be provided. He smiled and stacked my family's pictures before sprawling across the horsehair sofa. I moved the pictures to the floor and settled down beside him, pulling his arm around my shoulders, curling my fingers into his palm. Before us, the crowded room waited for arranging. Günther told me I'd be surprised at the garden of plenty that had been growing while we were involved with cold and hunger. He described as sources of unending wonder, American mail order catalogs that made available to the occupation, through their postal service, a world where Germans had few glimpses. He brought my fingers to his lips as he described how the discards from such a cornucopia of riches could make remarkable trading, and with American families already filling the refurbished apartments at the edge of the city, he expected a fair share would be passed on to him if he worked harder. He said that with transportation constantly improving, he'd come to Schwetzingen more often. Then he said that with my mother gone and Herr Ziegler's new appointment, it was time I gave up the room in Heidelberg and moved back to live with my family.

There was nothing to do except find his mouth with mine, losing myself in passionate kisses until Tomas and Inge came squealing down the stairs.

# Summer
## 1946

Unscreened windows opened to the sun let a persistent fly find packets of waxy paper Günther was unwrapping at Frau Schuler's table. On her stove, steam hung above a pan of leftover coffee he'd brought in a washed glass jar.

"Tell us about your recital, Günther." Frau Schuler brushed at the fly. "Was it well received?"

I flinched. Günther's performance the night before had hardly been a recital. He'd sung popular tunes with a four piece band at an American party whose leftovers were now spread before us.

"How could they not love me?" he said.

Each time he came he'd lost more weight, the circles under his eyes had deepened. I let my cheek touch his.

"That major Anna's dating was there with an American woman. Someone said it was his wife."

Anna had taken my keys to the place on Pfannengasse but she'd given them to a woman she called Irmgard. Irmgard lived in the room with an American soldier whose name was Nathan. I'd wanted Anna's friend to register the room in Irmgard's name but, recently, he was being cautious.

"Ummm. Your employer uses fine flour and many eggs." Frau Schuler held a pale square with coconut glazing. Her remark could have been critical or casual, the value of eggs and flour was still more than most Germans took for granted. Günther unwrapped a chocolate square for her inspection but before she did more than finger the texture she returned it to its wrapper. She confided she'd heard from neighbors that most American families had their own black market dealer. Günther only shrugged.

German families still offered Leica cameras, Zeiss binoculars, even pieces of a silver coffee service, to a willing farmer in exchange for what he grew or slaughtered. The farmer traded these to a black market dealer for cigarettes, the surrogate money, with which he bought what he could find and needed. The cigarettes had come to the dealer from an American who'd found interest in something a German family had surrendered. With my hand on Günther's shoulder, I poured last night's coffee into delicate cups, only half listening as he told Frau Schuler the Russians had broken another promise to send grain. If our farmers were to produce what had formerly been grown in the east, they needed seed, tools, fertilizer, a bull to breed a cow, a better wagon. He hoped men with larger suitcases were slipping these things across closed borders.

"Where is the American government in this?" Frau Schuler asked. "Is this their plan for our survival?"

Grasping his cup with both hands, Günther blew across the heated coffee. I sat down between them. Horst Wegner attended most of Günther's concerts, writing of his voice as a formidable instrument capable of filling the largest hall, adding on at least one occasion that with his personal charm and chiseled physique, he was prepared both visually and vocally to reach the top of his chosen profession.

Frau Schuler said she'd learned a woman was hired as a servant in each American household no matter the rank or size of the apartment.

Günther said, "The French are even more extravagant."

I closed my eyes. The delicacies on the table were only for the moment. Life could be hard again when winter winds blew chill. A servant? In an American household? Why not? I opened my eyes to see Günther stiffen.

Sleep was impossible that night with all my planning and I was up early, but before I'd accomplished all I had to finish before I left for Heidelberg, Frau Schuler had pushed open our front door. She wore the hat she'd always worn when traveling to the city. "I've supervised them all my life," she said. "I know how to be a servant."

I had no answer. Nor much to say on our slow bus ride into

town. I was only thankful her step remained firm as we descended, her voice strong as she read from a newspaper stacked on a rack in a central kiosk. "Trouble in the British Zone? With miners in the Ruhr?"

I drew her back from the path of a man who was striding forward with unswerving purpose. His bulky odious clothing was an accumulation from several armies. I'd seen such men before. Gaunt dirty pale men with little resemblance to anything human. Prisoners of war released for no clear reason these long months after hostilities had ended. They'd ridden great distances in open railroad cars, or clung to seats in wooden compartments at the discretion of attendants, making their way into the west from the bleak plains of Siberia, returning to families who believed them dead, eager to integrate themselves into lives that had gone on without them.

Bus brakes squealed. A staff car's horn was blaring. The man hadn't looked up as he plodded into the traffic on Gaisbergerstrasse. Frau Schuler's attention remained on the kiosk. "I guess American families wouldn't be coming to Germany in such numbers if the authorities thought there'd be trouble mining coal," she said.

We crossed Gaisbergerstrasse and climbed the few low steps into the Grand Hotel which was now the American employment office. A staircase curved up to the right. We followed signs to the left, to a part of the building above a municipal garden. A woman whose asymmetrical features seemed folded into a perpetual scowl, sat at an almost empty desk. I could see she was assessing the quality of Frau Schuler's clothes, the supple leather in the gloves Frau Schuler was fastidiously removing. "You have no income?" the woman said.

"No."

"Your husband?"

"Dead."

I thought this clerk must know clothes made little distinction. Frau Schuler would look different from a woman who fled to the west with a single suitcase, or a woman who may have been wearing her best when an air raid siren sent her into a basement but emerged owning only what was on her back. But what did this frowning woman think of the absence of a pension from a dead husband who, she must know from Frau Schuler's bearing, had been successful? I accepted two applications for employment and because Frau Schuler seemed uneasy in the new surroundings, whispered instructions while she copied answers in her meticulous, formal hand.

Early in the following month Frau Schuler received notice of assignment to a three room attic apartment across from the orchards on Quinckestrasse. A newly married corporal and his teenage American bride had agreed to need a servant only two days in each week. Such restricted work meant fewer meals for the servant but the compensation was the same as for full employment, and it also meant less waiting for unreliable buses on the ice-bleak days we knew were coming.

I wrote Günther that I was the one who should be making the long trek to the edge of Heidelberg to scrub floors in an American apartment, but I supposed we were lucky the dour woman in the employment office had been sympathetic to Frau Schuler. "Or to the professor," he wrote back.

Summer passed in a series of cloud shadowed days and it was time to shake our winter clothes from their storage boxes for yet another season. I took my mother's clothes to the barter market around the feet of the Madonna in Heidelberg's Kornmarktplatz and soon had a pledge of enough coal to take us into winter. The man who made the offer had assessing eyes and a deceitful smile, but I accepted because he surrendered the identification pass all of us were required to keep in our possession until we could get the coal to Schwetzingen.

Leaving for home, full of triumph, I saw the woman with two toddlers I'd spoken to during my first return to the city. Somewhat taller now, the children still clung to their mother as she extended a pair of high heeled slippers, trying to trade for shoes that fit her daughter. "It doesn't matter the condition," she kept repeating. Beside her a one legged man held out a pair of woolen trousers, a remnant of his Wehrmacht uniform the law would allow a woman to wear though a man could not. Then, in Hercules Square, I met Anna. During her usual exuberant embrace, she exploded into a tirade about military regulations that discouraged a marriage both of my tenants wanted. Nathan's company commander had called

Irmgard a whore, insisting that once in the states she'd leave her husband. Anna wanted to know how he dared say that. He'd never even met her.

Within days Anna was in Schwetzingen returning my keys. Before Frau Ziegler had made us a cup of *ersatz* coffee, we'd learned Nathan and Irmgard had married. They were in Bremerhaven awaiting transport. Anna's visit was short. Frau Ziegler found it exciting. I was left uneasy. Günther had to be told the room had become a burden but he'd written he'd be busy through the weekend, working first in the Kaiserhalle at a reunion of American veterans of battle, and then accompanying the equipment of the dancers who'd been the evening's entertainment, to Frankfurt where the military truck would be unloaded for another show. I was deciding how to approach our new complication while I sat in the music room idly playing tunes that were familiar. My fingers slipped into the theme from a film that was popular through the war, *Quax, der Bruchpilot*. With Heinz Rühmann. Behind me in his straight-backed chair, my father cradled his violin. He began to pluck above the bridge, each string in turn, occasionally twisting black tuning pegs on the narrow scroll until his D string snapped with a fine, taut ring. "Perhaps Paul can find another," he said.

"Paul?"

"I see so little of him lately. Is he that busy? He's a fine man, Renate. Intelligent, ambitious. Your mother and I will be glad when the two of you have married." I was beyond grief. I could only wonder where he was now. Perhaps my playing the old tune had dredged up a random memory. He loosed the ends of the broken string and folded the pieces into his pocket while I closed the piano, listening to the wind ruffle trees as it crossed the garden.

Later that day I told Frau Ziegler I needed to return to Heidelberg. She understood. She'd care for my father.

Anna was at my door in Pfannengasse shortly after I'd closed it heavily behind me. She entered like a whirlwind scattering my thoughts when I so needed peace. I suppose I sounded harsh when I demanded to know how she'd known to find me because she stopped and her expression darkened before she twisted away. She told me she'd seen me changing streetcars at Bismarck Platz.

She'd run all the way because I had trouble with the landlord. He'd let another woman use the room when he'd found it empty but was still demanding last month's rent. In another week I'd owe him two.

I pulled at a drawer in my stained bureau, staring mutely at the contents. I didn't want to deal with Anna. I sat down on my bed to remove my shoes before pulling my mother's black blouse out of her black skirt and stretching out on my bed where I smelled sweat and cheap perfume from other couplings.

Anna started in about a man she'd send around that evening and I put a pillow over my face.

"What's wrong with you, Renate?"

I clutched the pillow tighter.

"Renate?"

Frustration clouded my voice but it wasn't just with her. I had so much to resolve with Günther. I wanted blue skies and open fields and forests. I wanted the innocence we'd had back in the mountains. I said, "I'm not a body part for the American soldiers."

"What?"

"I can't. I don't want to be. I won't."

Her face flushed red beneath her makeup. "Is that what you think of me? Is that what you tell Günther?"

The pillow almost covered my face but I could see her pulling her bright coat around her, making no attempt to hide her anger.

"Take the man, Renate, and pay your rent. And never forget the police would like to know how you're living in two places."

I leaped up, angry now, red faced too, shouting at her to go on and report me like a loyal Nazi. Then what would happen to her friend at the housing office? She'd never get anther favor after he finished explaining.

Anna slammed the door.

I knew I should follow. Hurting Anna wasn't a resolution but another day was better. Today I had to rest. I had to plan. When I went to Günther in Mannheim, my thoughts had to be as orderly as I could make them.

I spent the next hours cramped in sleep on the small bed in my stale room but when a heavy knock rattled my door, I could still see light beyond my window. A second pounding brought me lurching toward the noise. A soldier pushed into my room. "You Renate?"

"Yes."

"I know Anna."

I couldn't believe she'd done this. The soldier was big above me, smelling heavily of cigarettes. He looked around before he yanked a drawer in my bureau, digging through the contents, demanding I get ready.

I said, "Get ready?"

He said, "You can't go to the club with me like that. You look like Ilse Koch ready for another flaying."

"Ilse Koch?" And then I remembered.

He said, "You Nazi sluts are all alike. I can find better 'n you washed up by the bridge."

I started beating on his chest. He caught my wrists. I started crying, great piercing wails of rage and indignation. Were Günther and I so damaged? Was there a congenital flaw? Are the camps a Pandora's Box now opened? My desperation turned to fear when I realized the soldier's face was white with fury, his breathing broader. I shrieked at him to get out of my room and after one long moment he began to back away. No sooner had he slammed the door than I hurled the black clothes I'd worn throughout the summer across my bed and pulled a pale blouse over my head, a thick skirt around me. The sky was darkening beyond my window. I grabbed my coat against a drenching and ran the length of Hauptstrasse to be at Bismarck Platz in time to catch the next urban train to Mannheim.

In the quiet, in the dark at the top of Günther's stairs, I had no plan but waiting as my thoughts struggled through a blur of soldiers. None of them had ever mentioned Germans who went to Jewish stores on purpose, brushing past Hitler's Brownshirts who stood at every entrance, or families who defied the Führer's orders and hid a Jewish friend for years. Had no one heard of the White Rose students?

Günther was suddenly beside me. He'd sneaked away to get some rest while the dancers had everyone's attention. I didn't hear. I didn't care. Dancers had no meaning. I demanded to know what kind of men were at that meeting. Were they like the men who came to my room on Pfannengasse? Arrogant savages, all of them, and the one I'd just thrown out the worst of all.

The padlock on Günther's door opened with an enormous snap and he stepped into the room before me. Sweat from his work was everywhere about him. "They are what you say. They are men."

"If you mean they're hung with testicles and penis, I should know."

Everything was suddenly slow motion, even our labored breathing. Günther flicked on a bulb hanging from his ceiling. He removed his coat. He opened his wardrobe but closed it again and his fingers dug into the wardrobe's ornate carving. Just when I thought he'd never turn around, he said, "You make no attempt to know them."

Now I was furious with Anna, blaming her for this hurt to Günther. I tried to explain why she'd sent the soldier but my words made little sense. The only thing he seemed to comprehend was that another man had seen me. He brought a box of tiny American pretzels from an upper shelf but only a drift of salt fell in his hand when he tipped it over and he slammed the box back in his wardrobe. "You surprise me that you've returned to Heidelberg. I thought we settled that through the summer."

I pushed around him, kicking the door of his closet when it didn't open, backing away from his accidental touch when he reached to turn the key. "Settled what? You just work harder and have your lessons."

"I'm doing the best I can."

Clawing through years of layered truths and evasions, I began raging about a document of occupation that kept most of us from working and couldn't stop even when hard lines formed around his mouth. He brought an electric burner from his wardrobe and bent to push its cord into the wall. I reached for cups and their saucers and spotted an almost empty bowl of damp saved coffee, realizing he'd been resorting to last winter's compromises so he could bring fresh to us. He said, "Don't even try to argue."

I hadn't meant to argue. I let the cups clatter to the table before I handed him the half dried coffee.

He said something about the Krupp plants being a waste of twisted girders but other factories were whole beneath the ruin of their outer shells. "Some that stamped out helmets for our soldiers are probably making pots and pans."

My gaze caught on his wet, worn shoes. The seam along one side was broken.

"Some that made boots are probably making shoes." He combined his coffee with water he stored in a tall glass jar. "Until we have real money, businessmen can't be expected to work for trading goods. Like you."

Like me? I hit the table. One cracked cup flipped from its saucer. "How can you talk to me that way?"

"How could you return to Heidelberg?"

I straightened the cup, intending to tell him I'd returned because Anna's friends had married, she'd returned my keys, but I heard myself saying my father had broken the D string on his violin. "He thinks I have a job that will afford another."

"He thinks? He thinks? I suppose he's right. That job you had in Heidelberg would afford another, but you should go back and smash his violin before you work like that again."

With his shoulders squared, his jaw rigid, I remembered him on another day with his shoulders sagging, his eyes blank and staring. He'd been telling me about being part of a detail that shot a boy soldier no older than his brother Konrad. The child was newly sent to a retreating army and acted foolishly because he was afraid of dying. I closed my eyes. I knew Günther as I knew no other. I knew his ambition, his desperation, the little pockets of emptiness that would always be beyond my filling, and I wanted him from the very essence of my being, wanted the response that was the essence of his being. I took the coffee from his hands to finish the task we both had started, telling him as I moved around avoiding contact, that we were being foolish. We were both tired. We were both upset. It wasn't important that I went to Heidelberg. He knew I hadn't meant to meet a soldier and I knew he hadn't meant to hurt me. I asked him why we didn't just acknowledge the unresolved tensions between us. Who were we trying to protect? Ourselves? From what? Each other? The percolator began a rhythmic th-rump th-rump behind us and I turned toward the sound, watching the darkening coffee fill a cracked glass dome. His arms slipped around me. I was surprised to feel him tremble. I said, "No soldier ever made me feel like a woman, Günther. Not like you."

With his face hidden, he whispered that I must believe he was trying. He was really trying, but he had to ask one thing. I couldn't let any man close to me again, not for any reason. Not until he found a place in his heart where his failures wouldn't defeat him.

I said, "Günther, there will always be men in my life."

"But not with any intimacy, not in your room. Oh God, Renate, I don't know what I'm saying. Help me. Please."

The motion started slowly, swaying, clinging to each other. "Are your eyes closed?" he asked.

I closed them.

"The day has passed, the night is warm, there is music from an old inn."

I wanted to laugh and cry. We were both so fragile, so grasping for a future. "May we dance a little?" I asked.

He dipped and twirled me in the space his room permitted. "We may dance a lot. Waltzes. Every waltz we dance together."

The last of the coffee hissed over the pot onto the red burner and he bent to close the control, calling the coffee new wine that would be waiting at our table. Or better, *Bowle*, with fresh strawberries in the bottom of our glasses. He lifted the pot and poured the last of the coffee into our cups. "Bowle will make us pleasantly drunk," he said.

I took a deep breath and asked if there were a small shop nearby where I might buy a D string for my father's violin. Günther put the coffee pot back on its burner. With his hands cradling my face, his thumbs smoothing across my forehead, he said. "One of the Americans will find it for you."

"Americans? Are they here, too?"

"Yes, they're here."

"Why?"

"Because they enjoy the night and the music." He straightened his bench and my chair before he leaned across his table and pulled the electric plug away from the wall. "I know an officer's wife. An artist. She'll know where to write for your father's D string." Rolling the cord around his hand, pausing before he dropped it into a drawer, the shadow of a smile crossed his face. "Of course, there is another way. We could kill a cat." At my gasp he added, "No, no. They're not all dead. At least one escaped the table of some fat Frau. I saw it yesterday near the Rosengarten. A scrawny yellow thing with a long curved tail. People followed wherever it went. It's true. I heard a child asking, 'What is that?'"

I covered my ears. I felt soft and loved and merry.

"I saw which way it went," he said.

How could I ever leave him? He was my core. Without him I was a shadow looking for my substance. I told him, no. Let the cat live. I'd rather ask his American friend.

He swept my chair back from the table and we sat down to finish the stale coffee before he returned to the Kaiserhalle to load the dancer's truck for its trip to Frankfurt.

# Autumn 1946

The rain started again as I returned to Heidelberg. At first it was just big drops against the windows of the empty urban train, but by the time I stepped out at Bismarck Platz, wind drove a torrent parallel to the ground. I ran, twisting into boarded storefronts. They gave no protection, not for me, not for the satchel with cigarettes and coffee Günther had provided for my landlord. My keys were in my hand when I reached Pfannengasse. Away from the wind, already finding some relief, I climbed the stairs. I didn't leave my room again until the storm subsided.

It was easy to slip into forgetfulness, to dream about the day Günther and I could finally be together. Before he kissed me and ran to catch the streetcar that would take him back to the Kaiserhalle, he promised our long nightmare was over. The rhythmic cadence of the rain against my window brought a sense of resolution.

The storm moved on during the night when I couldn't hear the silence. I awoke to a pale sun lifting above the hills behind the castle and pushed my window open to the freshness. Morning light reflected on a wash of unevaporated water caught between the cobblestones below me on the street.

Sudden voices made me draw back behind my curtain, the rasp of early gaping doors. It was Monday. The newly reopened market for horseflesh was readying for the week. I slammed my window and twisted the handle to secure the lock. Today I'd escape the sight of sinewy shanks brought from the country in creaking wagons, sharp odors from sausage stuffed in offal, the blood-caked whiteness of an apron on the butcher's apprentice. I dressed quickly, eager to be away before the first American automobiles blocked the incline of my tiny street. On Monday, the wives of American army men came to Pfannengasse in massive cars alight with polished chrome. They bought ground horseflesh to feed the blooded Schaeferhunde and Boxers they raised in their apartments.

From a box beneath my wardrobe, I pulled a sweater whose brightness had kept me from appearing in it on the street, nylon stockings Irmgard had forgotten, sheer underwear still in a wrapper from the Post Exchange. I stuffed everything into my two string bags and hurried away. At the narrow end of Hauptstrasse I darted past Karlstor, hoping to catch a train toward Schlierbach. In a valley on the far side of Neckargemuend, I was sure I'd find a better bargain but if I couldn't, I'd leave everything with Frau Schuler's sister. I wanted nothing more than to be rid of all reminders of a past I knew was now behind me.

Below Dilsberg, in one of the clustered villages away from the Neckar River, the foreign labels from the soldiers' store pleased a farmer's new young wife. Smiling gratefully, the old man filled my bags with fresh apples, cabbages, smoked meat. When the woman threw her arms around him, he added enough fresh eggs for my father and Frau Schuler.

Descending the train again in Heidelberg, I tried to balance my welcome burden but the bulging sacks were awkward and after the first block of Hauptstrasse, I left the crowded sidewalks to follow a twisting, wall-lined alley. In an open park across from the river I lowered my burden to the ground and rubbed where string handles had left red bruising on my fingers. A young American corporal sat cross-legged on a bench, staring out across the water. I didn't see him rise and take a few quick steps between us. "Ma'am, I c'n help with those," he said.

"No. Wait."

He twisted away, swinging my string bags back from where I'd placed them. "Hey, you speak English. Good. I c'n help." He hovered before me, his sun washed face above the familiar khaki as happily crooked as his grin. I was too tired to be angry but I wanted none of his intrusion. I tried to retrieve my sacks. I could carry them myself. He said, "No need doin' that."

His grin broadened when I hesitated and he took a few steps back, hesitating too, before turning across the street to a brick reinforced walk along the river. Had he been German and this the days now blurred by time, I'd have found his offer kind, maybe even courtly. Now I followed him across the street, shoulders slumping from fatigue, unburdened fingers stretching. He paused for me to walk beside him and I was ready to concede I'd be grateful for help in the long blocks before my room. I told him I didn't want to argue. "Good," he said. "I don't want that neither."

He said his name was Lewis, Bill Lewis. Four months before, he'd "shipped across the water" in a transport called the General Buckner to work at the 130th Station Hospital, a military hospital just outside of town. I was about to caution him about my eggs when he set the bags down, his comments never ceasing while he rearranged the contents. Lifting my bags again he resumed his loping gait. I smiled at the contradiction, the care and lack of caution, but when I realized I was smiling it was as if I'd walked into a wall. He glanced back while I was regaining my composure. From the satisfaction in his grin I guessed he thought his help had given me a needed rest. I could only hope my eggs were safer.

His enthusiasm was almost contagious as he rambled on about his train ride south. The biggest church he'd ever seen was right there at his elbow and they'd passed real castles on the Rhine. "Did'ya know grapevines grow right up the hillside?" he asked. "I'm a beer man myself but them grape fields sure was pretty." One of the men sitting near him knew the grapes were particularly good that year. There'd be a record harvest. He said he guessed he'd "haf'ta" try the wine. He put my burdens on the ground and rubbed the bruising to his fingers. "Don't tell me a little thing like you was figurin' on carryin' these bags all this way." His hat came off and his fingers rubbed through his sun-blond hair. Suddenly, his gaze was across the river, "Will you look out there? Those are some fine houses. That one's like a castle. No, a church. I'd like t' see inside." With the same breath, he added, "Do you mind me askin', ma'am, what's yer name?"

I surprised myself by answering without hesitation. I told him my name was Weiss. Renate Weiss.

"Pleased to meet you, Fräulein Renate Weiss." His grin broadened when he used the German term. "I like havin' a pretty lady t' talk to."

We strolled more slowly, pausing while my new friend switched my bags from side to side, stopping while he watched a single car turn into an alley. "How come Germans don't like cars?" he asked. I assured him we certainly did like cars but then he wanted to know why he never saw us drive one, just Americans' cars or taxis, and I told him during the war we gave our cars to Hitler. It was a patriotic thing to do. He stopped to think that over before confiding Americans gave their rubber floor mats. "It'd be hard to live without a car in Texas," he said.

At the small incline of the Alte Brücke, he darted toward the far side where the bridge had wooden reconstruction but looked back at the red stone ruin looming across the hillside above the old part of town. I asked if he'd been to visit our castle. He said no, but he was "plannin'," adding he thought it a shame America had bombed it.

I said, "Not you, the French."

"The French? Them, too?"

He didn't understand. I told him French sappers caused the destruction in the seventeenth century. Well, that and age, and his chagrin that he hadn't known the history gave me such a twinge, I was sorry that I'd caused it. I hurried to reassure him Heidelberg was only slightly damaged in the war. I didn't mention the zoo. I knew he'd ask about the animals and I didn't want to admit I hadn't cared enough to learn what happened. I did tell him about the townspeople who tried to save the bridge where we were standing and his hand trailed in silent appreciation along the ancient stone. He said he'd done some reading when he got his new assignment but apparently not enough, and we agreed assuming the war had caused the castle's damage was an easy mistake. "And it was a war. But with the French in the seventeenth century."

"Now ain't that somethin'. Us not even a country, and you already fightin' with the French. I tell you, Fräulein Weiss, everythin's so different. You'd believe it if you saw Bannock, my town in Texas."

Bannock. I tried to imagine a mother there. A father, too. A family who took him to a train with the same love and pride and worry my family had taken Hartmut.

He leaned out to study the bridge's wooden section. "Y' know, I don't believe what I c'n buy with cigarettes even when I do it. The fellows told me a bunch a them went holidayin' in the Black Forest with just two cartons. A whole three day pass with just two cartons."

His sun darkened knuckles rapped the joint where wood met stone. He said, "Cigarettes is rationed but the army gives us plenty. Too much for guys who keep from smokin'. I can't think what it was like when families sent extras here legal. Whole cases through the APO. That's the army's post office. Troopers must a got whatever they wanted with what came from stateside while money orders with a whole month's pay went flyin' home across the ocean."

I caught myself reaching for my shoulders across my breasts. Could I ever forget the mouths, the groping hands, the violation I felt each time a soldier found a rhythm in my body?

"Our captain says there's good reason to have no useful money. It keeps the natives quiet. What can they do? Always scratchin' to get by." His expression changed. "Oh, I don't mean you."

"I scratched some," I said.

He retrieved my bags and started back along the walk above the river. His unit had been required to watch Signal Corp films coming over on the Buckner. "Terrible films, Renate Weiss. Men lookin' like their insides was sucked out by a powerful vacuum. I tell you it turned my stomach. Some guys vomited. Our CO says the military don't want those of us who never fought a battle to forget what Germans are capable of doin'."

Just keep walking, I thought. Don't be tempted to mention shame. How many times before I stopped repeating? I directed him away from the river.

"Hey not so fast," he said when, at my building, I reached for my bags. "I want you to have supper with me."

"That's not necessary, Mr. Lewis."

"Corporal Lewis," he said and smiled. "You gotta be hungry, I know I am, and I still have questions."

I knew this corporal from Texas would take me to the Stardust Club, still the only place in town where a serviceman could host a German. I'd offer no excuses, but what kind of answers did I have for a soldier who was both interested and kind.

While I worked at the lock that always stuck for want of a drop of oil, I saw him glance at the plaster horse's head above the market's door.

"About that head," he said when I was back downstairs.

At the Stardust Club I was surprised he knew a trained and ready military governor had accompanied the American invading forces, initiating political reform even before peace had been established. He knew radio stations and newspapers were tightly controlled and books had been rewritten before schools reopened. He'd even heard about our Fragebogen and wondered if all that paper had been useful. When I told him three million of the questionnaires were put into German courts for disposal, his answer was a startled, "They weren't."

"Well, yes they were."

"You mean former Nazis is judgin' former Nazis?"

Gossip told of suspect judges who retained their jurisdiction while minor party members drew a prison sentence but my answer was that his government had tried to clear the courts before the questionnaires were turned over. "During the invasion a complete file of party members was found in a Munich paper mill waiting to be destroyed."

His fork clattered to his plate.

"Any person whose name was in that file, if not jailed, is now restricted to manual labor."

I expected further comment but he only poked at his food. "Were you a Nazi?" he asked.

I gasped but I thought he heard and I let my breath out slowly.

"I never met a Nazi, or anyone who fought the Americans. That's a joke around the barracks. All the men here fought the Russians."

Herr Weber, who'd owned the butcher shop in Schwetzingen, fought the Americans. He'd been taken prisoner and spent a year in the American west, washing dishes deep in soap suds in an Officer's Club at a place he called Fort Ord. I stopped. I couldn't tell him about Herr Weber. I was afraid Corporal Lewis had read about the Anatomical Medical Institute in Danzig, where soap was made from human corpses.

At a pause in our conversation Corporal Lewis mentioned language lessons. He said he'd been thinking about a tutor because the mandatory classes at the barracks went so slow. My English made him think I was a teacher.

I reached for my glass and sipped the water I always found on American tables. A teacher? Why not a teacher? My school English had been the most stilted kind of beginning but I was almost fluent after being with the soldiers. I told him I'd meet him at the American library. He should set the date and time.

"Hey, *bueno!*" he shouted. And then with that grin that revealed so many straight white teeth, "Nope. Wrong country. *Gut. Gut.*"

He accompanied me to the entry of my building and formally shook my hand. "Bueno!" I shouted as I took, by twos, the narrow stairway to my room.

"I'll be a good teacher," I told Frau Schuler on my next day's trip to Schwetzingen. "You can't imagine how eager this soldier is to learn."

I repeated this the next time I was with Günther. "You can't imagine how eager he is to learn."

"Wonderful news." We'd met as we were entering the former hotel lobby.

"I let him buy my dinner." On the step above me, Günther stiffened. "Stop it, Günther."

He bounded up a few quick steps before he waited.

"Be glad," I said.

"I'm glad for you."

"For us."

On the landing by his door, Günther put both hands on my shoulders. "Downstairs, when you said you met a man …"

"Günther, don't."

"Should we have talked it over first?"

"No. Not every simple action."

"It isn't simple, Renate. Not the way I feel."

"And how do I feel? He took me to the Stardust Club."

At his door, Günther fumbled with his keys.

"Günther, this is real work with real responsibility. Frau Schuler can't stay home, not yet, but all of us will feel less burdened."

"Of course."

"No student will see my room."

"I know that."

I rubbed the tension where it held across his shoulders. "Bill Lewis is so young. He's like you said, he wears a uniform but he's never been a soldier."

The lock snapped open and he pushed before me into his room. "What's young, Renate?"

"Nineteen. Twenty. No more than that."

"And you are what?" We were laughing when he kissed me but

I knew we'd taken only faltering steps the night when we were dancing. The peace I'd felt in my room listening to the rain was an illusion.

We shuffled from our coats and began the routine of finding his pot, stirring his dried coffee. His attitude changed. He was actually beaming when he told me he'd been accepted by a new voice coach. A refugee in the west who'd been a principal with Dresden's Semper Opera. A bit more must be paid him, but with more American families arriving almost daily, Günther was sure he'd find more work.

I smoothed my hands across his chest, reaching for his shoulders, smiling because I knew what I earned from giving lessons would make absolutely certain he'd have time to take advantage of his new lessons. "Just kiss me one more time," I said as I pulled his arms around me. "And I'll promise to bring my students to your next recital."

"Your students? More than one?"

"Many. Many. Corporal Lewis told me he has friends."

Bill's first lesson began with my pointing to a window, a door, the stacks of books around us. I said the words in German. Bill struggled with pronunciation. I pointed to the pen he wiggled in his fingers. I'd brought a copy of the *Rhein-Neckar Zeitung*, our local newspaper. The lead article was about American Secretary of State Byrnes' September 6th visit to Stuttgart, the first American politician to speak with German politicians present. The same information would have been in his newspaper, **The Stars and Stripes**, and I thought the shared subject would make it easier for him to pick out language similarities, but it was the political content that held his interest. Byrnes had called for the American government to abandon further attempts at limiting German production. He proposed linking two or even three zones for trading.

While I gathered my papers at the end of the lesson, Bill pushed into my satchel a manual prepared for soldier students and a dual language dictionary from the soldiers' store. Before making an appointment for his second lesson, he added his notebook and his pen. To my surprise, as we stood shivering on the sidewalk, he put a pack of Chesterfields in my gloved hand. "The other stuff is just to help you help me," he said. "This is payment for my lesson."

Walking back to Pfannengasse, my fingers caressed the small, slick pack. I brought it to my nose and caught a hint of the distinctive fragrance. Memories have to fade, I thought. They have to. But in my mind were other cigarettes in crumpled wrappers that had been tossed on my bedside table.

I had no time to write all this to Günther before, to our second session, Bill brought another military student, who brought two more. I was soon saving time for a high school student, the daughter of a physician for whom Bill worked. The child asked to have her lessons in her home.

"The first American home I've ever entered," I said to Günther. I was sitting beside him on his floor, at a long planned meeting, as he finished sorting pages of music according to the completeness of each copy. The evening stretched out long before us. Eventually, Günther rose and helped me up beside him. "Everything's better, for me as well," he said. "Horst Wegner has made a difference. I'm looking at offers from larger venues, other cities."

"Other cities?"

A sharp knock absorbed his answer. When he opened the door, a gnome of a man retreated back into the shadows. "The maestro sent me. He needs the music."

Günther pulled me in behind him. "Tomorrow. I told him I had plans."

"That's not how he understands it. *Mein Gott*, he thinks you're late."

Indecision clouded Günther's features until he dropped my hand and reached for the stacks of music. "Can you ever understand?" he asked.

I thought I couldn't.

"I'm sorry. I'm just so sorry," he kept repeating as he followed me down the stairs. When he suggested we set a date for our next meeting I told him I wasn't sure about my obligations but even as I said it I had no illusions. With all my other hungers, the strongest was for him.

Cold burnished the hills around the city until a storm tore at the reds and golds and ambers. I'd not been to Mannheim since our aborted night together and when I looked up and saw only leafless branches, I felt such loss. That same day, I'd received a postcard from Günther telling me the venue for the program he'd been rehearsing had been moved to Wiesbaden with the added possibility of a tour north to Kassel and into the British Zone. With Byrnes' proposal for linking zones not progressing beyond words on paper, Günther was looking forward to seeing what the British had accomplished.

Two additional families filled my time, talking, learning, trying to understand more than simple translations. I began to feel a shared heritage with these Americans, a European heritage that was older than the recent war. They were not my friends, my students, but friendly in a strange American way. One of Bill's associates, a fellow Texan, was troubled by our January elections. A weary librarian was already glancing from her watch to us when he wanted to know how America could let Germans vote less than a year after the war had ended. That was hardly time to clean the weapons. I tried to be quick in my explanation that the elections were just for local politicians who were meant to help with local issues. We were a land in ruin. There was no reason to worry that we had no machinery to clear the rubble, we had no screw drivers or nails or wire or spare parts. I said, "Think what it took to clean the water."

"I hear what yer sayin' but there's a Texas country mile between that and makin' government decisions."

I needed Günther's explanation about our longed for central government but such thoughts only added to my consternation. Günther's move had created disproportionate complexity. He wrote daily but his letters came in bunches. To arrange access to a telephone when he had like access was only possible on one occasion. And then he wrote that the tour to the British Zone had been abandoned because of problems with transportation. I brought that letter to my classes thinking to share his even German script, but after several Americans had handled it, I felt it written by a stranger. I was lonelier than I'd been since his departure. I cut short the usual after session conversations and hurried out into the cold, but by the birth house of Friedrich Ebert I was shrieking with delight. Günther was bounding up Pfannengasse toward me, his worn coat flying.

"I couldn't write. The decision to release me was just too sudden."

We'd never met in Heidelberg, he'd never seen my room, but my keys were in my hand. I asked how long he'd waited and told mim he looked blue with cold.

"Not blue, a rainbow, a pot of gold." In one great embrace he lifted me across my threshold. He said, "The audition was clearly mine. I knew it as I listened to the other singers."

Heidelberg's Christmas concert. I'd heard it was to be allowed again, in the Holy Ghost church not far from where we were standing.

"A hundred voices were finally chosen but I'm to have a solo. Me."

He didn't seem to notice the strangeness of my room, the bed I quickly straightened from the morning.

"I've come to take you to Mannheim. Those that left before me called my coach. We'll have time for just one toast before I catch a late train back to Wiesbaden."

A condition of his release had been that he'd get some rest and guard his voice for a program the following day.

The Wiesbaden contract released Günther into a vortex of irregularly scheduled rehearsals and the everyday jobs he still needed. I thought we'd share my room, but he thought he had to commute from Mannheim where, he said, employers were more generous. I ignored unspoken motives for this decision because when he walked the streets where I was walking, our separation seemed easier to bear. I said nothing about the solo singer when I mentioned the concert to my students, only smiled at my secret when their eagerness to attend sent them hurrying for Reichsmark when I offered to buy the tickets.

On the appointed evening, Bill arrived first. He came gathering fistfuls of the winter's first snow, looking back in delight at the footprints he was making. Others crossed from the *Haus zum Ritter* where the Americans had a restaurant. Our mood was festive and friendly as we sought shelter from the snow laden daylight behind thick stone walls. Rosy trim on soaring vaulting led to a gallery where Günther would soon stand and sing.

"If this is a church," one of the children said, "where's the altar?"

"And a picture of Jesus?" his brother asked.

"Hush," their mother cautioned.

Music stands scraped across stone flooring as the men of the orchestra gathered. They were formally dressed with only an occasional muffler hiding a stiff shirt front but a cello player, his white hair long around his shoulders, wore an overcoat against the cold. Then a hush, the miracle of anticipation as the maestro raised his hands and music was everywhere around us. Strong. And full. And growing.

> COMFORT YE,
> COMFORT YE, MY PEOPLE

Gunther sang with a trumpeter as his partner, each corner resounding with the joy of Handel's music.

> KING OF KINGS,
> AND LORD OF HOSTS
> HALLELUJAH! HALLELUJAH!

"That was great," my students said as we left the church, our faces flushed from the cold and the memory of the music.

"Thank you."

"Thank you."

"Come with us." Bill lifted his face to catch a flake still drifting in the air.

"I'm meeting a friend."

"One of the singers?"

I nodded.

"That's even better. We can tell him? her? How great it was."

"How much we appreciated the opportunity."

I told them my friend and I had other plans and they disappeared into the darkness as the snow came full again. The city was a blend of white. I waited by a back stairway where Günther had said he'd leave the building, my every nerve alive to the moment we'd be together though I thought it would be later. Surely he'd want celebratory time with the other singers but a door burst open in a flash of light. Then closed. Günther grasped a rail as he leaned out above me.

"It was wonderful," I whispered.

He leaped over the rail, clutching my hand, fingering the fabric of my glove. A sudden gust from off the river sent us hurrying away, brushing at our eyes if a drifting flake caught on our lashes. Günther extended his hand for my keys as we turned into Pfannengasse, laughing when I dropped them, dipping with me to scoop them up in a handful of snow. He wiped each key before he unlocked the building. After the second door, he slipped both keys into his pocket.

In the quiet, in the dark, he hung our coats. He stirred tiny lumps of coal I'd plucked hastily from a roadway. His hands on my blouse were gentle but with clear purpose, pausing only to lift in quiet submission when mine reached down his sleeves to remember the suppleness of his skin, the tautness of his muscle. He uttered a single sound as we threw our final garments toward the chair, a long breath that was almost a moan as we moved toward the release that had been so long denied us.

In the darkest hours as night approaches dawn, a series of shrieks from across the hall brought us from exhausted sleep. A door slammed. Heavy bootfall followed and the outside door fell shut below us. "Do you think help is needed," Günther whispered.

Before I could answer, soft slippered feet moved toward the toilet in the hall.

"I find it hard," Günther said, his hand was on my shoulder with a rhythmic tightening, letting go. "My own special demons are in this room. I keep trying to defeat them but I find it hard."

The remains of the night were filled with fingers, tongues, caresses, probing. A hand pressed lovingly against a mouth to quiet an ascent. Daylight glowed beyond my window when Günther finally asked if this were the only place I'd brought the soldiers. When I nodded, he threw the covers from our bodies and leaped out of bed. "Then I claim this place as mine. I came here and I conquered." Triumphant as a Wagnerian hero, he reached for his shivering Isolde and brought me up to stand beside him. "Later we'll find a smith who'll make me keys so we can share our stronghold."

I led him back to bed, bringing the covers around us before I spread my hands across his chest, his waist, his loins, caressing to life my affirmation, moving up with my legs on each side of his body to cement a triumph I thought we had accomplished.

That afternoon, Günther found a smith who, despite all government restrictions, would make a copy of my keys without the landlord's knowledge. With them Günther could come to our room when he was able, leaving a message if I weren't there, or a gift he thought would please me, or sit in the chair with wooden arms not giving in to the demons that still danced around him.

# Winter
## through Spring and into Autumn
## 1946-1947

The new year exploded in a winter more paralyzing than the one before. A new currency was talked about, but not attempted while the Reichsmark's value dropped to worthless. A German economic council, struggling to initiate exchange between the American and the British Zones, had to work within an economy in such a state of degradation recovery seemed impossible. Then, temperatures dropped lower than had ever been recorded. Electricity was cut to designated hours, gas to selected days and only to the time of cooking. When the stealing of wood soared out of control, trees were rationed. Four trees for two families, but any individual cutting a meter of wood from his allotted tree to warm his family, was required to cut an additional meter to warm the offices of our struggling local government.

The rivers froze, not just the Neckar but the Rhine. And in the Ruhr, the mines shut down. Miners, suffering from malnutrition, were too weak to carry out their duties. American food sent to feed the occupiers was diverted in a futile attempt to meet the caloric allotment for the population.

Across all zones, a merciless snow kept falling until bus drivers in aging buses abandoned their vehicles in the streets. With no transportation and conditions impossible for walking, I clung to my room, seeking warmth beneath my blankets, ignoring gnawing hunger by planning elaborate lessons in my head. When the unrelenting cold absorbed the fuel set aside to warm the victors, my students arrived at the library bundled into woolen layers and stayed that way throughout our time together, making jokes about blankets brought to offices where secretaries typed awkwardly with gloved fingers. The only glimmer of light in all that darkness was for Günther. Defying plummeting temperatures, audiences in increasing numbers made the extraordinary effort to hear him sing.

In February, the Neckar flooded high into the city leaving a stench of rotting logs and sewage as it receded. I trudged around in a kind of inert animation until one day on my way to meet a student, a military three-quarter-ton truck from the Headquarters Motor Pool almost ran me over as it turned across the sidewalk and disappeared through a narrow passage between two desolate buildings. The shock of such a near collision with the only driver on the street raised me from my stupor. Frustration exploded into anger. Having time before the lesson, I charged after the truck's foreign driver, ready to confront his irresponsibility, but in a cobblestone yard behind the buildings, I saw a soldier and his female helper, who'd been passengers in the truck, climbing an unpainted outdoor staircase toward what appeared to be activity on an upper floor. Hesitation was for the less desperate. I plunged after, pulling myself up by a slippery railing as I struggled to keep my footing. On reaching a small landing, I yanked a wooden door. The couriers had disappeared into a windowed office but a balding man whose patched blue workers' coveralls did nothing to disguise his unmistakable authority was coming toward me from a room jarred by a pulsing din. Behind him a group of women, hands warmed by gloves with cut off fingers, sat around a table folding, stacking, stamping recently printed papers with a worn medallion on a long smooth stick. The god of caprice had flung a bolt of hope and hit me. In response to my stream of questions, the man nodded. Yes, this was a functioning business. Yes, a vacancy happened now and then. He said he didn't mind if I checked with him, but not too often. My step lightened. My shoulders squared. I even smiled when I passed the army truck's foreign driver. I couldn't wait to write to Günther.

By March, the city emerged from its long, dark winter with permission for peacetime's first parade. Günther was in Heidelberg for the celebration. As we walked the crowded blocks of Hauptstrasse, we listened, unbelieving, to the beat of martial music. An American oversight authority controlled all music played in public, so the cadence was particularly unfamiliar. We were delighting in this sign of progress when I saw Bill Lewis bounding toward us, his camera clicking in all directions.

"The man from the hospital?" Günther's frown was in his voice.

I wouldn't be deterred. "Günther, Bill." I used the familiar when I introduced them. The men shook hands but Bill's attention was already on a group of children wearing festive *Lederhosen*. Each child waved a streamer-wrapped stick topped with a giant pretzel. The stark whiteness of a hollowed egg filled the center of some pretzels, others held a small apple. When one child bit into his apple, Bill was beyond containing. "Will he mind if I take his picture?" he asked Günther.

"He won't know," Günther said. "He's too excited."

Bill leaped across the street for a better angle.

"Bill? Günther?" Günther asked, but he was smiling.

"The American way," I said as Günther pulled the end of my scarf and tossed it across my shoulder.

The band was coming. A waving, smiling *Bürgermeister* led the way. Behind him, among other overcoated marchers and a few horse drawn floats, were pairs of revelers wearing cone-shaped costumes. Each cone covered in dry straw, signifying winter, was accompanied by another cone covered in branches of evergreen from the forest, flower-pocked with new spring's promise. Crowds followed these dancing figures to Hercules Square where the straw stacks were abandoned and ignited. Across growing flames, as I cheered and clapped, I saw Anna cheering and clapping between two uniformed strangers. Air Force officers from a different part of the zone. She nodded when she saw me but she didn't wave. Günther didn't notice. I knew I should mention this chance encounter, and, in a way, that's what I wanted, but Günther's attention was on a crush of children throwing their sticks with streamers into the fire. He leaned down to whisper that this year would be different. One day soon he'd show me yellow flowers because he happened to know where, last fall, bulbs had been planted. I remember shivering in reflected heat.

April erupted into a sea of apple blossoms, from Quinckestrasse in our city all the way to Weinheim, and daffodils bloomed below the windows of the Americans' Stadtgarten restaurant. By May, the world turned green. In June, the government of the United

States, acknowledging that such deprivation as the two winters just completed couldn't be allowed to happen again, rescinded the original document of occupation denying economic recovery and George Marshall, an American general and diplomat, announced the European Recovery Program. America would assist the defeated as well as the victorious nations.

July was hot and dry.

With other campers, Günther and I spent our nights on the banks of the Neckar, lying beside small inverted V's of canvas, our arms around each other. He told me the time had passed when we just endure. He was ready to set goals, to search out opportunities. Stuttgart's State Theater was preparing an opera season and he was confident he would win a contract if he could secure permission to travel to that city. He promised, when he'd been successful, we'd have the wedding he wanted for me, with a horse drawn carriage to bring me to his side in a church with soaring vaulting, his friends to sing. He said Frau Schuler would have cake made with fresh eggs and creamy butter and everyone would dance until the early hours of the morning. Then came a long, dry August. The worst winter had been followed by the worst summer and drought reduced the yields of farmers. For one more year, Germany faced a threat of famine as the months passed into the third winter since the war.

# Winter 1947-1948

*I* heard the knock on my door with a measure of indecision. With no student scheduled during several training days when the American military would be confined to barracks, I'd intended to spend time in Schwetzingen with my family, but as the afternoon darkened and eastern winds grew more intense, I chose the protection of my room over the bitterness outside. I'd been reading while the last of the coal in my stove turned to ashes, thinking I'd put my book away when the glow was gone and go to bed.

The knock came, impatiently, again.

I glanced at my watch. Not Günther. He was in Mannheim readying for his move to Stuttgart. He'd been granted permission to participate in the opera auditions but before he left, he was earning what he could by caring for a pregnant Boxer dog in an American household while the owners were away. The knock came louder one more time. I opened the door. A length of body, a turn of head, some spark of recognition drew a startled exclamation from me. "Paul? Paul Schuler, is that you? No, it can't be." I started to close the door.

"It is Paul," the apparition answered.

He stood above me, a great mangy wolf of a man whose clothes hung on his frame like a molting winter coat on a carnivorous animal. His boots were wrapped in newspapers and strips of cloth. Then, as if the animal had caught scent from the air, he spoke again. "I've come a long way, Renate. I have to sit down."

He shrugged me away when I tried to help and a stench from the wild followed. Pulling a tight Russian cap from his head, he slumped onto my chair with wooden arms. He said he'd looked for me at the station, adding, "My mother came to Heidelberg, meeting every train. She'd only kissed me once when I asked for you."

He couldn't have gone to Schwetzingen and returned in this condition. "You left your mother at the station?" I said.

A sharp cough brought him leaning forward until a string of spittle stretched from his mouth to his baggy quilted trousers.

"You left your mother at the station?" I repeated.

His eyes snapped open, staring roundly up at me. The coughing spasm left him. "Seeing me alive was all she needed."

I'd forgotten how pale his eyes were and how hard, but I remembered how I'd longed for his and Hartmut's greeting when I returned from Aland Nord.

"My mother tried to tell me why you no longer live at home. She didn't have to say. Before I was back across our borders, I knew of the victorious American army, their bands, their entertainments, their degradation of our German women." His crusted fingers curled against my chair as he described the woman from across the hall who'd let him in downstairs, her soldier client with her. His breath was gone but eventually he added, "The winters are very cold in Russia. One forgets the winters are cold in Germany, too."

I searched this exhausted stranger for the man whom I remembered, the neighbor I'd worshiped with a schoolgirl's anguish, my brother's childhood companion.

He said he'd had one bath since his release. Before that he wasn't sure he could remember. It was too late for a bus to Schwetzingen, too late for anything but ministering with what I had to offer. I told him there was a toilet in the hall. No bathtub on this floor. Abruptly he was standing again and his attention turned to my basin in the corner. The remnants of his padded coat, a *Luftwaffe* jacket, a tunic shirt, his baggy quilted trousers all dropped beside my bed. I was startled by the brazenness with which he exposed his body but in the crowded closeness of my tiny room I couldn't look away. He was thinner than he looked in layers of clothing but he still had the stiff-backed carriage of a soldier. I saw the strength that had allowed him to survive.

"Tell me, Renate, do your soldiers bring you soap? It's been years since I used soap."

With the familiarity of one accustomed to very little, Paul bathed in my porcelain bowl. He used the towel I offered. The dark teeth of my comb snapped in his matted hair and he tossed it back onto my bureau. I asked if he wanted something to eat.

"I want to sleep," he said and crawled, naked, into my bed.

While fresh cold water filled my largest vessel, I separated Paul's clothes with the toe of my shoe, aware there could be vermin. Scraps that could be dry by morning, I lifted to the water before I recognized the futility of that action. His clothes were only fit for burning. After hanging what I'd dampened, I sank into the chair with wooden arms and slept fitfully through the night in the room beside him.

I was slicing bread when he awoke.

"My clothes?" Sleep clawed at his voice.

"They may be damp."

His feet dropped over the edge of the bed and he sat with his unkempt head clutched tight between his fingers while I arranged bread and cheese on a plate, but before I'd placed the food on the table, he'd pulled a layer of clothes over his body and disappeared into the hall. He returned to sit with his back to me, forcing handfuls into his mouth, belching. I turned from the sour odor of his breath and added ersatz coffee to slowly heating water. I was too upset to ask about his mother but she was hardly from my thoughts. I asked him about himself.

"You want to hear how we fought the Russian winter in lightweight uniforms because victory had been ordered by summer? How flesh peeled from our hands on the frozen barrels of our rifles? How our feet were black when our boots were cut away?"

I busied myself with my utensils.

"I could tell you how our bodies crawled with lice until we were crazy from the itching. When our medical supplies gave out, our scratches were a magnet and what could've been resolved with a drop of iodine turned deadly. Life is very simple then, Renate. A matter of avoiding scratches."

This is Paul, this is Paul, my mind repeated. I poured his coffee. Between tepid gulps he said remembering the fresh clean odor of my flesh had kept him alive in hells that stank of unwashed bodies, my whispers drowned out sounds of others moaning. He said only dreams of me kept him alive until the Russians gave him a train ticket to the border. I was too horrified to contradict his imagination but when he stood and thrust his arms through the padded sleeves of his foul, stained coat, I reached for mine. His claw-like fingers stopped me.

"Paul, I must."

"No."

I knew I should be more insistent, he'd left his mother at the station, but underneath his rigidity I sensed a growing anger. He reached for his boots. I handed him the still damp wrappings.

His heavy footsteps in the stairwell faded to the street and I hastened to my window, hiding behind my curtain to watch until his hulking, lurching, stranger's back had disappeared. Then, pulling on my own dark coat, I went immediately to Mannheim.

"My God, Renate, could there be a worse possible time?"

Phone service was still difficult between cities so I'd waited until Mannheim before using the phone number Günther had given me to call if I needed him. Before I'd finished explaining, he'd told me to meet him at his room. I waited on the street. The look on his face as he hurried toward me warned me that the demons I'd thought forgotten had brought him from his duties. I wanted to approach the problem with restraint but as we climbed the stairs, words kept bursting from me. He must have seen these men returned from Russia. Not fed or with new shoes like the ones sent back from France or Britain. Surely he could imagine what it was to know one. The only thing I could think to add as he worked the padlock on his door was that Frau Schuler must have told him where I lived. How else could he have found Pfannengasse?

Günther's room was chilled from being empty so neither of us removed our coats as we plunged into the routine of putting cups on his table, looking for his coffee, but Günther stopped before we'd finished. In words clearly forced to calmness, he said he wasn't making accusations, he was trying to get a picture, but Paul came to me right from the station? "You let him in? Okay. But he cleaned himself there in your room? Why didn't he go upstairs?"

"I don't know. I told him where there was a tub."

"I'm not implying anything, Renate, but he stripped naked in your room?"

I had no other answer. I told the truth.

His face was impenetrable, a photo caught in time. "Then what did he do?"

"Nothing. He went to sleep." It all sounded so unbelievable. It'd been unbelievable for me the night before.

Uncompromising lines were narrowing his mouth as he bent to plug a heater into the wall. Rising slowly, he hung his coat on a peg beside the door. As I shoved my gloves into my pocket, I told him I'd slept in the chair. He stared at the sky beyond his window.

With the space heater finally glowing, I unwound my scarf, hanging it and my hat on top of his. "I was little more than a child when Paul left for the university, Hartmut for the air force just months after. Hartmut was dead so soon."

"And your brother's death obligates you to help Herr Schuler?"

"Paul was my playmate."

"A playmate, Renate? I'd guess he expects more than to be a playmate."

Some choices are impossible to explain. At that moment, I found it necessary to tell him Paul said only dreams of me had kept him alive. All at once, Günther was holding me, pressing my head against his shoulder, telling me he'd be less than honest if he pretended Paul's return didn't disturb him but if Paul's dreams were just of me in the six years since he'd seen me, those dreams wouldn't be erased by a few days talking to his mother. I brought his face toward mine, my fingers digging at his tension, pleading that Paul's life had been such hell. I couldn't hurt him. I couldn't hurt his mother.

"I don't want you to hurt them, Renate, but I don't want you to hurt us, either." His kiss was hard, possessive, but he couldn't stay. He'd had unexpected phone calls and the colonel wasn't a man to understand if he wasn't with the dog as they'd agreed.

The room was suddenly in motion. He swung his coat across his shoulders, trying for a smile as he pulled my hat down over my ears. He said he wasn't making threats but I had to understand. He wasn't ready to live again with others. Last night was no less than I could do for someone I'd known from childhood, "But please, let's go at this slowly. And together."

I tightened my scarf and adjusted my hat to a jauntier angle, not feeling the lightness I was forcing in my voice. Günther would see. Frau Schuler would civilize her son again. I even suggested

Paul would return to his studies as soon as he learned the university was open.

Still tense, he asked me not to return to Heidelberg if I weren't expecting students. After his family returned on Sunday we'd go to Schwetzingen together. I was relieved not to be returning to my dank room. In Mannheim, among his books and music, I could believe he'd have a chance to sneak away again but after he'd leaped into a streetcar that would take him back to the American houses, I wasn't sure I was ready for his leaving. Plagued by Frau Schuler's anguish as she rationalized her son's behavior, I watched his streetcar disappear.

On Sunday I awoke to find a heavy snow had fallen. Great swollen mounds had formed against the window bringing the possibility that clogged roads would delay Günther's military family. Many times as the morning lengthened, I pulled at his door, listening in the stairwell, but heard only other doors scraping across high sills on lower landings. The newspaper on his table was ten days old. I'd read all of it already but I read it one more time to fill my waiting. No Europe wide recovery plan, as proposed in June by General Marshall, had been established but General Clay's summer directive giving us more political autonomy had raised hopes and increased cooperation with the British. My gaze drifted back to the snow filled window.

The door burst open and Günther entered, bringing the chill from outside with him. He leaned back against the door, short of breath from taking the stairs by twos. The colonel had new orders. He'd be leaving for Frankfurt in the morning and he wanted Günther there to help his family.

I remember taking Günther's coat, absorbing the chill and the dampness. I didn't have to ask if this would interfere with his audition, I knew nothing could change that. I asked about the dog. Günther's laugh was a welcome relief. He said I should give him time to catch his breath and use the toilet. On our way to Schwetzingen he'd tell me how relieved he was not to have been a veterinary midwife.

In Schwetzingen we had a brief visit with my father, then Günther took a moment to toss snowballs at Tomas and Inge. They'd run screaming around a corner before he put his arm around me, pulling me along in a slippery hurry. Disappointment actually slumped his body when, at Frau Schuler's, we learned Paul and his mother had gone to Kleingemuend before the snow had started.

"They took a suitcase," one sister said.

"Her son's so handsome." The other giggled.

I liked the sisters. They'd been good tenants for Frau Schuler, young and cheerful, pretty in a bouncing, repetitious way, and at least one thought Paul handsome, but Günther's grip had tightened on my hand. "Something else that can't be helped," he said as the sisters closed the door behind us.

I pulled a low, filled branch, scattering snow in a silent fall. "Of course Paul's aunt would want to see him, but didn't you notice those pretty sisters? They seem ready to take care of Paul."

Günther's smile reassured me.

At my father's, Tomas and Inge leaned from my former bedroom window waving and shouting until their mother drew them back inside. Günther hadn't planned to stay for supper but when I asked, he said, "If it's early." He'd have to clear his room in case he went directly from the colonel's needs to Stuttgart, leaving what he couldn't carry with his teacher and I felt that added separation of his music. A divide not of our making already widening before we met. As I worked around the kitchen, he asked me to spend a few days with my father. If he couldn't be with me when I confronted Paul, he'd like to think the two of us were with Paul's mother.

"Where are the others?" my father asked as we settled at the table. So little was left of him. His slight body. His drifting mind. I wondered if he knew the meal was early. "I'll stay some nights with you," I said and Günther nodded.

We helped my father to the music room when the meal was finished and left him sitting in his straight-backed musician's chair, his violin high on his shoulder. The fingers of his left hand raced along the neck though his right hand hung limply.

Günther's grasp tightened across my shoulder when, behind us, my father's bow caught two low strings, double stopping, before brilliantly evolving into an athletic exhibition I'd thought him no longer capable of playing. A crystalline arpeggio followed.

"I've not heard him play before," Günther said. "I hadn't realized he was quite that good." The violin slipped into plaintive minor tones, a song that was eastern in its longing. "What could have been in his mind as the years went by and he had music only as a hobby?"

I tried to memorize the length of him against me, storing for the future the way his hand found the back of my head when we kissed. I had just these moments before he left for Mannheim.

A cold fog clung to the city the day I returned to Heidelberg. Not a soft fog. Not sweet smelling as the fogs of spring. It hung in the streets along the river, absorbing the length of alleys in an acrid mist. The Schulers hadn't returned from Kleingemuend while I was with my father but I'd begun to believe the problem of Paul's returning would simply take care of itself. My thoughts were on Bill's language lesson, planning ways to approach the coming Christmas season.

I went directly to the library.

Bill was delighted with my stories and struggled to tell me tales, in German, of a Texas Christmas. His vocabulary was so improved, I was sure he'd found a German girlfriend and was pleased with my imaginings as, after our session, I maneuvered along the gently sloping sidewalk. I paused at the tunnel to the printer. With a regular job in addition to my students, and Paul helping, surely Frau Schuler could stay home even with Günther leaving. I wanted that for her. I hurried into the cobbled yard and climbed the outdoor stairs. Inside, the foreman in his patched blue clothes smiled when he saw me. "I thought of you today," he said. "Your persistence is rewarded. After the new year we'll have a vacancy in assembly."

I wanted to shout above the clanging presses, hug this man with his ink-stained fingers and kindly face. I stumbled back down the stairs. No word had reached me from Günther, no visit between Frankfurt and Stuttgart, but a regular job, with regular pay, was the best kind of news to tell him when he returned.

On Pfannengasse my building was clammy from the days of snow. A shriek of laughter filtered through the walls. I knew Günther had been in my room when I touched the light. Red apples in a bright blue bowl were on my table and a note scribbled on the back of yellow paper wrinkled from his pocket. The note said he couldn't wait or get to Schwetzingen. His employer had returned to Heidelberg for a briefing, bringing his private car with Günther driving so he could go to Mannheim. The dog had seven puppies. With traffic slowed by fog, Günther had time just to bring the apples. He could possibly return once more before Stuttgart if he were sent for the dogs, but if we missed again he'd write as soon as he was able, as soon as he had an address.

I crumpled the note and threw the yellow paper across the room. Then, fighting tears of anger and frustration, bent to retrieve it. My first thought was to return to Schwetzingen and force some kind of resolution with Paul but I couldn't leave Heidelberg. I couldn't chance another miss with Günther.

Paul came two nights after Günther left his apples. He didn't knock. He rattled my door and stood clean-shaven before me in clothes he'd worn to Tübingen where he'd been a student. His expression was not cold but bloodless. "You came to Schwetzingen to flaunt your lover." He slammed the door behind us.

My fists were little use against his wiry strength as he backed me against my basin. When his hand thrust up my skirt, I began to cry.

Günther was in Heidelberg the next morning. I was across the river, needing to walk in the hills in early morning darkness, needing to suck clean air into my lungs. When Paul left, my only thought had been to get away. I hadn't noticed his sweater thrown across my chair, his scarf across my dresser.

Günther had spent the previous evening trying to keep warm in his employer's car while the colonel and his lady lingered at a formal reception. The pickup for the bitch and her puppies had been scheduled for the following day and Günther had spent that idle time in planning. If he left Frankfurt before dawn's light made the streets seem safer, he could be in Heidelberg and steal a few hours with me. He'd be taking a chance driving out of his way in an American's car without permission, but this would be his last trip before his move to Stuttgart.

I knew he'd been in my room when I saw his keys in the bright blue bowl he'd brought to hold his apples. There was no note, no other sign, and then I saw Paul's sweater. I ran from the room, directly into the woman who worked the room across the hall. She smiled over her shoulder at another soldier. Yes, she'd seen Günther. Yes, he'd asked about the stranger. She laughed when she told me the old man who lived in the room above me had really confused her answer. He'd come downstairs when he'd heard them in the hallway and confronted Günther with the complaint that he'd been kept awake all night. "Noisier than usual," he'd said.

"Then last night wasn't the first he's been here?" Günther asked.

"Oh, no. It's like he lives here." The old man with his watery eyes hadn't seen the difference between Paul and Günther, and my other neighbor's client was in too much of a hurry for her to offer a correction.

Ignoring the futility of searching for Günther there, I went immediately to Mannheim. A woman had taken his room. "I never met the man who lived here," she said.

I pounded on each closed door.

"The young man who lived in the attic did mention his move. He seemed quite pleased."

"He works very hard, you know, and he has lessons."

"I didn't realize he was gone. Did he get permission?"

I sought his coach and pleaded for an address, clutching my hands together, fighting not to grab his shirt front and shake the information from him. His face glowered with suspicion. "Herr Lange will tell you all you need to know. He must devote himself to music."

"To music!" It was the wrong thing to say, the wrong way to say it. The former singer from the Semper Opera closed his door.

I escaped to Luisen Park, seeking comfort in a place where Günther and I had walked together, but night soon darkened pathways and more snow threatened. I fled back to a corner near his building where I could see a light in the window of his room beneath the eaves. Standing there, growing colder, I tried to force my desperation across the terrible abyss of his absence so Günther would hear and understand. Knowing he'd never return to Pfannengasse, I went to Schwetzingen, giving no thought to what I'd tell the others, no thought to when I'd return to my students.

Through that night, I lay awake in sweaty darkness, struggling through a haze of unremembered dreams. I knew I was in my bed, in my room beside the kitchen, but I kept trying to believe Paul's assault had been a nightmare. Günther was in Mannheim. I recognized this wasn't true and sank back into semi-consciousness, screaming in my head. My father's shuffle in the hall told me others were waking. Soon I'd hear the Zieglers. I'd lived in this house too long, with its illusion of tranquility, to believe I could speak of rape or rage or other dirty secrets. A well-learned need for dignity was all I had to cling to. Taking in great gulps of morning air, I threw back my covers, freeing my feet to search for slippers beside my bed. I reached for my robe which lay across it. I'd tell the others I'd come home to rest. My students had canceled classes through the holiday season. Günther couldn't believe what he was thinking. He would write. He would return. Or I would go to Stuttgart.

I hurried making breakfast in the kitchen before the commotion of Tomas and Inge could assault me, but my father was slow, he lingered with the children. I felt the house contracting.

I was on the street that linked our houses the first time I met the Schulers. The two of them, mother and son, were animated, beaming at each other. In fine pre-war clothing, they looked very much what they once had been, the family of a distinguished professor.

"Renate," Frau Schuler called from a distance. Paul nodded politely as they approached, smiling the smile that was so central to his charm. I was stunned by the denial in his actions but managed to respond, edging along the fence to accept their greeting, flinching as Paul took my hand and bent to kiss my frost-red cheek.

Frau Schuler covered our clasped hands, looking from one face to the other. "Is something wrong?"

"Nothing's wrong," Paul said.

I longed to shout my accusations but I only twisted my hand away.

Exuding tenderness as he took his mother's arm, Paul said they'd found the day not too cold if they moved briskly. They were walking to the castle. He asked me to come with them. He even touched my shoulder. I don't remember my excuses but I do remember Frau Schuler looking back before they reached the corner.

I fled to the small salon where my father was oblivious to my returning and snatched a book to turn the pages.

Laughter preceded the Schulers on their return. They came up our walk, to the broad stone steps, the wide front door. They knew the door was open. Frau Schuler was already calling as she entered. I must come to them that evening. They were planning a simple meal but special because we could be together. Paul ignored my mute refusal. "Your father, as well," he said.

Frau Schuler enclosed me in a warm embrace. "Of course you're coming, and of course we include your father."

I couldn't look at her. I couldn't look at Paul. Time had collapsed. I was a child again, the little sister. There'd been no war, no years of deprivation. Hartmut would be at the dinner and my mother. Professor Schuler. Gerda would bake a cake for me to carry.

"We'll see you at six," Frau Schuler said as she and Paul walked back to the street that linked our houses. "Come early, we'll chat while you help me in the kitchen."

I sat on my bed in my room beside the kitchen, listening to ordinary noises, trying to find calm in the familiar. Nothing I'd ever say or do could give Frau Schuler the agony of knowing what had happened. I even convinced myself I'd fought so hard because the stranger who returned from Russia assaulted memories I didn't want to change. As I moved about getting myself and my father ready, I decided I'd go briefly to Heidelberg. So few lessons were planned before the holidays, my students would accept any reason if I canceled. After the new year, after I'd started my job at the printer's, after the newness of Paul's returning had passed, that was time enough to confront him, and if Günther hadn't written, that was time to go to Stuttgart.

Frau Schuler's American employer had released her through the holidays and I detected joy in her telling about the crowded visit in Kleingemuend, but I heard something guarded as well, something unreal about the way she didn't even glance in my direction. In the kitchen she apologized for not having found me before she went to meet Paul. The message she'd received from a neighbor who had access to a phone was too unclear. She couldn't miss a possible arrival. I longed to put my arms around her, to tell her I understood, but her hurt was so deep I couldn't bring myself to touch it. "Renate, he was different at my sister's," she said. "Has he been all right with you?"

I concentrated on the settings I was gathering for the table.

"Answer me, child. Have you seen a difference?"

I let my breath out slowly. "Yes," I said, "I have. I told Günther Paul needs his mother."

Her relief made such a difference in her voice. She asked about Günther and I told her I hadn't heard. "Ah, that's the reason you've been distant. I was worried it was Paul." I loved her so much, I made a silent vow to be forgiving of her son. I even tried to greet him with affection when he entered the kitchen, urging us to hurry. His mother spread the *Eintopf* she'd been stirring across a platter. "Men are too impatient," she said.

But through the days that led to a bleak Christmas, the child in me returned. A frightened child, a child in a child's season trying to be good. Many times each day, I checked myself in the small, cold toilet room beyond the kitchen, forcing my fingers against my body for a sign of menstrual flow, raging at the thought of Paul when there was none. My life swung between an apathy of disbelieving and frantic animation. For hours, I'd do nothing but curl into my bed. Then I'd erupt into a vibrancy, an absurdity, a fury in which I bolted to the street, searching strangers' faces. I wanted to berate Günther because he'd left me. I wanted to find solace in his arms. I wanted to attack Paul, clawing at his smile. I returned to the castle gardens, to the lake now edged with ice. Pacing. I drove my thoughts back to summer, when lilacs bloomed, to fall and the harsh red of a Japanese maple. Near the Moorish Pavilion, where American officers had their illicit club, I broke a twig from a tall thorn tree and a thorn pierced my finger. The blood was from a stranger. The lethargy returned.

Günther's note arrived in the week I could no longer deny I was pregnant with Paul's child. It came in a plain envelope with a temporary address. The auditions had been more competitive than he'd imagined. His days were very full. But in his exhaustion, in the turmoil of his leaving, he'd neglected our promise to be open with each other. He was sorry if his selfishness had caused me pain. He'd come to Heidelberg as soon as he was able.

I read the letter twice before I folded it away.

I wouldn't resume my language lessons. My students had asked too many questions about the *Lebensborn* society, Hitler's Spring of Life society, among whose duties to the Reich had been to provide a meeting place for officers from the elite forces and dedicated young women willing to produce racially pure children for Germany's future. In my panic I searched for the joy I'd always been told these Lebensborn women had. I needed the security of a past when Hitler's horror of abortion forbade the process for Aryan women. I imagined loving the baby, loving the baby's father as when our parents expected us to marry. But even in my isolation and confusion, I recognized the absolute necessity of returning to Heidelberg when the holidays were over. The job I'd been promised at the printer's would begin with the new year.

Each day, each early morning through the bitter weeks that followed, I hastened from my room, moving through streets, ice-bound in the shadows, to my job in the hidden courtyard across from the university. An occasional café had opened where food could be bought with an exchange of ration coupons, but random acts of political extremism accompanied this progress. On the white side of a university building, built by American benefactors before the war and now military classrooms and an American movie theater, tall black letters suddenly appeared:

# GO BACK TO AMERICA

An innocuous 88 painted here and there throughout the city was less blatant.

The eighth letter of the alphabet.

HH.

The old mandatory greeting.

I brought to Schwetzingen a carefully lettered card that'd been passed to me by a stranger one crowded afternoon on Hauptstrasse. Frau Schuler read it aloud.

**"Ami, go home. German students will be free."**

We were sitting at her kitchen table, Paul hovering above us. I told them the cards were distributed by isolated groups but were a worry. Paul contradicted. "I'd have said a truth."

These Sunday afternoons, in the kitchen's warmth, I searched for ways to tell the man across the table I was pregnant with his child but it was as if spoken, the words would make the fact more irrevocably true. Instead, I spoke of my work, of the range of former wealth and education in the women who sat beside me, of how the shop's surprising survival depended on printing a regularly updated version of an American telephone directory for the ever increasing army of occupation.

Before Paul could speak, his mother shook his arm.

At the printer's my wage included coarse bread brought by an apprentice in the morning. More bread and a bowl of watery soup later in the day. As January passed, I ate little else. My weekends in Schwetzingen stopped when more than weakness from a pregnancy I'd been trying to ignore kept me in my bed. I had fever, pain, nausea I'd guessed was only partially due to the growing baby. Through uncounted days, I faced the wall, reality a wisp I struggled to bring forward. I barely heard the knock on my door but managed to call out, "Not locked." The words left me coughing.

Paul was explaining as he entered. His mother was worried. She'd have come, but the wind, the weather. He wouldn't let her.

"Go away." I was lucid, angry, wiping saliva with the back of my hand.

"I won't."

I started choking, bringing up the bile. Paul reached for the porcelain bowl I'd been using. He held my head while I retched and gagged, letting the slick yellow drain from my mouth, rinsing the bowl when I was finished, placing it back beside my bed. He wrung a cloth at my basin in the corner and patted the damp across my forehead, across my mouth still sour. "Go away," I said.

"Let me help," he said.

His pale eyes were soft with a concern from the years when we were children, before the lines in his face had deepened. I needed help so badly. I asked him to go to the printer. Speak only to the foreman who might understand if he were asked to hold my job. Paul rinsed my glass, brimmed it with fresh water, and put it close so I could reach it. With gentle intimacy, he gathered my hair away from the pillow. I felt comforted when he told me he had a meeting but would stop back before he returned to Schwetzingen.

From the meeting he brought thick hunks of bread and apples, a piece of pungent sausage he quickly closed back in its wrapper. He found a knife to core an apple. "You should keep something in your stomach," he said. "And drink all the water you can keep down."

I told him he sounded like his mother.

"It's where I learned." He smiled. He said the last bus wouldn't wait but he'd be back tomorrow. As he shrugged into his coat, I repeated my request about my work. He didn't answer.

In the next days Paul was in and out of my room with news about my father, his mother, excited about the meetings in Heidelberg he attended almost daily. He spoke of the federal government Germany had been promised. The last London conference had failed to produce one, but he was confident there'd be another chance.

With surprising skill, he prepared what he brought for us to eat. Cutting, chopping, cooking on my heating stove with wood fuel he found somewhere. Until my strength returned, he spent many daylight hours in my room. He read, he talked to me of Germany's future. He bathed my face as my fever ebbed. Once from the depths of a briefcase he always carried, he brought three red cans, displaying them on my bedside table. "From Anna," he said.

"Anna?"

He'd met her after one of his meetings. She was with a friend of his named Max. It was only by chance he'd mentioned my name. His smile wavered as he told me her face was made up like a whore. That was such an old fashioned way of thinking. When our calorie allotment had been increased and food was actually available, women were freed to think about how we looked and we wanted to look pretty. Makeup had a growing acceptance.

Paul told me Anna lived on Akademiestrasse, near the Pferde Platz. He thought she was working for some colonel. With a knife, he punctured a lid on one of the red cans and pried it open, adding water after reading directions. "She said to tell you the soup is not from Heidelberg but from the days when you were walking home."

I lay back against my pillows. Those days were from another life. They happened to other people. I'd finally destroyed Günther's only letter, abandoning the solace I stole from tracing his pen strokes with my fingers. He'd not come to Heidelberg as he'd promised. I needed to plan for a different future. Paul's touch was not like Günther's but it was firm. I no longer needed his help but because I needed his part in that deeper past, I let his arm support me as he spooned broth between my lips. One day I told him to keep the keys I'd given him. There was no need for him to stop using my room before his meetings just because I felt strong enough to return to the printer. The time was close when I could tell him the whole truth about my illness. And tell his mother.

Large flakes were intermittent in the air the morning I returned to work. They seemed almost random beyond my window, but when I pulled the downstairs door behind me, wind off the ice-clogged Neckar tore at my coat. My lungs stung from the cold. In a protected corner of the Hay Market, I leaned against an overarching building before following some laughing students who were crossing toward the university.

Beyond the presses, in the room filled with their din, another woman was in my place folding printed papers. I knew the uselessness of protest. A space left empty on any bench would soon be filled by someone who needed the work as much as I. Paul's failure to tell the foreman was bad enough, but not to tell me of that failure was insulting. All feeling of closeness left me, all feeling of trust. On Hauptstrasse, a streetcar filled my presence. Its blue side glistened. Faces peered down from breath-dimmed windows.

Paul was in my room. He was hanging his coat above the stove for drying. A canvas sack, lumped with coal, was beside the chair, a newspaper on the table.

"You didn't tell them!"

He unpacked the coal into my rusted bucket before spreading the newspaper across the table, turning pages slowly. "More demands for real money," he read aloud.

"You let me get up this morning and walk through this weather for nothing. Look at me, Paul. I'm soaking."

He shrugged. "It was demeaning work but I suppose compared to whoring you didn't notice."

I threw my coat across the chair and sat heavily on its dampness before leaning forward to remove my shoes, my anger growing. I shook my thick stockings across my bed.

At the scraping of Paul's chair, I looked up and recognized the conflict. In me he saw our country's degradation and yet he wanted me for all his loathing. He told me there was no need for me to work. He'd provide for all of us.

"How?" I asked. "From your mother's wages? You accept your

mother's money as if you were a student. You kiss her cheek as though her sacrifice were nothing. Look at her cheek, Paul. Look at its color. Can you understand what being a servant has done to her?"

"Leave my mother out of this."

"I can't. She's the reason the rest of us keep living and she does it on her hands and knees scrubbing floors in an American apartment." I took my coat from the chair and hung it in the broken closet. He was as much a whore as I'd been with the soldiers.

"I have a job," he said.

I steadied myself against the closet. "I don't believe you."

His laugh erupted at my denial, retrieving the charm, the casual confidence, the handsomeness of old. He said he worked for our future chancellor, Gerhard von Rautner. Von Rautner would rid Germany of our enemies, kill the cancer of occupation. His lean body sank back, half-sitting against the table. I could feel his eyes following me, absorbed in the way my body moved as I took the kettle from its place on the back of my stove and added icy water.

Von Rautner met with Paul's group at the *Blaue Reiter*, a beer hall on Hauptstrasse, just beyond the Kornmarktplatz. The place had always been notorious for its tiny rooms and secret meetings. I sat down to wait for the heating water and pulled a quilt across my shoulders, furious that Paul was having trouble forcing his attention away from my breasts which were full despite the gauntness of my body. "Get out of here," I said.

He turned to face the window.

"Get out of here, Paul."

His fists tightened on the sill before he retrieved his coat from where it hung drying. "I have a meeting," he said.

I didn't want to leave the haven of my room but I couldn't chance the turmoil of Paul's returning. I threw my toothbrush into my knapsack, my comb, some clothes that were loose enough for wearing. I'd go to Schwetzingen. I'd find his mother.

Across Hauptstrasse I quit the jostling throng for the calming byways of the city, abandoning the uselessness of anger as agelessness closed in around me. Wandering an oblique twisting way toward the buses, my attention was caught by white letters on a bright blue placard above my head. Akademiestrasse. The name tore at my memory. Akademiestrasse. Anna's street.

I hesitated only briefly. Any lodging would be in Anna's name. Even if an American paid the rent, no American could claim a German apartment not assigned by the military's housing authority. I pulled my coat around me and started walking back from Pferde Platz, peering at names in the weather's darkness, reading each mail slot beside each door.

A. Wehrhahn.

I caught the foyer door as another tenant hurried out into the cold.

On each broad landing as I climbed marble stairs, I read more names engraved on brass plates slipped into shining brackets.

Anna Wehrhahn/Charlie Dobbs.

I pushed the bell.

"Is that you, *Liebchen*?" It was Anna, calling out in bright clear tones, her high heels clacking across wood flooring. And then, "Renate! My God, Renate! After all this time!"

Weakness seized me. Disbelief. I leaned back to grasp a stairwell railing before I said I'd come to thank her for the soup.

Anna was all fluttering confusion. "Of course. The soup. But how did you know where to find me?"

I didn't want to think of Paul, I didn't want to speak his name, but beyond Anna's open door I saw refuge. I told her Paul had mentioned a street. I looked for names. It didn't matter, Anna wasn't listening. Her eyes were going from my face to the canvas pack I carried and back to my unkempt hair beneath a woolen cap I'd worn to school. I said Paul had a friend who knew her.

"Max. I know. Max Jaeger. He works in accounting down the hall from me at Schmidt's." A silken robe outlined Anna's body. Her high heeled shoes were satin slippers. I could see she was trying to hide her amazement while, with her hand, her arm, her body, urging me into a room of patterned rugs, thick pillows, deep chairs. She took the pack I carried. I gave her my hat and coat. I guessed there was a bedroom beyond this central hall, maybe two. I imagined a divided bathroom, a kitchen with shelves for storage. I fought an intruding picture of the crowded place on Pfannengasse, the always dirty toilet in the hall.

In an area separated by an archway, Anna put my sack on a burnished table. She told me it was good to see me and pointed to a pillowed chair. Settling opposite, her arm along a line of wood that backed a sofa, she said she didn't know Paul knew her address.

My fingers dug into the softness of the chair. I said, "I didn't know you worked for Schmidt. Paul thought you were a maid for some colonel."

Anna laughed. "That makes him hopelessly out of date but I had good times with my colonel." She leaned forward, her hands gathering at her silken garment. "You look terrible, Renate."

"I've been ill."

"Of course."

I knew Anna was curious, but this was all too strange, too early. With all that happened in between, I wondered if the comradeship of our days along the trail was still important. Now, needing rest, my hair pulled back from a face I guessed was pale, I knew I was more vulnerable than she was then. I looked up to see her brighten. She'd had good times with the colonel's son as well when he visited from West Point. She was laughing, telling me about the time the father wanted his son to take the general's daughter to a celebration of their Fourth of July. "Such a fuss the boy was making," she said. "It was just a dance." I settled back, grateful that Anna hadn't changed as much as her surroundings but I was brought upright when she shouted, "Idiot!" After a moment of misunderstanding, I realized she was imitating the colonel's tone as he defended the general's daughter as a lovely girl, one his idiot son should be proud to escort to any party. Then, as suddenly as she'd laughed, Anna ceased to smile. The general's daughter was a pig. With all her fancy manners she was a pig, driving around in a big car and telling the military police who stopped her to arrest her if they dared. "And do you know what? They don't dare because that sniveling little prick who's their company commander won't back them up. The general takes him to the private hunting areas. That's all he wants. To hunt. He doesn't care to enforce the law."

I shook my head against the pillows wondering how few answers I must give and still lose myself in Anna's chatter. When she lapsed into silence, I said her stories sounded just like Paul's.

"Do they?" she said. "It's only that the general's daughter is such a pig. Oh well." She pursed her lips, lifting an arched eyebrow at me as she asked if I knew what the boy did that night. The night of the big dance after his father and mother left for the celebration. I knew because I knew how easily Anna used her body but I shook my head. She said he'd come to her room in the attic and asked her if she cared to talk.

"And you let him in?"

"Of course."

"And he talked?"

"He was pawing at my dress before he'd said ten words."

Suddenly, I was resentful of the fresh stylish person who sat before me, resentful of the room with its tall ceilings. I didn't want to share the intimacy of her revelation but I said, "You slept with both the father and the son?"

Anna clapped her hands. "And the old man is better. The old man is better than his twenty-year-old son." She sat forward, thrusting out her arm. "He gave me this watch. The son. On the back it says: 'With Gratitude.' Imagine. I asked him why he didn't have our names engraved and he got all red in the face. It was really funny. I think by then he knew about his father but he didn't quite believe it."

I admired the proffered watch. "And of course you didn't tell him."

"Why should I?" Anna's shoulders lifted in a familiar shrug. "The general's daughter went to the Bodensee with a count who tends their garden. The old man told me just before he fired me. He insisted Klaus was a fake. He's wrong you know. Klaus is a count."

"He fired you?"

"He had to. His wife found out." Anna smoothed the ties of her robe along the sofa. "I felt sorry for her. She was fat from too much cake and lazy as a farm sow but she was nice to me."

I escaped back against the pillows, folding my sweater around me as Anna droned on about how the colonel's wife had come home unexpectedly from one of her meetings where she helped the orphans. Her husband was supposed to be at work but he was coming down from Anna's room zipping his pants or something else as stupid. Anna didn't know it happened. She worked all the next day and didn't suspect, even when the woman's door was locked. "She slept a lot, and she had headaches." The colonel told Anna when he came home that evening. Anna guessed he was surprised to find her but before she left he gave her several cartons of cigarettes he'd been saving for a camera.

I pushed away from my chair, conscious of my scuffed shoes still damp from the streets, my coarse skirt held together at the waist by pins, a skirt too short for the new style, never meant to be washed in water and washed too many times. Anna's gaze followed and I wrapped my sweater closer.

She said she was at the Blaue Reiter with Max when she met Paul. She'd been asking Max's advice about the best way to tell Charlie she'd been fired. She and Charlie had only started dating and she was worried he'd hear some rumor. Max told her they were looking for someone who spoke English at Schmidt's and that was exactly what she needed. Charlie didn't like her working as a maid so she let him believe the new job was the reason she quit. He was so pleased, he agreed to pay for an apartment so they could live together.

I pressed a window open, my sweater falling free.

"Renate, are you pregnant?"

I leaned out listening to the city. A distant dog was barking.

Anna came to stand beside me. "I heard Günther no longer lives in Mannheim. Why would he leave if you're pregnant?"

I closed and locked the window, fighting back my anger. After all my resolutions to forget him, to feel such emptiness on hearing his name. I told her it wasn't Günther's baby. Her startled outcry was exactly as expected but she only shook her head when I told her it was Paul's. She asked if that were the reason Günther left and I welcomed back my rage. I didn't want him. I couldn't want him. I wouldn't have the hurt he gave me. I told her no, Günther had planned a move to Stuttgart for some time.

"And you chose to stay with Paul? I don't believe you."

The relief started in my shoulders, spread to my hands clinging tight to Anna's. I told her everything, raging sometimes, crying, all. I even told her that in some ways they were both alike. Paul forgot nothing, not the battles, not the smallest deprivation in Siberia, every transgression he believed the Americans were making. Günther was the same. "He can't accept the past either. His or mine. I felt raped a second time when he left me."

Anna pulled me to the sofa. She said she was surprised at my lack of understanding and asked me to think back to that first winter. "The last thing any man needed was another defeat and what did you hand Günther? Your Americans shook his manhood. Then just when he got rid of them, you produce a former lover."

I saw no use in trying to explain Paul had never been a lover. I told her Günther wrote from Stuttgart but I didn't answer.

"Dear God in heaven why not?"

"What could I tell him?"

"The truth of course."

"Confront him with another man's child in a letter? Anna, please."

Her eyes rolled up. A heavy sigh escaped her.

"Anyway, he said he was coming to Heidelberg and he didn't."

"Then we'll go to Stuttgart. Let me find him for you. I know people you can't imagine."

I held my sweater out to expose what had been so unsuccessfully concealed and asked if she really thought Günther needed to know this. At first I didn't understand her answer but she must have thought I was agreeing because her enthusiasm heightened until I realized she was explaining she was ready to help me with that, too. She knew a place that could rid me of the baby. I pushed away from the sofa, fighting again for an illusive past where the world felt safe. I couldn't have an abortion. My breasts were already tender, waiting to be suckled.

"I find it strange you'd keep a baby from a man who raped you," Anna said. "Are you sure you're not doing this to punish Günther?"

At the window my forehead touched the glass. The cold reached down inside me. I realized I was beyond accepting any reason except the one I wanted hidden even from myself. I told her Günther needed this chance in Stuttgart. He needed a real beginning. He didn't deserve the turmoil of Paul's baby.

"You love him that much?"

I didn't answer. I didn't even nod. I couldn't until the

weakness left me. "I love him more than that," I said.

Anna rose and put comforting arms around me.

"Paul took care of me while I was ill," I said.

"So what does this caring man say about being a father?"

I told her I hadn't told him and she pushed me away. Her arms flew wide above her shoulders before falling limply to her sides. She said she worried about me with Paul. She didn't know him but she knew Max. She knew Max's friends. Maybe I shouldn't tell him.

I said, "I'll have to. Soon. I plan to tell his mother when I reach Schwetzingen."

Anna tightened the ribbon around her waist, a visual shoring up we both needed. She said, "Of course. His mother. Well, we'll both feel better if I make tea." A telephone's sharp ring caught her in the hall.

I turned back to the window, wondering at the luxury of a private telephone. Anna's contacts had always been with clerks and secretaries, they couldn't have manipulated orders for a telephone's permission. I wondered who or what was Charlie Dobbs that he could do it. I touched a porcelain bowl that held a flower, the frame of an oil painting. Before a gilded mirror I grasped under where the baby rested and curiosity held me. In other days I'd taken a different satisfaction in my body.

Anna returned with porcelain cups on an inlaid tray. She put them on the table. The phone call was from Charlie. He'd been called away on temporary duty. She took my hand and led me to the table, insisting that I stay the night. With plenty in the kitchen we wouldn't have to go out in the weather. She said she needed time to tell me about Charlie, the funniest, most intelligent, most wonderful man in the whole wide world. She truly loved him, and the amazing thing was that he truly loved her. She stood behind my chair and wrapped her arms around me. Her silken robe was soft against my face, her perfume obviously expensive. "You'll be doing me a favor, Renate. Please. I'm lonely when Charlie is away."

I could do little more than nod, blinking, clutching my cold-roughened hands together. I knew that when Anna had told me all there was to know about Charlie, we'd talk about

Günther, lovingly, fully, glorying in his successes and in his future. Only Anna could understand how that future would be mine although I wouldn't share it. But before we slept, I'd tell her about Paul. The other Paul, the young Paul I thought of as the father of my baby. Perhaps in the telling, I could find a way to help myself and help his mother.

# Spring 1948

Like Anna, Frau Schuler recognized my pregnancy the first time I was with her although, I admit, I was trying less to hide it. Without my floundering around for any kind of explanation, she assumed I'd turned to Paul when Günther left me but when I told her I hadn't told Paul he was going to be a father, she was furious. She insisted he be told and that done, that we marry.

I chose to tell Anna in a letter. I wasn't sure I'd be able to fend off her objections if telling her in person. I wrote that Paul and I had talked. We'd reached accommodation. A municipal ceremony was planned for a fortnight Thursday and I asked her to attend me. Paul would ask Max. Frau Schuler was preparing a small gathering for after. Her sister would come from Kleingemuend, my father, ours and the Schulers' tenants. I told Anna she'd like the sisters.

The ceremony was held, not the planned Thursday but the next. Anna and I, Paul and Max standing before the city magistrate in the red stone building beyond the Hercules fountain on the Rathaus square. I tried to ignore the rush of memories that almost overwhelmed me. I tried to think only of a different future.

The ceremony was brief. Almost sterile.

Mother Schuler cried when it was over.

# Summer 1948

My days became segments of unconnected time strung together by routine chores. Cooking. Cleaning. Caring for a shadow of the man who'd been my father. As I stood at our kitchen table chopping carrots for a festive midday meal we were preparing to honor a promotion Herr Ziegler had earned in his Labor Service unit, I longed to be walking among the apple trees with their profusion of white blossom. I needed the resurgence of their pristine beauty in the gritty world around us, but even more, I needed the illusion I was a proper wife. Chopping carrots was part of the charade my life had become. I'd already set aside soft dumplings to be added to a simmering chicken Mother Schuler had bargained for in a local market. In this fourth summer since surrender, refugees still lived in ruins, many wearing rags, but every tillable space had been producing and fewer of us were going hungry.

My husband had been invited to our celebration, but the day before Herr Ziegler had told Paul's mother he'd seen Paul hurrying into Heidelberg's station. Being in uniform, with a Military Police patrol behind him, he'd been able to satisfy his curiosity with a quick question to the ticket master. Paul was on his way to Karlsruhe. We were left to imagine why, and to wonder if such a short trip included a quick return. Dinner preparations were near completion when he burst into the kitchen. A stylishly tailored coat hung from his shoulders exposing the shimmer of a striped silk tie. I watched him preen. He'd been absorbed with himself since we were children. He would covet a popular image of fashion even while disdaining its display in a proliferation of slick magazines handed down to those hungry for such publications by the American victors. He kissed his mother's cheek, then mine, and swung a leather suitcase onto my table crowding my clutter of chopped carrots. From it he brought a woman's coat the color of a reddened sky by morning and draped it across his mother's shoulders. She lifted the elegant shawl collar against her face, only partially hiding an expression of concern that matched my own. The color, the cut were American, like Paul's suit.

"You don't think it's bright for an old woman?" she asked.

Paul told her to find a mirror, see how beautiful she looked, and she hurried from the room.

Paul was far more clever than I at trading. We'd often laughed about his triumphs but such clothes weren't spread out in barter markets. I wondered where he'd found the coat, where he'd found the suit that he was wearing, but with his anger often near the surface, his life away from us was his own.

He handed me a newspaper-wrapped package before swinging his suitcase to the floor. "Be careful," he said as I unwrapped it to a cone-shaped core of irregularly shaped lumps of pale, almost dusty chocolate. I put a fragment in my mouth. Paul closed our hands around the remaining pieces. "Try to understand," he said. "What it was like to fight so hard to live, and do it, what it was like to long for love ..." He didn't finish.

Our married closeness was a source of such ambivalence to me. The nights we spent together in my bed beside the kitchen, Paul cried in his sleep, cursed, flailed about before he bolted to his feet and paced the floor. I longed to help that Paul, my childhood companion, but in quiet moments in the garden or if I allowed myself to glance toward the moon on a clear unclouded night ...

Mother Schuler returned without the coat. Paul asked no questions. "Someday I'll bring you Belgian chocolate," he said to me.

Herr Ziegler and his lively family exploded into the kitchen. Paul's courtesy bordered on extravagance as he kissed Frau Ziegler's hand but his gaze settled on her husband. The last time the men had been together, Herr Ziegler had aroused Paul's anger with his compassion for Jewish prisoners the Ziegler's had seen in guarded files as they fled across the Warthegau. Now Paul wanted to know if Herr Ziegler was aware of what was happening in Berlin.

"You mean the lack of access?" Herr Ziegler asked and Paul began another tirade about Russians driving the Allies from their enclaves in the western sectors of the city. This wasn't a discussion in which I'd be expected to take part. A wife's political views were expressed through her husband. I gathered my mother's favorite dishes and escaped toward our dining table but the men followed, my hapless father between them. As I spread plates around the linen covered table, Herr Ziegler insisted the western Allies were only being tested and Paul shouted, "A test? A test? The British have evacuated their women and children." Creeping red reached his ears as he cursed the Russian soldiers who invaded each train after it crossed into a narrow corridor, the only approach allowed to the divided city.

Herr Ziegler gleefully pointed out only documents were provided to a few Russian boys and I secretly wondered if he enjoyed taunting Paul since the rest of us were so cautious.

Paul said such protection was given only to the Allies in their special coaches. He had names of German men and women who disappeared after being taken from the trains by Russian soldiers.

Herr Ziegler pointed toward the ceiling.

We'd all heard of a plan to build an air bridge. I wondered what kind of a bridge could possibly provide for Berlin's two and a half million civilians. Even the American's General Clay had admitted he didn't think the chance of success was worth a snap of his fingers.

Paul said, "With the Soviets planning military maneuvers in the air above the city, soon only birds will approach Berlin."

Mother Schuler entered, holding out a steaming tureen. Frau Ziegler followed with Tomas and Inge who brandished a heavy ladle. My father rose at the women's entry. Herr Ziegler settled him back in his chair but Paul wasn't finished. He threw a handful of dirty Reichsmark on the table, "Then the Soviets issue their new money, and insist we use it in the West because the Amis leave us floundering with this."

"Sit down Paul," his mother said.

I spread a napkin across my father's vest, drifting away from the conversation. I didn't want to hear their speculation about Russian and American armies gathering on their respective sides of the Fulda Gap, holding maneuvers, watching each other. But when Tomas and Inge began to wiggle, Paul touched my arm. "The chocolate?" he said and I hurried to the kitchen. Behind me he was explaining the chocolate was part of the Marshall Plan for German students. "The little ones like it I suppose," he said. "University students call it glue for the soul."

Herr Ziegler accepted a chunk for each child, urging Tomas into a bowing thank you before the children bolted toward the stairs. When their parents followed, Paul brought the pale red coat from the hallway stand and held it for his mother.

"That man is unbelievable," he said when he returned from escorting her home. The jacket of his American suit had been replaced by a sweater. "Is it possible he believes the Americans can do anything about a total blockade? With an air bridge?"

I leaned wearily against the sink and his features softened.

"Remember when we prowled this room with Hartmut, waiting for a taste of sweet with Gerda baking?" he said.

"You and Hartmut took my treats and kept them from me."

"We didn't," he said but he was smiling.

"You did. You two always teased me. Gerda had to help when she heard me screaming." I needed these moments when he seemed caring and in some strange way, I thought he needed them, too.

"Will you come to Heidelberg with me?" he said.

I pushed hard against the baby's stretching. Paul's child.

"What I did that night was degrading for both of us. I've apologized. I've tried to make amends."

From somewhere beyond explaining, I heard myself say, "You'll take me to one of your meetings? I want to meet von Rautner."

Suspicion narrowed his pale eyes but he nodded.

A soft rain fell the morning we left Schwetzingen, growing more persistent while we waited for a streetcar that would turn up Hauptstrasse. Paul removed his coat and wrapped it around my shoulders, retrieving it only when we reached the room. He'd learned the trick of locking the closet.

The evening he relented and took me to one of his meetings, we approached the Inn of the Blue Rider through another downpour but as we pushed through the door, the weather retreated before the dissonance inside. Shrill voices and clattering glasses, shifting benches across a wooden floor. Smoke was thick above each table where an American was sitting.

Paul led us to another door opposite the kitchen. He knocked and waited before proceeding into a smaller room, dimmer than the first. All eyes turned in our direction and a vague movement started, a clearing of space on a bench at the room's single table, but before Paul stepped across to take his place of rank opposite a man with steel-rimmed glasses, he gripped the hand of each one present. I followed. A few looked up with curiosity as they shook my hand.

Von Rautner was a thick man in a dark serge suit. Startlingly blue eyes looked out from beneath a slicked-back thatch of graying hair. His square, groomed fingers circled a heavy-handled stein of beer, lifting and replacing it in a wet mark soaking into a cardboard coaster. The movement was not a hurried one. Nothing about him spoke of nerves. The movement was careful, deliberate, done with great attention and great care while his eyes followed every move of everyone around the table.

Von Rautner's first words silenced the murmuring our entrance had created. "Who at this table believes the West will ever accept Germany into a community of nations? Peace has created a dangerous new world. Despite De Gaulle's posturing, France, is gravely weak. Great Britain not much stronger. Some think of America as a tail for the British kite but that isn't true. The United States is the power."

"The Soviets?" The question came from the end of the table, from a giant of a man with bushy eyebrows and a full red beard. A slender woman beside him lifted a length of hair and brought it forward reminding us of Germany's rightful place as the beating heart of Europe.

Von Rautner nodded. "History teaches us that two great powers will compete in a trial of strength. Whether they use arms or economics is of little interest."

I studied Paul's face. Grown older of course and with an added hardness, but his pale eyes were shining with the fire of his youthful dreams. "The Allies are beyond giving concessions to each other. We must make this disequilibrium our advantage."

"Without real money?" A pale man across from us had the aesthetic look of a student. He wore steel-rimmed glasses not unlike von Rautner's.

"Ah, there's the question," von Rautner said. "The long-awaited currency reform."

The bearded man said, "Marshall promised help last June. It's almost June again. The American Congress is appeasing their people by moving away from wartime spending."

Paul accepted clean steins from a woman who'd left the room to get them. He put one in front of me and the woman poured beer from a foaming pitcher already on the table.

Von Rautner lit a cigarette he'd picked from a white Lucky Strike package and Paul nodded toward the image of burning money. "How much longer must we depend for our survival on handfuls of American tobacco?"

The pale man said, "In the British Zone factories are refurbished while the Americans dismantle what is left of ours and send them off to Russia."

"Perhaps we can trade those refurbished factories for the Ami's Bavarian scenery." The man with the full red beard raised his beer toward the others.

The others laughed.

Paul frowned.

Von Rautner waited until all quieted. "We live in a time not unlike that after the Great War. We starved then and got Weimar for it. Ask yourself. Was democracy a solution? Learn."

"And choose a leader who can raise Germany, like a phoenix, from its ashes," Paul said.

I sank within myself. Professor Schuler had used those same words in referring to Hitler. What was there in Paul and his father? Brilliant both of them, but ready to break down the rule of law with deception, manipulating every mistake until it was perceived as planned. The room closed in around me. Like Hitler, would this group ignore signed treaties and use military solutions rather than diplomacy? Would they invade privacy as a means of control and discourage rational thought by withholding information? Would fear be mistaken for patriotism?

The student was saying something about the black market.

Paul said the black market was a giant fraud. The Americans could stop it at any moment, but why would they? Their soldiers grew rich supplying the product.

"That proves their government is dishonest," a forceful woman said.

"And weak," from somewhere down the table.

"The Soviets are better."

Paul turned. "The Soviets are stupid beasts."

Von Rautner took a last penetrating drag before pinching his glowing cigarette between his fingers. He cautioned Paul not to undervalue his enemies as he dropped the cigarette to the wooden floor, grinding the butt beyond recovery, paying no attention to the student leaning sideways, inhaling deeply as a last wisp of smoke drifted away.

The bearded man said, "If we don't want to be Russian communists, we'd best plan well."

The woman beside him said she'd rather die a Russian communist than live with the Americans' Morgenthau Plan. Her partner laughed and kissed her hand. Others joined in his laughter.

I continued wordless the rest of the evening, watching Paul bend forward as the discussion grew more intense. So much about him was like the student who came home from Tübingen. His casually tailored jacket. The leather patches on his sleeves. I struggled to remember his arguments with Hartmut. What had he believed that I was too naïve to understand as I listened in worshipful silence?

Eventually, he rose and touched my arm. The group stood and a clash of heels cut through the din around the table.

On the rain emptied street, I struggled to match Paul's stride, finally grasping his arm, demanding he go slower, questioning if he'd learned anything from the past. He'd learned German armies could conquer Europe from the Urals to the Atlantic. From the Arctic Circle to North Africa and the Near East. When I mentioned defeat, he said, "Not the next time."

On Untere Strasse we stepped across a rivulet that had formed where the cobblestones sloped toward the center. I asked about von Rautner.

"He was a professor. Until the Americans took away his right to teach."

"A professor? Here? Did he know your father?"

Paul didn't answer. He rattled our keys.

I was the first in nightclothes, the first to fall exhausted into bed. I'd no wish to argue further, but I was curious about the Morgenthau Plan. The name had sounded familiar.

Paul laughed, as had the others. "Morgenthau is the American finance minister. A Jew who gained his power catering to that Jew Roosevelt."

I shook my head against the pillow. Nazi practice had been to use religion as a denunciation.

"Morgenthau wants to build a fence around our country and castrate all the men. Germany is an industrial nation. He wants to make us a potato field."

I curled away, exhausted. With my face to the wall, I didn't see his features harden, see him cast his final garments toward the chair. He didn't flinch at my quick movement of rejection, my protest of illness and fatigue. His hands moved inexorably up my body inside my gown, pulling me toward him, positioning me on the bed, telling me a proper wife would agree with her husband. I clutched the worn sheet in both my hands, compelling my mind into a hidden valley of the past, remembering for the first time in years the lightness of my glass dancers.

In the morning Paul left the room before me. "For a mission," he said. I asked if it were to Karlsruhe again. The slightest hesitation let me know he'd heard.

I went to Schwetzingen, walking. The rain had cleared the air. A wild musing prompted the thought that Paul could become so involved with this new radical movement, he'd forget me if I stayed quietly with my father. I used a telephone in a shop around a corner to call Anna. "Leave him," Anna said.

"Not now. Not with the baby. I'll talk to his mother."

"Two German officials came to the office and asked for Max."

"That isn't Paul."

I told Mother Schuler I was frightened by what I'd heard. She was frightened, too. I said the only solution was to insist Paul live at home where we could listen for his easy answers, contradict convenient lies. His mother said, "He's a grown man, Renate."

Her dignity wouldn't let her participate in my probing but I was beyond any reservations. I traced gossip about Paul's travels to a neighbor whose brother was night clerk in a Karlsruhe hotel that housed American workers. With his sister's cooperation, I confronted the man on his next visit to Schwetzingen. That his was not an elegant hotel must have annoyed Paul. The clerk described it as rather common quarters reserved for lower ranking workers. Paul visited one called Thelma. I found that quite ironic. Paul had such trouble pronouncing words with the th sound, no matter how he practiced. There. Them. Those. I'd helped him often. The clerk described Thelma as soft and plump and clinging. Not Paul's type. But then he wasn't there for love although I never doubted that he found that, too. He was there for von Rautner's information. The colonel Thelma worked for was a liaison from the air force. He'd recently been stationed in Berlin.

Paul went to his mother about my absence.

"Disconsolate," she said.

Their visit found me in the music room, playing while my father sat in his musician's chair, his head tipped back, his mouth a round, dark hole. I heard them enter the outer hall and began playing harder, long runs with both my hands, and chords, deep chords, minor. Paul leaned across my shoulder. He'd dressed for the occasion in an open shirt, a sweater I remembered. I could smell the freshness of his body. "Does your father even hear you?" he asked.

My fingers drifted into a melody we'd sung as children. *Hänschen klein, ging allein in die weite Welt hinein.* Little Hansel goes alone into the big wide world. "Sometimes he holds his violin, but he never plays." I turned from Mother Schuler's anguish to tell Paul his friends were dangerous.

He answered that I wasn't married to his friends.

I asked him to stay in Schwetzingen. Help his mother. Be a father to our child. I stopped. I was beyond pleading. "Try crossing von Rautner, try doing something that makes him angry."

Paul looked toward his mother. "Von Rautner's out of town. I can't just disappear."

Tomas and Inge were playing on the curving stairs as I'd once played with Hartmut and Paul. I heard the young Paul's voice.

Stop that, Renate.

And I had stopped.

Come on, Renate.

And I had come.

Give that to me.

And in worshipful silence, I'd done as he had asked.

I looked into Paul's pale eyes, their loneliness a hunger. I told him I'd come to Heidelberg but only until von Rautner returned. When he did, Paul was to sever all connection.

Mother Schuler fixed a snack of bread with sausage and carried it to the table in the small salon where the four of us sat in an oval of silence, lost in thoughts we didn't share. She broke soft centers from the bread and gave them to my father.

The countryside slid past an open window on the bus that took us away from Schwetzingen. Waldorf in the distance. Leiman, without stopping. As we approached Heidelberg, Paul lifted my hand. I let it lie limply in his until he brought it to his lips in Günther's gesture. At the busy oval in front of the railroad station, he grabbed it again. "My God, Renate, look."

In the wide forecourt before the station hundreds of people were gathered in little clusters, gesturing to each other, pointing at an ominous speaker newly erected on a long, dark pole. It was so like an ever present system used in the days of Hitler, I almost expected the familiar fanfare that preceded special announcements.

"It's the money," Paul said. "What else could it be? After three full years, our military governors are preparing to announce new money."

I said we should tell his mother but Paul was right, it was too late.

"Von Rautner's been warning us for weeks: clear your depts. Fill your shelves with anything that's useful, buy a burial plot." He chuckled at von Rautner's humor. "When the Allies decide to act, our Reichsmark will be more than obsolete, they'll be a liability." Hovering behind other passengers impatient to leave the bus he added. "They're telling us on a weekend with no official available to answer questions."

Near the arches at the entrance to the station, we saw the man who sat near the end of the table at the Blue Rider. The man with the full red beard. Paul's hand lifted in recognition just as the speaker in the square erupted.

> STATE, LOCAL AND PUBLIC AUTHORITIES WILL BE ALLOWED NEW DEUTSCHMARK EQUAL TO THE SUM OF ONE MONTH'S REVENUE. BUSINESSES, SIXTY MARKS FOR EACH EMPLOYEE. OTHER FUNDS, HOWEVER NOW INVESTED, ARE CANCELED. AT DESIGNATED POINTS AROUND THE CITY, INDIVIDUALS WILL BE GIVEN FORTY DEUTSCHMARK IN AN EVEN EXCHANGE FOR FORTY REICHSMARK. ANY REICHSMARK BEYOND THE INITIAL FORTY HAS A VALUE ONE-TENTH OF WHAT IT HAD BEFORE.

"That's economic savagery," Paul said.

The man from the Blue Rider shook Paul's hand. "Now the battle begins, with a reunited Germany as the prize for the currency that finds acceptance in the rest of the world."

Both men were in such a state of agitation, I guessed neither recognized that I was listening although the bearded man's thick hand enveloped mine. He told Paul to hurry back to Karlsruhe. The Soviets would surely close Berlin completely and von Rautner would want to know what the Allies were planning to resist that pressure. Their hands locked one more time before they hurried away in opposite directions.

Paul and I crossed to the Ploeck, cutting diagonally above the Pferde Platz to Hauptstrasse. "Why now? Why now?" he kept repeating. "What else do the Amis suspect could happen behind the security of an absolute blockade?"

Breathless from jostling through the crush of people on the street, I reminded him he'd made a promise but he struck one hand into the other. "Can they be afraid the Russian bear is ready to gobble us up? And who will help them then? The British?" He laughed.

When I pulled him to a stop, he glanced back down the narrow street as if surprised we'd left the station but his voice was firm. He said the currency reform was too important. His plans must change. At our room he slammed the door. "I must find von Rautner."

In the mirror above the bureau, I studied Paul's reflection, seeing in the shadow on that scratched surface all my hopes, my disappointments. I turned and we stared at each other across the tiny room. "I thought you said von Rautner was out of town."

He didn't answer.

Finally I said, "I'm going to Anna's to wait for the next bus to Schwetzingen. You find von Rautner and tell him, today, that this is your last meeting. I'll return one more time, but only to help you pack."

I didn't look back. I just closed the door behind me.

Through the next week Paul was back and forth to Schwetzingen, raging at Herr Ziegler about the direction our country should be taking, arguing with me about relinquishing the room. His mother stood in ashen silence, controlling tears I knew she shed when the rest of us were absent. Late in the week, Paul agreed the room could go.

The afternoon I rode the bus in from Schwetzingen was hot, uncomfortable and dusty. Paul's suitcases, though yet empty, dragged against my shoulders. I was later than I'd hoped but my first stop was at Anna's for a welcome rest, a relieving drink of water, and to seek her help in removing my name at the housing office. "Anna, please. I'm late. Paul will be getting angry."

"Let him."

"We don't need the room. He's left von Rautner."

"He lies."

The harshness in Anna's voice didn't surprise me. The disheveled hair, the nightclothes she was still wearing, were the surprise, and that Anna had been drinking. In the times I'd been there since the wedding, I'd never found her in this condition, the windows closed on a stifling day, her fine apartment airless. I told her one more time that if she'd tell me what was wrong, I'd try to help, and she answered one more time that nothing was wrong, though, clearly, that wasn't true.

"Charlie?" I asked.

"He'll be here later."

I had to leave, I had no choice. The arguments with Paul had been too bitter. His decision to return to Schwetzingen too recent. Pfannengasse would just have to be locked and the formalities taken care of later.

The suitcases were awkward as I hurried through the crowded streets but I didn't slow my pace until I stepped into our lower hall and could lean against a wall in quiet darkness. At the top of the stairs the door to our room was open to chance breezes. Paul was sprawled across the narrow bed. Thinking him asleep, I eased the suitcases to the floor and slumped into the chair with wooden arms. Paul's voice burst into the room. "I have a mission." He didn't move except to speak. "Did you hear me? I said I have a commitment. For tonight." He stiffened onto his back, half sitting against the pillow. His chest was bare against the summer weather.

My carefully formulated plans vanished in a wave of loathing. For Paul. For myself. For trying to believe he was capable of changing. Even with the door wide open, the room was a prison. I glanced at my watch. It was hours until the next bus to Schwetzingen but I couldn't return to Anna's, not with something happening there with Charlie. I told Paul I'd find a café. "I can't wait here."

Paul's gaze followed the noisy meandering of a fly against the ceiling but I could see the way his mind was working. A woman in my condition alone on the street? He vaulted from the bed. "Only American women appear in public places with their bellies all distended. A good German woman wouldn't put herself on such display."

I crumpled back into the chair, assaulted by ordinary noises. The fly. A streetcar's distant clanging. Someone arguing in the room upstairs. Paul leaned against the open window, trying for control as I was trying. Would we always be so ambivalent with each other? He told me he wouldn't miss his appointment but he supposed he could take me to a café. It was better I not be seen alone in my condition. His concern was almost funny.

He went into the hall to use the toilet and I rose to stand in his place by the window, staring out into the still, dank air.

Some of the heat left Heidelberg in the long summer twilight but the narrow confinement of Hauptstrasse was heavy with close-packed bodies. An occasional American car was the only traffic until the clamor of a streetcar passed us by. My thoughts were with Mother Schuler's torment at this last failed attempt with Paul, yet a nagging alertness kept me watchful, searching faces when a stranger brushed my arm. I stumbled away from Paul, out into the street, where I looked back toward the crowded sidewalk.

"Paul, it's Günther." The noise on the street was magnified and painful. "Günther! Wait!"

Günther turned. His eyes found mine.

"Günther. Oh God, Günther." The heat was clawing fingers holding me back, the crowds an adversary. "Where have you been? Where did you go?"

"Everywhere. Nowhere." He glanced toward Paul.

Paul's jaw tightened. "So this is Günther Lange," he said.

"Herr Schuler." Günther extended his hand.

Paul was forgotten, my body, my pain, all the anger when Günther hadn't kept his promise to return. I wanted to melt into his body so we'd never be apart from one another but only grasped his hands. He seemed different, taller even, thicker, in clothes I didn't remember but an old stiffness in his body made me sick with regret. I told him Paul and I were on our way to drink a glass of wine and asked him to come with us. He said he wouldn't intrude. I said it was no intrusion. We wouldn't stay long, Paul had an appointment. I was pleading but unashamedly.

Paul said, "You may join us."

Günther glanced from Paul to me before he said he'd come if we let him buy the wine. I made no attempt to veil my relief. I was close to laughing, close to tears. I asked where we should go.

"The Arnold?" Paul said.

Günther laughed out loud. "There I'll not buy the wine. I'm not wealthy, nor am I a fool." He turned us away from Hauptstrasse into a silent alley behind the university, all of us walking just a pace apart in the cobbled street. I sought words to erase the months since he'd left me, to interrupt his looks at Paul, twisting the gold band on my finger until Günther watched that, too. He said he knew a place at the end of the Anlage, above the train to Heilbronn. We could sit on a porch that was cool and quiet and he could afford to buy the wine as well.

The café was near a fraternity house. Students sometimes came to drink and sing. Paul said the military had taken a fraternity house he knew. Nine American women had displaced thirty men.

I shook their arms, gaining through this touch some return of my elation. I told them we'd have no political discussion. I wanted to feel like Fasching. Mardi Gras. Carnival in Rio.

Günther laughed. I believe he was making an effort for the evening, trying to please me in spite of himself when he said, "And your costume? You are a snake?"

Paul was calm but he stopped walking, his face a darker shadow on the shadowed street. "If you imply that a woman in her condition shouldn't be in public places, you forget, Renate is not a proper German woman."

Günther staggered, staring at Paul before turning to me. "I apologize. I was meaning to be funny. I wouldn't offend you or your husband, but it's obvious that you …"

The pain on his face was more than I could manage, a catalyst that turned my pain to anger. "Stop this! Both of you! Say no more!" I grabbed their arms and started walking.

We crossed the Anlage to a finely graveled promenade beneath broad chestnut trees. At the last steep street before the castle, celebratory laughter reached us from a café further up the hill. Günther led the way around crowded tables in a garden, through an empty barroom to a porch where long trails of vines dropped over a wall to railroad tracks below. Only a scattering of patrons found this place. A single American soldier with a German woman, an earnest German couple. In a corner three tables had been pushed together for a group of American soldiers hunched in conversation over steins of beer.

Günther ordered wine as a train on its way to Heilbronn stilled conversation until the last car disappeared into a tunnel beneath fine homes on the hill. Scowling, Paul gestured toward the single soldier with the German woman just as the soldier's supporting arm slipped and he fell forward, toppling glasses that drained wine onto the floor. "Animal," Paul said, hissing.

"Take it easy, buddy." An American from the crowded table unwound his length from a lyre-backed chair.

"Straighten him up, Iverson," someone at his table said.

With neither haste nor reprimand, the man called Iverson pulled a garrison cap from the drunken soldier's epaulet and straightened it on his head. A brief search produced a ten mark bill and he threw it on the table. Someone at his table shouted that was pretty generous and Iverson said the woman probably deserved it. As he half pushed, half helped the drunken soldier toward the deserted barroom, he told him to head straight down the Anlage until he reached a taxi near the station and have the driver take him to a pro station before he took him home.

Paul leaned across our table. "Do you know they have prophylactic stations on the street? That they give passes to companies as a reward for avoiding disease? If you're bothered by their arrogance, think of them lined up for one of their short-arm inspections."

Günther accepted a slim bottle from the waitress and filled each glass. "I find the Americans quite different from what you're implying, Herr Schuler." He thrust the bottle across the table.

Paul's attention came back to us. "Because you've found an easy life in your work for them?"

Günther's hands rubbed along his corduroy trousers, clenching into fists above his knees. He said he remembered one day that wasn't easy. He'd been preparing a yard for planting behind one of the grand houses closer to the castle and hadn't stopped, quite literally he hadn't stopped until the entire area was turned, stones were gathered into piles, and clods flowed evenly beneath his rake. He drained his wine and quickly poured another. When the resident officer's wife was told the job was finished, she left a door open when she came out for an inspection. "The aroma from their evening meal makes my gut churn, even now. I was that hungry," he said.

Paul brightened.

"She gave me a pack of cigarettes," Günther continued. "What I expected, though I'd hoped for more since I'd not been offered lunch. I left with what she gave me and had gone three blocks before I realized the pack was opened."

Paul snickered.

Günther shrugged. "I can still hear the cellophane crackle as I jammed that package in my pocket. Two damn cigarettes. It's what you give a porter for carrying your suitcase, what you leave a waiter after a meal. I tried to think what two cigarettes would buy. Some bread? A cup of ersatz coffee?" Günther stretched involuntarily at the table. "I kicked at the first thing I saw. A mound of rock beside the road." He laughed as I imagined he laughed the night of the story. He'd sat down on the rock to coddle his bruised toe wondering if two cigarettes would satisfy a doctor as he put one of the crumpled cigarettes in his mouth. It curved down as if it were frowning.

"And you turned it up so it would smile," I said.

Günther hit the table. "I did, Renate. For a fact. You know me well." He lifted my hand, fingering my knuckles. I saw Paul watching. Günther said he lit the cigarette with a wooden match he'd found while weeding and the second from the first. "That one burned quickly because it'd lost tobacco in my pocket."

Paul tapped an extra cardboard coaster in a rhythmic drumming on the table. "Two cigarettes for a full day's labor. Your officer's wife was no doubt a Jew."

Günther dropped my hand.

Paul said, "I suppose you admire the Jews as well, Herr Lange."

Günther's metal chair scraped back on the stone flooring. "My employer in Stuttgart is a Jew. General Trautman. I find him fair and honorable, a good officer, a good man. Sometimes I wonder how he feels assigned to duty here in Germany."

"Why would you wonder that?" Paul said.

"You deny the concentration camps, Herr Schuler?"

Across the room, the soldiers glanced up from their drinks and conversation as Paul's voice rose. "How many times must I explain? The bodies in those pictures are our dead, our dead. We had to have someplace to put what was left by the Allied bombers."

"So we carried them to common graves, miles from any city?"

With a glance across his shoulder, Paul quieted. "What do I care about the Jews?"

Günther said, "You should, Herr Schuler. You should care about the Jews. You should care what was done in the name of the German people."

Paul said, "I care about Germany. I work for the day our national flag can fly again."

Günther emptied our green bottle before holding it up in a signal to the waitress. As she hurried toward us with another, he told Paul, "Just because I've reached accommodation with the Americans, you've no right to think I don't love my country but I scorn your feelings about a flag. What is a flag? A piece of cloth. Originally man chose it for its color." He tipped the chilled bottle over each glass. "To me, everything that speaks to our lives must serve a higher purpose. Sound. Color. Form. Movement.

They're our universal language. They're meant to unite mankind, not foster isolation. I paid a price to learn that enemies are interchangeable."

"And I didn't pay?" Paul's face darkened. "Next time will be different."

"Don't depend on a flag, Herr Schuler. There are those of us who won't fight again for colored banners." Günther lifted his glass and held it out before him. "Auf Deutschland," he said.

Paul came to attention still sitting at the table. "Auf Deutschland," he repeated.

I looked across the room where my glance caught that of the man his friends called Iverson. "To Germany," I said.

Iverson lifted his amber glass of beer. "To the good old USA." The chorus went around his table.

Paul stood. I reminded him I was going to Schwetzingen and he asked if I was expecting difficulty finding my way there. Günther interrupted before I could react. He said he'd driven the General's wife and daughter to Heidelberg in their private car. They were staying with friends, but they knew he was from this area. They'd given him permission to use the car if he needed transportation.

Paul said, "Well then, Renate?"

Neither Günther nor I looked up as he left us. We drank in an unnatural silence until Günther tipped the bottle over our glasses and only a last drop clung to the rim. He glanced toward me with a silent question. I shook my head in answer and he gestured to the waitress for our bill.

On the Anlage, beneath the sheltering darkness of the chestnut trees, tiny rounds of gravel crunching underfoot were the only sound until far ahead we heard a band that played for dancing. A woman sang. As we drew nearer, a muted clatter of dinner plates on linen-covered tables reached us from a company grade officers' restaurant. Glare from a fenced area for their parking caught Günther's puzzled frown.

"Is this where you left the car?" I asked.

"No, I left it by the old Stardust Club. We've come too far." He forced his hands deep into his pockets as we crossed toward a senior grade officers' hotel but grabbed my arm to pull me back when a long official car turned into the walled enclosure.

Across from the Ploeck, where blue buses stopped to take on passengers before trips beyond the city, an anxious group at curbside assured me the next bus to Schwetzingen was overdue. I told Günther that gave him a choice. I certainly could find my way from here. He stopped walking so suddenly I stepped into his back and was overwhelmed by the sudden bulk of him against me. "I don't want you to leave, Renate. I don't know what I want."

We passed Hauptstrasse and a long dark block of empty storefronts before we turned right along the river. At the entrance of another guarded lot Günther produced his authorization papers. A uniformed Labor Service guard checked them against a green license plate on the indicated car before he let us proceed beyond the fencing. At the long, sleek automobile Günther held my door. He fumbled with the keys before unlocking the driver's side.

Beyond Bismarck Platz and waiting streetcars, I told him I was surprised Paul made no fuss, he was usually more controlling, and Günther answered that he guessed Paul knew we were fairly limited in our activities right now. He'd have me back tomorrow. I couldn't let that pass. I said I was leaving Paul even before this happened.

"This happened, Renate?"

"Yes. Finding you."

We drove in deeper silence, Günther occasionally swerving sharply though there was no other traffic on the street. He turned onto the Autobahn, following the red glare of a single light before turning away past planted fields to the beginning of Schwetzingen's houses. When we stopped beside the iron fence on my tree-bare street, he reached across to push my door. I expected him to withdraw into the shadows behind the wheel but he opened his door and followed me along the drive. "This is difficult for both of us," he said as he shoved the car keys into his pocket. "But I can't leave before we settle things."

Tell him, I thought. Tell him about the turmoil of the past months, the terrible isolation after the initial waiting. Say my marriage was only my retreat from the reality of his leaving. Dear God in heaven, tell him while you have the chance that there is no life without him. A cloud crossed the moon. I pushed the door, feeling him close behind me, feeling his hand reach toward my arm as if to guide me through the darkness but before we touched, it fell away. "There was a time we agreed to be candid with each other," I said.

Hidden in the shadows, he leaned back against the door and I heard his fists hit once against the panels. "You want me to be candid?" he said. "You have a husband. I met him and I don't like him."

"How can you speak like that when you just left me? With nothing, less than nothing, not even where to find you." His hand pressed quickly across my mouth and we both looked up the stairs, alert to those who could be listening, and toward my father's room at the end of the hall. "Nothing mattered after you were gone," I said more softly.

Günther led me into the small salon and closed the door.

"You wrote just one short note," I said. "I was sure you'd write another."

He said, "I had no words to put on paper."

"Then why didn't you come to Heidelberg? You said you would, but then you didn't."

"I came," he said.

I gasped.

"It hadn't been long. The first I could get away. The old man who lived in the room above you opened the downstairs door and from inside where I was standing, I could see someone at your door using a key. My key, Renate? You gave my key to Herr Schuler?"

"What you saw was nothing."

His pain was everywhere about him, in his face as he leaned forward, even in his anger. "The baby isn't nothing. We both know it isn't mine. Where is your responsibility in this? You're the one all big with another man's child. I'm telling you I don't understand why you didn't take the same precautions we were using."

"Günther, this isn't fair."

"You want to talk about what's fair?"

"Paul gave me no more choice than you gave me in leaving."

"I gave you no choice?" His voice was a harsh whisper. "What choice did I have the first time I came to see you and found Herr Schuler's presence in your room?"

"Your choice was to believe in me. Günther, he raped me that first night. That's when I got the baby. Did anyone tell you I was crying?"

I sat down on the small-armed bench that was on one side of the square table, my breathing short, uneven. When Günther sat heavily beside me, his hands clasped out across the table. His chin was on his chest. He told me it was more than what anyone said. He could see intercourse in that room. He could smell it, and I wanted to know why he couldn't see the anger, smell the rage. Why couldn't he think there was an explanation? He came alive as he remembered seeing Paul on his next visit. He said he'd cursed the day we'd met out there on the mountain. He'd thought he could never kill again but he knew that if he went upstairs, he'd kill us both. So he ran. For days, demons in his head demanded his revenge, but then at night he'd call my name. Eventually, he wrote the letter. "Why didn't you write back?"

"You said you were coming to Heidelberg. Could I put on paper what you couldn't? Think what I needed to explain."

He seemed to sink within himself, drawing me forward so I could hear. He told me his first auditions were a disaster. He was really facing failure, eating only what was offered, sleeping where he could find warmth. "Our love was from that same hostile world, a world that seemed best forgotten as I struggled deep in it again. I'd failed so miserably to keep you from the soldiers, I convinced myself Herr Schuler was better able to take care of you."

"Can that be what you think I wanted? To be taken care of? Is that why you left me in such pain?"

"You think you're the only one who feels pain?"

Watching his loved, familiar profile, longing for the flavor of his flesh, I told him he was such a part of me, he couldn't imagine how I felt when I couldn't find him, and he said I couldn't imagine how he felt when he thought he had to stay away. Only our breathing filled the silence until I brought our hands together, twisting my fingers between his until he gripped them. "Günther, I was so alone, I needed you so badly but you'd left me and I didn't understand. You didn't go when I went with any soldier. Why when you thought Paul ...?"

His grip tightened. "We weren't like the soldiers, Renate. Animals. Copulating. When I touched you I was speaking as surely as if I were using words. It's about love, Renate. You didn't love the soldiers, but once you loved Herr Schuler."

I spread his hand, his palm exposed, my palm hovering above it. "Then tell me you no longer love me and I'll say no more."

His hand slipped away. "I'll be honest. I find no peace, I have no quiet moments. If I don't stay busy my thoughts go back to times we were together but it's as though I'm only remembering how I loved you." His life was different now. He'd stopped scrambling for a living. He drove for the Trautmans because they understood about his singing and never interfered when he was trying for a contract. The General said it made him feel like a patron of the arts. "I sing in increasingly important houses, to critical acclaim, and there's a chance I'll move to Munich to work with Wolfgang Meisch."

I touched his hair, grown long around his collar. "Don't disappear from my life again."

Gently, he brought my hand back to the table. "Just like that? We make a threesome with your husband, all living separately from each other?"

I almost smiled. I said we could write. We could be friends.

"Not friends, Renate. We're not suited to be friends and you have another responsibility." He touched my swollen body and I grasped his hand against me, searching for connection, pushing until I knew he felt it, too. The baby couldn't come between us. I wouldn't let it, but he drew his hand away. "Isn't it ironic? Just when I've reached a point in my career where those people we were could be together ..." He twisted his watch to catch an illumination from the dial. "The ladies have planned an early start tomorrow. I have to get some rest."

Günther kept an unbreachable distance between us as we walked through the hall and into the warm night air. He had the keys to the General's car in his hand when he touched my shoulder.

Alone in my room, across from the room where my family had long played music, I relived every moment of the evening, every gesture, every word. I kneaded my shoulder to remember his touch. This time I knew where he was in Stuttgart. With General Trautman. If he went to Munich, there was Wolfgang Meisch. My life was complicated with Paul and the coming baby but those two words, Trautman, Meisch, for me they made a future.

I was on the first bus to leave Schwetzingen the next morning. My eagerness was not for facing Paul alone in the room on Pfannengasse, but after a sleepless night of planning, I wanted him not to have possession of a few things that were mine: clothes I could wear when the baby was born, some books, a piece of my mother's jewelry. On the slow ride into town I relived the night before, trying to feel Günther's arms around me.

Even now I become unsettled if I think of Paul racing down the hill after he left us, into the Anlage, across narrow streets to Hauptstrasse. With luck, the number five streetcar was rattling toward him from where the main street narrowed, its headlight piercing the encroaching darkness. His practice was to leap aboard as a car was moving, pushing forward in the sudden glare of its interior, steadying himself on the back of each seat. I can find myself twitching at whatever I happen to be wearing, hiding a pregnancy no longer there, if I try, again, to fit into a whole the irregular pieces of information we had about him. Thelma's room was just above the hotel's entry. The night clerk's sister had reported that. Paul never knocked. He swept inside, and Thelma would be instantly upon him, pulling his arms around her thick waist, kissing him boldly in full view of anyone who passed. I enjoyed picturing her as overweight and even slightly sweaty. I wanted to think Paul was sacrificing for his cause. He'd brought such pain to me and to his mother, such humiliation, I didn't want to give him any pleasure, even in my imagination.

Awkwardly descending from my bus, I could see Paul leaping from his as he had entered, with the streetcar moving. Perhaps anxiety had gripped him. Perhaps he'd found only shining American coaches on the first track, the one that commonly held the train to Karlsruhe. Running again, he'd have had to search for an aging compartment, raging that such a coach was the only way a German was allowed to travel. If he started his run in the wrong direction, the train would leave without him. Americans wouldn't let a German walk back through their sections of the train.

I felt a sudden pain across my groin as I made my way through the crowds toward a streetcar that would turn up Hauptstrasse. What I wanted from the room seemed less important and I began hoping Paul had missed his train the previous evening. If he'd been forced to wait for something later, perhaps he was still in Karlsruhe. I tried to concentrate beyond the streetcar's window, watching Heidelberg pass by. A determination to have confidence in our new Deutschmark had gripped a newly cohesive West Germany despite a still flourishing black market, and boards were gone from storefronts. Polished windows caught the morning light.

On Pfannengasse a veil of smoke drifted high into the stairwell, unmistakably from our room. I rushed upstairs. Paul was sitting, naked, in the chair with wooden arms, staring at me through the murk. His stained underwear trailed out across the floor.

"Paul! What's happening here?" I twisted a window open.

"It was that blond woman. That Molly in her tight sweater."

That made no sense. The woman's name was Thelma. He scooped his underwear into our overburdened stove, blowing hard to renew the flames on what I could see was the smoldering shirt and trousers he'd worn the night before. He answered my demands to know what he was doing by saying it was no concern of mine, but there'd been a fight.

"With the woman Molly?"

A startling hand sent me sprawling back against the bureau. I could feel the print of his fingers rising white across the redness on my face. "I'm sorry," he said, but he didn't reach to help me. "The clothes don't matter. Von Rautner will see ..." He froze at his mention of von Rautner's name.

Slowly, as I would ease around a wounded animal, I opened one of the suitcases I'd brought from Anna's the day before and packed the things I'd come for. Paul was right. It was none of my concern. Only his mother mattered.

On the slow return to Schwetzingen I was consumed by Mother Schuler's anguish. She'd have expected a celebratory breakfast and come early to our house around the corner. Frau Ziegler would have told her Paul wasn't with me the night before. Perhaps she'd mentioned Günther. I'd left home too early to know Herr Ziegler had been on patrol near the station. He'd seen Paul running from the streetcar.

After talking with the Zieglers I wanted a few more pieces of the puzzle before I saw Mother Schuler and went directly to our neighbor. It was only by chance it was her birthday and her brother had come home after last night's shift. I resented his swelling with importance as he confirmed Paul was somewhat later than usual the night before. Another woman had gone to Thelma and Thelma let her stay. The clerk said he could usually tell when Paul was expected. On those nights Thelma asked him to turn all visitors away. Perhaps she thought Paul had changed his mind and wasn't coming. That didn't sound like the woman I'd imagined. She would have waited. Certainly alone. An emergency had drawn Paul to Karlsruhe. An unexpected mission for von Rautner.

The clerk said that after Paul had started up the stairs, he'd snatched a message left hours earlier for another tenant he knew was absent. An excuse to follow. The visiting woman, surely Molly, was on the floor by Thelma's phonograph looking through a stack of records. As the clerk hovered in the hall, he'd been startled to hear Thelma introduce Paul as Captain Howard. Molly's bright-tipped fingers had caressed her neck as she'd repeated, "CAPTAIN Howard?"

Paul had been caught in a stupid lie. One punishable by incarceration. A little fabrication that he was Captain Howard, perhaps in the army's Counter Intelligence units to explain his civilian clothing, was certainly just for Thelma. It could be disavowed until she'd introduced him to a second witness and he hadn't found the courage to deny it. The clerk was so pleased with this bit of information, he demonstrated how he'd walked back, feigning a limp, pausing to rub his ankle by Thelma's open door. He'd seen Paul fumble at his pockets, telling "Telma" he'd smoked the last of his cigarettes, asking if she could spare one. Molly had risen from the floor, her long legs unfolding slowly. The clerk heard her mimicking, "Telma? Telma?" as she moved toward Paul, taunting him with a hissing thhhhh sound. The clerk said she was close enough for Paul to feel her breath, her breast against his arm, as she offered him a cigarette from one of those heavy silver cases most Americans carried. When he wouldn't accept, she tapped one on the cover and let it catch in her red lipstick.

The last thing he'd seen was Paul step away from Molly to accept a cigarette from Thelma and reach for a heavy silver table lighter, but he'd paused out of sight on the stairwell, listening for any last bit of gossip before bolting back to his station.

Molly was downstairs soon after. As she passed, she told the clerk she had a bad taste in her mouth and was going to the officers' club to kill it with some good American whiskey. I could only guess what Paul was thinking. That a woman like Molly would know he wasn't American, just as the room clerk knew. And Thelma. Fat, dull Thelma, maybe she knew, too. But if he put his hand to Thelma's face to move it away as she came toward him, he might have touched the wetness of a tear. That would have been a reason for his staying. My neighbor's brother said it was after midnight when Paul left Thelma's room. He said he was sure. He was watching the clock, feeling anxious for his relief's arrival. At midnight, it was already his sister's birthday and he'd promised to catch the late train to Heidelberg. I wondered if Paul had watched a clock as he rolled about in Thelma's bed getting the information for von Rautner. He needed to catch that same late train for him to be in the room when I found him. I know he needed his fingers on his notebook to record every detail of what Thelma told him. I was the one who burned the book when I found it in our room.

I've no way of proving my supposition, but I believe Thelma never knew she was being used, or even suspected Paul was other than a man who loved her. The night clerk said she was a quiet, almost reticent person before she met Paul. She must have been consumed by grief when he stopped coming. Or perhaps, like Anna, she'd consoled herself by drinking. As far as I've been able to discover, she never responded to any police investigation, but I'll bet she was sweating where her hand touched Paul's as he led her toward the bed.

I remember little about the week that followed, except a reclusive Mother Schuler, an absent Paul, a pain that kept me counting each time it seared hard across my back. My time of confinement was still a month away but I was anxious. I'd seen the midwife and been told everything was in order. A pain in my lower back or across my groin was to be expected. But in the long twilight of one of those sultry days that sometimes come in summer, the heat had me wondering if it was time to contact her again. I'd opened all the windows, trying to catch the slightest stirring, and heard my name shouted before I heard the front door open. I wasn't intentionally slow in responding. Walking was uncomfortable and awkward. I reached the hall as Mother Schuler stepped back outside. "Are the Zieglers about?" The windows of the upstairs rooms glowed in the semidarkness.

"Not downstairs."

"The kitchen. Quickly."

In the kitchen Mother Schuler leaned against the door as it closed behind her. I braced my hand against the table as I eased into a chair, glancing at the headlines of a newspaper she'd handed me. The beaten body of an American woman had been found in the ruin of Karlsruhe castle. My hands were ice though I was sweating. I knew it was Molly and that stains from giving her a lethal beating had forced Paul to burn his clothes. I wanted to read more but Mother Schuler turned the paper to a second page. Another body had been found, in the woods below Heidelberg's castle. A man. His hands bound. Garroted. A member of a Labor Service unit making a routine inspection behind a senior officer's quarters had stumbled on the corpse in the darkness of early morning. The police found no indication of who had dumped the body. A preliminary investigation had determined the murder was committed elsewhere.

Memories filled the kitchen. The comfort of the massive stove on winter afternoons. Extravagant odors from Gerda's baking. Hartmut. Paul. The excitement of so much promise. I rose to put my arms around Paul's mother.

"The authorities brought the paper," she said, her regal self in full control. "Perhaps it was the war. Perhaps the deprivation of Siberia. Perhaps he was trying to please his father."

"What will you do, Mother Schuler?"

"I shall claim the body. He is still my son."

Paul's daughter was born to me that night, alone in my room beside the kitchen, when the heat broke and the rain beat down, while my father slept and Frau Ziegler didn't hear me calling. I'd staggered to bed right after Mother Schuler left me and lay there alternately frozen to my toes then sweating from what I couldn't tell her. My water broke when I stepped from my bed to make a cup of tea. The gush between my legs was such a shock I lay back down thinking I'd call Frau Ziegler but I must have lost all sense of time. When I awoke, the pain was so intense and steady, not rhythmic and with breathing space as I expected, that I turned on my side thinking I'd let it pass. By the time I knew I had to make an effort to get help, my bed was slick with blood and the pain was so powerful I could do nothing except push to birth the baby.

When he found me in the morning, Herr Ziegler ran to tell Mother Schuler and summon the midwife while Frau Ziegler cared for me and my new daughter. Tomas and Inge hovered in the hallway noisily excited.

Katarina was a beautiful baby, and healthy, but she cried with such a lonely wail. In a strange way comforting that aloneness was solace for our fears. But the police came only once to each of us. Perhaps they thought it futile. They had so many questions and we had so few answers. I've always suspected the police weren't really trying. Paul was one of the trouble makers they were happy to be rid of and who of us would prompt them? Not me. Not Mother Schuler who deserved what solace she could salvage. The night clerk? His memories of other police investigations were still too fresh. Von Rautner? Hardly. But within our home and the Schulers' kitchen, our search for answers became obsessive. Mother Schuler bought the Karlsruhe paper daily at the kiosk where she changed buses from the one that brought her from Quinckestrasse to the one that brought her home. She had no way of knowing we were reading the paper in different ways as we devoured the news together. She searched for some hint of what had taken her son to Karlsruhe. I followed the continuing investigation into Molly's death. That investigation was very different from the one for Paul. The police in Karlsruhe found a range of witnesses who produced new information almost daily. One man had come upon a couple in the bushes. He'd heard a woman moaning but, being drunk, he'd thought it was from passion. He'd asked the man stretched out across her body if it weren't strange to be making love there in the bushes and been told nothing was strange after the Russian front. A carload of soldiers heading for the barracks had almost run over a man who'd stumbled out into one of the wide spoke-like streets emanating from the castle. A blast from their horn had sent him lurching back across the patchwork of vegetable gardens around the ruin.

Twice the newspaper published pictures, but never one of Thelma. As offensive as it may sound, that left me consumed by a need to see, to know. I went to the hotel on a day I knew the night clerk wasn't working and stood in the hall outside what should have been her room. The door never opened.

When I left the hotel, I walked the way Paul must have gone, passing the flat triangle of the Fiat building, cutting across deserted throughways with park-like divisions in the centers. Before an overgrown area that was much like one of the pictures in the paper, I thought it could be here Paul encountered Molly. I imagined him glowing with charm in spite of his need to hurry, perhaps even telling her that Thelma and he would have joined her at the club if she'd said where she was going. If Thelma's name hadn't sounded as it should, Molly would have taunted him with the thhhh sound again, or drunkenly reminded him that Krauts weren't allowed in the Officers' Club except as servants. I could feel his horror as he stumbled backward up the traffic divide, sharp branches gouging at his thighs. I hope Molly followed voluntarily. I don't want to think he planned what happened.

I wondered when Molly became convinced a man as handsome and charming as Paul wanted something more than sex with Thelma. I wondered if she told him she would turn him in. It was certainly something like that that made him hit her. The newspaper had reported signs of struggle. I recoiled from the thought of Paul's long legs straddling her body as he lifted her head with the power of his blows and wondered when his groping fingers had closed around a rock. The newspaper said the murderer had used one. He'd pulled her thin sweater over her battered head and tied it with the sleeves. That was how they found her.

Because there was never any witness from the station, I guessed Paul hid below the tracks, frantically filling his notebook until a northbound train stopped above him. Fate was in his favor. He'd plunged into a coach other than the one the room clerk had chosen. Slumping low on his wooden bench, praying there'd be no security check of bags and papers, praying a sour odor in the dark coach would mask the sour odor of his clothes, he probably feigned sleep among other sleepers until an hour passed and he heard the soft call of a conductor, "Heidelberg …"

The focus for his mind could only have been von Rautner's violent disapproval.

# *Autumn*
## *1948*

"Renate? Renate?"

I hurried to open the door at the sound of Anna's voice. I'd not seen her since my confinement and the only card I'd sent to let her know about the birth hadn't been answered. I stepped outside and she pressed into my hands a package tied with yellow ribbon and a pound of American coffee in a tall commissary bag. At her side, wearing the semi-dress uniform the Americans called pinks and greens, was an American officer. Along the curb beyond Frau Schuler's fence was a highly polished dark red American car. I smiled and tried to hug my friend but Anna pushed beyond me saying the man behind her was Charlie Dobbs. Her voice was loud and strident. Anna had been drinking.

Charlie Dobbs removed his stiff visored hat and grasped it with his elbow. His dark eyes beneath a brush of short blond hair met mine directly. He made no response to Anna's rudeness, no wink, no nod, but something was happening behind his eyes. They seemed to darken as his gaze moved from me to Anna. I felt awkward with Anna making no attempt to ease the unfamiliarity between us and echoed something Günther said to me after I'd confessed curiosity on entering an American home. "It's just a place where people live, Lieutenant Dobbs."

To my surprise his cheeks flamed with a mask of scarlet but a lopsided grin twisting his features relieved my consternation. He put his hat into my reaching hand. "The name's Charlie," he said.

Across her shoulder Anna said they'd been to her sister's in Mannheim and to Charlie's company in Seckenheim. The air was so, she called it absolute, she'd told Charlie she wanted to stop for her friend Renate. My postcard had arrived some weeks before and she thought I must be ready for an outing. Smoothing strands of pale hair, she pranced past the grand salon, the stairs, only glancing at the closed door of my bedroom beside the kitchen. She said they'd flown to Heidelberg where she had these things for me and reached back to pat the packages she'd forced into my hands.

"Thank you, Anna, Lieutenant Dobbs," I said.

Charlie's face lifted in his half-turned grin.

"Charlie," I corrected.

In the music room Anna jerked a cord hanging below a lampshade made of polished tortoise but as soon as the light flared, she collapsed onto a short settee and put her head back against an embroidered cushion. Charlie sat in my father's straight-backed chair, his curiosity settling on the black wood case that held the violin. He asked if I played. I told him no, the violin belonged to my father, a gift he'd given himself with award money from his research. I told him my father played quite well, or at least he did, and asked him if he played. "Once," he answered, his grin lifting a corner of his mouth.

"Would you like to play now?" I asked. The violin was a Guarneri and I'd often thought it was played too little.

"What?" The abruptness brought me arching upright. "I can't play here. I only played in a high school orchestra with other kids whose parents made them practice. I was never any good." His blush was crimson to his hair roots. I couldn't help myself, I liked Lieutenant Dobbs. I liked his easy embarrassment, his honest confession, his awkward smile, the caring way his whole body leaned toward Anna as he was speaking in spite of her failure to look in his direction. He asked me about the baby and I found it easy to describe how beautiful she was, how quickly she was growing. When I told him she was just past two months, he grinned again, that grin that must mean so much to Anna. He said two months was a little young to help me with the violin.

Anna's face was rigid. Her eyes closed. Only when I asked Charlie if he'd like me to make some coffee did her eyelids flutter. She said she'd wanted him to take us for a drink but he refused no matter how she pleaded. The lieutenant's discomfort was apparent.

I wanted to tell him it didn't matter but Anna had his full attention. Her eyes had opened and fixed on him. Charlie said he'd like to take us sometime, but not today. He couldn't. He was on duty soon. Anna said, "He works at Campbell Barracks."

"Campbell Barracks?" I asked.

Lieutenant Dobbs settled back into his chair, pinching the sharp creases in his trousers. "You called it Grossdeutschland Kaserne. The army changed the name to honor an American hero."

"A man who killed a lot of Germans," Anna said.

I wondered about preliminaries to this confrontation, perhaps going back to that day in Anna's apartment with the windows closed, the curtains drawn, the stifling air and the anger. Charlie said he'd hoped Anna would leave the place where she worked now and come to work with him. A new exchange was being installed in the Signal Office basement and he thought with her English and experience, she'd be a cinch for a position. Anna was suddenly alert, her feet flat on the floor. "Renate can work a switchboard. She supervised us in the German army."

Charlie turned to me. I nodded. He explained the Signal Office worked twenty-four hours daily, seven days a week, so shifts were constantly changing, but the pay for telephone operators was probably better than for most who started at the Barracks.

My fingers slid along the yellow ribbon around the package in my lap. If I had a regular job, with regular pay, Mother Schuler could finally stop her commute to Quinckestrasse and perhaps find peace in caring for Paul's child. She needed that. She needed time. She needed to see for herself the hope in other people's faces with the continuing miracle of new stores opening. A wave of food buying had engulfed us through the summer. A wave of personal adornment followed with merchants polishing windows to display dresses, underwear, trousers, shoes. Clothes were still rationed but we in the West were buying with real money replacements for what we'd worn too long through the final years of war and the years of depravation.

Anna clapped her hands. "Well then, you see. We've solved a problem for you."

"Now wait a minute," Charlie said. "I can't guarantee a job." His eyes had lost their luster. "You've papers to fill out. You need a physical. I suppose a test. If you're really interested, you'll find your answers at the American employment office in the Grand Hotel."

"I know the place," I said. "I'll go tomorrow."

"They'll want her," Anna said. "Renate will be the best operator at the Barracks."

"Now there's a recommendation," Charlie said.

With new brittleness in her voice, Anna added, "Charlie likes to help people. Telling you about this job can be his last good deed before his transfer."

Before I could ask if he were only leaving Seckenheim, Charlie said, "I'm going stateside."

The urge to take Anna in my arms as I had so long ago when she seemed a frightened child was almost overwhelming, but the child was gone. The woman had chosen drink and silence. I shuddered as I remembered the absolute joy with which she'd described their future that night in her grand apartment. We're all so vulnerable, I thought. So eternally looking for that other to complete us, yet so brutal to each other. The restrictions the Americans placed on marrying a German had been easing through the years but obviously Charlie wasn't taking Anna with him.

Katarina interrupted with a cry.

"The baby?" Charlie asked.

I nodded. My breasts felt full and almost painful.

"Good lungs," he said.

Anna led the way across the hall, averting her face until the lieutenant opened my door and she swept into my room. They reached the crib together. Charlie put one finger on a wooden rail for gentle rocking but Anna swooped the baby from her crib. "Don't cry, little one," she said as Kati cried louder. "Don't cry. Don't cry. Charlie has found your mother a job at Campbell Barracks."

After I'd told the Zieglers what I was planning I spent the rest of the day with my father, playing the piano, positioning his violin on his shoulder, hoping he'd find solace if he tried to play.

I took Kati to Mother Schuler as soon as she was home from Quinckestrasse, putting the baby in her arms as I told her about Campbell Barracks. I hadn't expected her to cry. I'd have thought there were no more tears in her.

At the employment office I was familiar with the forms, the

interviews, the tests. I applied for a position at the new switchboard in the Headquarters Signal Office as Charlie had suggested and felt almost anticlimactic as I accepted access papers for entry to the compound, further clearance to the restricted area of my assignment, a punch card for meals in a German workers' mess. Mother Schuler quit her commute to Quinckestrasse even before Frau Ziegler offered to help when I worked nights.

Within days of first hearing about the opportunity, I was approaching Campbell Barracks from a blue streetcar on Rohrbacherstrasse. Holding in check the memories that played with my emotions, I plunged into a profusion of khaki-colored trucks and buses, civilian cars of every color, long, black limousines with ranking officers sitting upright behind their German drivers. I'd dressed carefully in my pleated skirt and a sweater with some color, hopeful and confident that I was well prepared. Across from an entrance below high arched windows, I eased my breath out slowly. Two military checkpoints with a busy street between. The checkpoint on my left seemed the quicker of the two but an American military policeman on duty ignored my approach even though military personnel and civilian workers were rushing past in both directions. He glanced at every pass but not the papers I extended.

"Excuse me, sir," I said.

He looked up.

"I need to ..."

He dismissed me with a wave.

"But ..."

"The other side."

"What?"

"Krauts enter on the other side."

A lesson, I thought. Entries for the Allies and entries for us. Humiliating, but just a lesson. I folded my papers and turned to face the traffic. Another policeman was clearing cars that passed him, barely pausing. Lesson two. Except for an occasional khaki-colored limousine, the cars had American drivers. I looked more closely. There didn't even seem to be a German riding. In those days before recovery, the difference was there for everyone to see. It had much to do with clothes, of course. The shoes being most apparent if they could be seen.

I retraced my steps toward the streetcars and walked the length of the double entry on the opposite side of the street. A short, thick Labor Service guard checked workers on that side. "Your papers." He spoke English but his accent was clearly from the East. I answered him in German. He spoke again in English. "Wait. You'll have a turn." Lesson three. I was back in a world where authority was absolute and obvious.

A worn briefcase was opened for inspection, a purse. Everything was lifted from a leather suitcase. At a lull the guard reached for my papers, jerking his thumb to indicate the part of the building above us as he finished reading. He told me the entry to the Signal Office was around the corner to the right. I'd be checked again inside the door.

Beyond the shadow of the entry, a series of double-storied buildings surrounded a broad parade field. The largest American flag I'd ever seen flew from a giant pole. With my shoulders back, my step determined, I pushed the heavy door around the corner. An American military policeman lounged against a counter. He straightened when I entered but only glanced through my papers before he shouted up a flight of stairs, "Hey Gamboli, take this Fräulein to Sergeant Miller. Save me callin' Fred."

A soldier, looking much like all the others, was halfway up a flight of stairs beyond the MP's station. A full-toothed grin brought his face in focus as he glanced back down and raised one arm in triumph. "Come on little lady, I'll take you anyplace you want to go."

Unmistakable sounds of working switchboards came clearly from the basement but I went where the MP pointed to meet Gamboli on the stairs. His fingers played across my back before they curled around my shoulder, dropping only when we entered an office where a stubby woman in the uniform of the Women's Army Corp was leafing through a drawer in a tall cabinet of files.

"Sergeant Miller's always busy." Gamboli squeezed my arm.

"Hold on, Gamboli." Sergeant Miller slammed the drawer and accepted my papers, explaining with frankness I found startling that it was impossible for her to help me at the moment. The telephone lines to Karlsruhe had been vandalized again and the CO was waiting for the names of the men on duty. She turned to a man who seemed supported by his uniform as he hunched behind a desk at the back of the room. "Hey, Fred, get ..." Sergeant Miller glanced at my papers. "Get Renate's picture taken for her pass, then get back here on the double."

Fred smiled.

The Headquarters Signal Office stretched out in long corridors of hard, ridged flooring. Empty gun emplacements cut deep into thick stone walls. I knew these buildings had housed a Wehrmacht unit through the war and I looked about with curiosity.

After an identification picture was taken in a closet-like room on the second floor, Fred continued along the corridor although he was quick to explain that as a switchboard operator, I'd not have access to this part of the building. A snack bar was in the attic but I'd not be able to use that either because payment was in military script, that money I'd encountered only rarely. At a long room whose arched windows I'd seen directly above the entrance, Fred leaned around the door to wave at an American woman sitting at a desk in a far corner. By the end of that first day, I'd learned that without a pass that had to be countersigned by the Military Police on duty, I'd be restricted to the basement and the German workers' lounge unless an American was with me.

Sergeant Miller raised her hand for patience when we returned to her office. She was listening to a tall sergeant bent over her desk. "I know, I know," she kept repeating. The man from the night at the café with Paul and Günther, the one who sent the drunken soldier to the taxi. I didn't realize I was staring.

"I see you've spotted Iverson already." Gamboli had reentered the room from behind us and was hovering close enough to whisper in my ear.

"Down, Gamboli," Fred said.

Gamboli persisted. "All the ladies go for him. They go out of their way to pass his door. He works in Fault Control, but with you in the basement, you won't have much chance. No chance really. He doesn't like Kraut ladies." Gamboli said that I couldn't look at the boys in the code room either. "They're off limits to indigenous personnel lovelies." His eyes removed my cotton sweater, my heavy shoes before he added, "But a looker like you should have no trouble with the other jokers in this building."

Sergeant Iverson straightened after patting a sheaf of papers on Sergeant Miller's desk. His frown turned to a questioning flash of recognition when he saw me.

Sergeant Miller said, "Fred, I need you here. Gamboli, you take Renate downstairs and introduce her to the shift chief."

"*Oui, mon capitaine*," Gamboli's arm was already looping across my shoulder.

Down the stairs, past the entrance, down another shorter flight of stairs, Gamboli introduced me to a harried-looking little man who quickly introduced me to Johanna, the chief operator on duty. Dark up-swept hair framed her strong German features above a ruffled blouse that looked foreign. "You'll find this a good place to work." Johanna brushed at a striped skirt she'd inset with bands of solid fabric in a not-quite-successful effort to match the current length in the fluid postwar dresses of the American women. "You'll find a few of the men quite forward, but pay no attention. They mean no harm."

"I met Gamboli," I said.

Johanna laughed. "He's another matter. You'll get used to him."

The long, low-ceilinged switchboard room seemed almost familiar with operators wearing heavy headphones, pulled in close to flashing panels. Only a haze of voices speaking English was different. I tried to count. Twelve? Fourteen? women working plugs and switches. Johanna's right, I thought, I'll get used to this, and I won't wonder if Günther would be pleased, I won't hear him laugh at my misgivings. I'd had no word from him since the night at the café but in a newspaper a neighbor gave me for another reason, I'd seen an announcement of a concert in which he'd sung. The concert was in Mannheim. The date was past. I smiled at Johanna.

Winter began to spread its cold across the plains and daylight came late on rain-soaked mornings before my work changed to begin late in the afternoon. I came to work as others left the Barracks. It was an easy adjustment. I just went to bed a few hours later and slept a bit longer in the morning. Then the shift changed to begin when others were in bed. Only the Command Building and the Headquarters Signal Office were tenanted at night, the rest of the Barracks dark, the parade field silent. I found magic working as the hours changed to morning. There was a slowness, a closeness that wasn't there by day. After a long, dark shift, I'd come home to lie in my tall bed in my room beside the kitchen, listening for my daughter to awake, rumpled and damp from sleeping. After Mother Schuler came I'd sleep a few more hours before the three of us took our daily stroll, Kati in a black, high-bonneted carriage that once held Paul. Schwetzingen still had boarded storefronts with empty interiors and locked entries, but it also had the wonder of electric irons, typewriters, clocks in an assortment of lighted windows. We paused before a bedding store to admire large, square pillows, draped sheets, the feather fullness of new eiderdowns while I talked about my work at Campbell Barracks, confiding that German and Americans worked side by side but we weren't colleagues in the way I remembered from Aland Nord. There wasn't even a place within the confines of the Barracks where we could share a cup of coffee. A jeep approached on the narrow street, fouling the air with its gaseous exhaust. I hadn't mentioned a worker in another building who wore a faded Star of David on his new clothes. He claimed every German was responsible for the death of his wife and daughter. The jeep disappeared around a corner while I struggled to integrate the now into the years before. We could buy fresh food in markets. We had warmth on chilly mornings. A new eiderdown was for sale on the corner. Yet I yearned for the innocence of those days with Günther and Anna in the mountains. Anna had no money for the apartment after Charlie left so she returned to her sister's in Mannheim. The last time I saw her, she was still working for the man named Schmidt but I knew that couldn't last, not with the way she was drinking. I'd tried to tell her I'd help if she came to work at Campbell Barracks but she wouldn't listen. She was cursing Charlie, weeping at his leaving, swearing she'd never love again. She said Charlie had been her warning. She said she had to prepare for the time men turned away, for the time there was no interest when she walked into a room. I paused before a window of beautifully handcrafted dresses. Anna had always been so beautiful, and everybody loved her. I wondered if they loved her now.

*Munich, 19. October 1948*

My dear Renate,

    I met Anna, to my very great surprise, in Augsburg. She was there with a German businessman named Schmidt. With time on her hands, she chanced to see my name in a newspaper announcement and came, alone, to my concert. After, she sought me out. I find her changed, mean-spirited almost, but that concern is for another letter. Of course we were glad to be together but so little time. I was catching a late train back to Munich so she came with me to the station and we drank wine until we parted.

    Renate, what do I say? My condolences are most sincerely given. Loss is always painful, and the manner of Herr Schuler's death must have been particularly difficult for you and for his mother. But congratulations are in order. You have a daughter. Anna tells me you named her Katarina for Frau Schuler.

    If you've spoken to Anna, you know I have permission to leave the country. A master class has been arranged with Carlo Montuoni. That's right, in Milan, with Montuoni. But I can manage a day, a few hours really. A night train from Munich will allow me time in Heidelberg before I connect with another train through Karlsruhe and on to Italy. My trunk will have been shipped ahead.

    Please don't read more into this proposal than the surface. I find it arrogant and unfair to both of us even as I write, but if you can find it in your heart to do so, meet me at the station in Heidelberg at seven Sunday morning. If you choose not to be there, I'll understand. I can even believe it might be better, but I can't not mail this letter.

                                   Günther

I was early at the station. I saw him first, stepping out of a compartment, looking across the crowded ramp for me. I didn't run to meet him. I wanted to hold as long as I was able this moment of recognition, the indisputable knowledge he was here for me. I'd found him so soon despite the surge of soldiers from the first class coaches of the train. I could spare this time, savoring him walk toward me with the same unhurried grace that I remembered. Then he saw me. He caught my hand and pressed my fingers to his lips. He said, "When Anna told me, I couldn't stay away." I told him to stop talking, just let me hold him and he laughed that wonderful soaring sound that filled me with such joy. "I can't do that, I want to look at you."

I hid my face against his shoulder absorbing his night on the train, the wonderful cold of morning. "Not yet. I hardly slept last night."

He lifted my hair from behind my collar. "Renate, I've seen you worse, remember? You hadn't changed your clothes in weeks and were sleeping on the ground."

"I remember everything," I said.

The platform was clearing quickly. The last of the crowd was disappearing over a path that crossed the tracks, through the station, and out beyond the arches. Near the corner where buses took on passengers for their trips beyond the city, Günther must have felt my hesitation. "We'll take the time," he said. "I must meet your daughter."

Mother Schuler was waiting, Katarina a blanket covered bundle in her arms. In one sweeping motion Günther shrugged from his coat, tossed it back across my reaching arm and was cradling the baby while he shook Mother Schuler's hand. Lifting the blanket from her soft face, he said Kati was the first he'd seen so small, since his brothers, adding, "She's the image of her grandmother."

Mother Schuler's breath caught sharply. "And Paul?"

The hallway filled with shadows. I turned to close the door knowing there was no closing out the past. When I turned back, Günther was kissing Mother Schuler's cheek.

Mother Schuler had set our table with rolls warm from the bakery, butter, and jam she'd made from berries gathered in the woods. Brown eggs were waiting to be boiled with small cups to receive them and tiny spoons. She told Günther she thought he might be hungry and was rewarded by his arm around her shoulder and another kiss on her flushed cheek.

Kati's soft fuss became demanding and I took her in my arms. "She needs her mother," I said, but in my room, away from the warmth in the kitchen, I let an unfathomable aloneness overwhelm me. Günther and I had been silent during the ride from town, just sitting close together as if there'd been too much to say. He'd seemed so much stronger in his successes. Different in a way I couldn't quite explain. I finished the restless feeding and hurried back to the kitchen in time to hear him say he could almost smell the future. In a voice thick with his excitement he was telling Mother Schuler about his possibilities in Milan. Perhaps he'd be there only long enough to sing for Montuoni. He'd heard about an open contract in Verona and there was a chance he'd study in America as well. Some of his American friends were urging him toward that.

I lifted a spoon but didn't move to crack the egg Mother Schuler placed before me.

"The baby?" Günther asked.

"Sleeping," I said.

Mother Schuler pushed away from the table, gathering her porcelain coffee service onto a polished tray. She cautioned that the life he'd chosen promised no security and Günther's hand covered mine. It wasn't security he wanted, it was a chance. He knew he had the talent but what he did right now was so important. Every choice was a different direction. If he chose correctly, he could fly into the future. If he was wrong, his career could be limited forever. As she put the tray into Günther's hands, Mother Schuler asked if he could live with himself if that happened. I knew his answer before he said it. "Not if I've been timid."

In the small salon I spooned coarse granules of raw sugar into our fragile cups, the spoon a fleeting spark of silver in the ebony depths. Günther stood behind me, his face hidden. He told me there was no punishment worse than leaving me again. He hurt inside just to think how long it would be before we had the luxury of time together, but his visa was almost impossible to obtain, the master class had been arranged. He couldn't let this opportunity slip by and hope to find another. "I'm afraid," he said. "Afraid as when I couldn't look for you in Heidelberg, afraid as when I discovered you had married."

I was afraid, too.

"But this is right for me, I know it."

Mother Schuler knocked before she entered. "Your father's waking, Renate." Our coats were across her arm.

In Heidelberg Günther and I took the funicular to the Königstuhl, escaping the crowds and the restlessness they added to the city. Clinging to each other, we walked back down to the castle where the remnants of scarlet from a Japanese maple carpeted in remembered brightness what had been a moat. Beyond the crumbling munitions tower, we followed a long wall to a corner of the garden and looked out over the city: the Kornmarktplatz which had held the markets of desperation, the Holy Ghost Church where Günther had his early triumph, the Pfannengasse. My room was finally abandoned. I reached out to catch a leaf lifting in a wisp of breeze, questioning our past. Günther's answer was that the rest of his life wasn't enough to erase the monumental madness but he'd stopped expecting to find a reason. He'd found some peace. He'd learned he could be happy.

Drizzle from one dark cloud sent us down into the city to find shelter in a café, drinking coffee until we had just time to reach the station. As we passed an American hotel, a young resident with uncombed hair sat by a window opened to the freshness. He was practicing from Bach's suite for cello, pulling his taut bow across long strings as he leaned forward. Günther paused to listen.

"Your universal language," I said and I felt better.

Beyond the arched entry to the station, as the round lights of his approaching train pierced the gray daylight, Günther said he wouldn't tie me to a promise however much that was what he wanted. He was going far away. How long he stayed depended upon how often his visa was extended. After he'd kissed me one more time he said, "What would we have if I stayed here? Another walk in the woods?"

We found a compartment. Wooden. German. Empty, but for an elegantly dressed older woman whose eyes never lifted from her book. Günther lowered a window to grasp my hand as the train crashed back, pulled forward, dragged our hands apart, leaving me with my arm outstretched until the last coach disappeared along the track by which the train had entered.

A dull sun broke through a patch of clouds as I returned to Schwetzingen. Mother Schuler was busy in the kitchen, with Kati sleeping on a mat beside the stove. "Günther gone?" She glanced up from a deep pot heavy with the scent of *Sauerbraten*. Though the room was warm and I was not, I couldn't stay there trying to be cheerful, talking about a future I couldn't yet imagine. I escaped to the far side of the house and stared through a narrow window. Günther had said I should go on with my life as the force of the train pulled him away. "You are my life," I'd shouted as his reaching hand grew dimmer in the distance. But was I trying to hold a shadow? With all the partings, all the pain, with an indeterminate time before us, could that really be my answer?

# Winter
## 1948-1949

Sergeant First Class Johnson Bonamaker flashed his pass to the military policeman at the ground floor check point just inside the door of the Headquarters Signal Office and, with the confidence of one who is sure of military discipline, started up the stairs. His uniform was pressed sharp along the creases, neatly tailored against his frame. He was tall and straight and smiling and he was black. I was on my way to the German worker's lounge and drew back against the railing to let him pass.

The strong scent of a numbered cologne newly advertised at German counters brought me from my stupor. "Would you believe it?" the scented woman said.

"Believe what?" Johanna came up behind us.

"A black man. Here. In the Signal Office," the woman answered.

Gamboli appeared. "What are you ladies saying?"

"A *Schwartze*. Here."

Gamboli laughed. "Black meat for you hungry ladies," he said.

Off and on throughout the year since the American president had signed an order forbidding military segregation, I'd been haunted by the times I didn't rush to Eva's side when other children called her names I found abhorrent. I remembered exactly the tightness in my throat, the heaviness in my body, the fear I'd be judged as different from the rest, and I'd grown relentlessly determined not to be a child again with any willingness to go along with what others might be saying.

The scented operator said she'd seen such men before. She'd seen one near the American swimming pool on Vangerowstrasse and asked if it were possible he went in the water with the others. Both she and Johanna looked to Gamboli for an answer but at that moment Sergeant Miller called from her office, "If that's gossip going on out there, I want it stopped."

Massive furnaces heating all of Campbell Barracks had been fired when the sun had left the summer and on days like the one of Sergeant Bonamaker's arrival, with unseasonably mild weather, the building was oppressive. In the lounge I splashed cold water on my face before using a strong-smelling yellow soap the army had provided. Johanna came to stand beside me, holding her wrists beneath a rush of cooling water. "I understand for us he will be shift chief," she said.

The other woman entered and locked a booth.

I liked Johanna. I'd found her intelligent and fair, but I knew I wasn't ready for the place where a conversation with these two might take me. I escaped back into the hall, literally blundering into Sergeant Miller who pushed a file folder toward me. She asked if I'd return it to the new shift chief on my way back to my switchboard. She couldn't find Fred and I could save her climbing one more flight of stairs. Damp glistened on her forehead. Her heavy winter uniform had been loosened across her breasts. "Put it in his hand," she added. She mentioned his name.

I made a small fan of Sergeant Miller's folder as I walked back downstairs. I was almost grateful for the errand. It gave me another chance to test my resolve, but at the door of Sergeant Bonamaker's office old discomforts seized me. He was alone, pulled in close to one of two desks in Radio Repair. The other one was empty.

"Sergeant," I said and then, after clearing my throat, "Sergeant Bonamaker."

"Yes, Frau Schuler."

I was startled to hear my name and steadied myself against the door frame, mumbling something about Sergeant Miller wanting me to put these papers in his hand. He stood, not quite as tall as I'd imagined when I was clinging to the stairwell. His face was polished by the heat. He seemed to be appraising me through round steel-rimmed glasses balanced low on his broad nose but in a friendly, nonjudgmental way. Curiosity restored some of my composure when, under thick glass on his desk, I saw carefully positioned copies of the small photos taken for identification on everyone's first day of duty. Sergeant Bonamaker had lettered a name beside each person on his shift. He asked if I'd like a Coca Cola. While I mumbled something about not having American money, his head disappeared behind his desk and he brought two green bottles up from the floor. He'd bought one for Gamboli but his clerk was off somewhere and he put the frosty bottle in my hand. He lifted the second to his forehead saying I could take mine to the break room if I liked.

I lowered myself into a chair opposite my new shift chief's desk and, while he leafed through Sergeant Miller's folder, drank the cooling unfamiliar effervescence. When I finished I put the empty bottle on his desk.

A heavy downpour broke the brief spell of warmer weather the day I spoke to Sergeant Bonamaker again. He came upon me early in a day shift's afternoon as I was standing in the quiet of a lower hallway, my forehead pressed against a window, my gaze following patterns of dingy water rippling down glazed panes of glass. With what I can only remember as genuine concern, he asked if he could help. I was irrational and fuming as I embarked on a rambling account of how I'd left my lunch on the bus that morning. I hadn't eaten breakfast either. I'd overslept in the dreary weather and spent too much time searching for protective clothing before taking my daughter to my mother-in-law. Behind his steel-rimmed glasses, Sergeant Bonamaker's eyes were darker than any I had ever seen. The dim light in the hall accented his blackness. When I finally paused enough for him to speak, he was almost apologetic. He hadn't meant to intrude. He'd thought I might be ill. He asked if I'd forgotten my card for the German mess as well.

"Forget it? I destroyed it," I said.

"Do you mind my asking why?"

With what dignity I had left, I told him we weren't allowed a knife or fork in our mess hall and I refused to eat with a spoon. I know my laugh was nervous. "Your military police must think I'd attack you with something sharper."

He said, "A minute ago, I wasn't so sure myself," and smiled a smile that was all white teeth and friendliness and humor.

Suddenly I was telling him that on some days it wasn't just the spoon, some days I wondered why it was necessary for us to walk through separate entrances, why even in this weather a German couldn't ride in or out of any gate except as a hired driver. I was already sorry I'd started, but long pent-up resentments kept pouring from me. I told him I found it quite demeaning that every German bag was searched while Americans could bring anything through any gate in the trunks of their cars.

In the stairwell voices climbing toward the snack bar interrupted and then faded. He said, "You lost a war, Frau Schuler."

I said, "And because of that I've been a lot hungrier than I am right now." He was already bringing a piece of occupation money from his pocket, urging me to take it to the attic and buy myself a sandwich. I backed against the window, the rain was hard behind me. I said I hadn't meant for him to give me money. He said it was a loan, part of his supervisory duties. I'd work more efficiently if I'd had my lunch. We both knew it was illegal for me to have occupation money and I questioned whether his offer was a test. Now he was the one offended and trying to make amends. I surprised us both by asking if he'd eaten. Perhaps if we ate upstairs together. He told me to take the money. I said I wouldn't do it. He asked if I knew what would be said if we went upstairs together. The same thing that, long years ago, children would have shouted if I'd run to Eva Steynor's side when those other children taunted.

Bonamaker told me he had a hunch we were much alike and his hand came toward my shoulder but dropped before he touched me. "All right," he said. "I haven't eaten. I'd like to buy your lunch."

We climbed the remaining flights of stairs to the attic and stepped into a line before a square-legged table supporting a box of change in paper pieces. Light from a glass display case of sandwiches on thick white plates was the brightest in the room.

"Hey, Chris," Bonamaker said as the line moved forward.

Chris Iverson turned away from the only other German present, a man behind the counter who was counting paper change into his hand. "John," he said. He nodded to me. Crumpling his change into his pocket, he accepted a brown sack of food to carry to his office. As he passed he pressed a short jab into Bonamaker's shoulder.

Bonamaker bought two ham sandwiches on pale bread and two cold bottles of Coca Cola. I followed him to the back of the long attic where he put our tray in the center of a small table pressed against the eaves. Neither of us spoke to the other Signal Office personnel who watched us, glancing up from their lunches, chewing.

Bonamaker's invitation to talk with him in his office came just days after our work shift changed to begin late in the afternoon. He'd caught up with me as I was walking toward the lounge on my first break. He said he'd been staring at an empty desk since we came on duty, he couldn't even invent things to look busy and did I want to talk? Since our lunch over sandwiches in the attic had shown promise, I followed him to his office where we took our next faltering steps in a verbal dance. I smile to think how easily I use that analogy. It was a dance. Rather formal in its execution but pleasurable and intimate. Full of dips and stumbles. Often on each other's toes. I'm not saying Bonamaker's physical attractiveness was lost on me. His strong masculine appeal was giggled about by others, but from the very beginning there was nothing sexual between us despite the surreptitious glances that followed me each time I left my switchboard. I didn't care. I'd already given up on the mindless chatter in the break room. Before our shift changed to working through to very early morning, I was bringing crusty rolls from a bakery near my home and different kinds of sausage for us to share in the time set aside for a mid-shift meal. He brought oranges and once an even more rare banana and supplied the ubiquitous Coca Cola.

After one of our meals, I was returning what we hadn't eaten to my basket when Bonamaker leaned back in his chair. "Were you really afraid of me?" he asked.

I listened to the wind keen through the underpass which was the Barracks' entry, to the blowing rain against his window. After that first moment in the stairwell, anything resembling my former fear was so alien to me that another question leaped into my mind. I'd almost asked it once before when we were talking, but the phone's ring stopped me. Sergeant Bonamaker had kept repeating, "Yes, Fred, yes, Fred. I'd suggest you come to me first in the future." The moment for my question was lost in the receiver slamming hard into its cradle.

I folded my towel across my basket. "I was never afraid of you," I said. "But I've sometimes wondered what it's like to be a Negro."

His expression didn't change but an unexpected stiffness gripped his body. My hurried clarification that we knew about President Truman's integration of the forces didn't erase his frown and I worried I'd been rude.

No, I wasn't rude. Every time he shaved he saw his face was different but I should watch my terms. The military was desegregated. It wasn't integrated yet. He groped across his pockets before opening his desk drawer to find a new pack of cigarettes and, with unnecessary concentration, picked at a red tab until it released a cellophane cover. He said the government couldn't legislate his humanity, he was born with that, but we both knew the opposite was true. Look what my own accomplished. He peeled the foil wrapping from a corner and forced out a cigarette. The clicks of his lighter produced a flame.

What my own accomplished? I almost said we had no blacks in Germany but that wasn't true. Before I was born, a French government, angry with a floundering Germany's failure to pay reparations after the Great War, had sent Senegalese and Moroccan soldiers to occupy the Ruhr. The teenaged children of these soldiers, born to German women, disappeared in the early days of Hitler. I made my protest anyway. "We had no blacks in Germany."

He said, "But you had Jews."

Now my body stiffened. Racial purity, natural law were not original with Hitler. All Europe talked eugenics. Hitler just put ideas in practice with Nazi scientists using elaborate tools, measuring the length of noses, the circumference of heads, to make racial designations. I said, "The solution to the Jewish question wasn't the totality of Hitler's planning. He spoke of remodeling all of Eastern Europe, turning the people of those countries into slaves to serve a master race of Germans."

"And of course you never questioned."

Mother Schuler once told me she and my parents had ignored what they didn't want to know. They'd maneuvered through appalling explanations. I said, "I suppose your President Truman is trying."

Bonamaker drew deeply on his cigarette, brushing at the smoke which curled upward when he exhaled. "No. Truman made only the rawest kind of beginning. The answer to your question about being a Negro in the United States must be it's something like being a German in Germany today. I realized that the day a guy from The Signal Officer's office had me on the carpet. I was informed in no uncertain terms that Germans aren't allowed in the attic. Remember the day we ate up there together?" His gaze followed a hazy pathway to the tubes of light where smoke still lingered. "Think about it. This is your country, but it isn't. You're bound by attitudes and rules, if not written certainly enforced." He said that even in the capital of his country where he grew up, he didn't eat where a white man eats or stay in his hotels. He rode behind a line in buses. He laughed, a harsh unfunny grating. "Don't you find it ironic that the world's greatest democracy fought the world's greatest racist with a segregated army?" He crushed his cigarette into his ashtray. Curls of tobacco spread across the glass but he kept twisting. He said when he'd joined the army, he'd hoped he'd be judged by the color of his blood and his willingness to shed it rather than by the color of his skin but it didn't always work that way.

I was moving toward the door when he said he wanted to share a secret. He'd taken an incongruously red cloth he kept in his desk drawer and was polishing his glasses. He said he'd had it with the military's black units being led by white deadbeats who couldn't make it elsewhere and wanted to be part of a change he knew was coming. He'd applied for and been accepted into Officer Candidate School.

I clutched my basket handles. A black officer receiving salutes from white soldiers? Was there no end to how deep my racist indoctrination went, how long it lingered no matter how I raged against it?

"I leave Germany after the first of the year."

My ears rang with the comments others must be making, the unrealistic characterizations not unlike the Nazi's hooked-nose Jew, and I tried to remember Herr Steynor's even features, imagine a grown-up Eva's beauty. I looked into Bonamaker's black face. He was waiting for my answer. I said, "I wish you could meet a friend of mine."

"I can't?"

"He's off in Italy, following his dream."

I wish now I'd offered him congratulations, I didn't even shake his hand. I should have asked about ambition, about dreams that give the future meaning. Instead I mumbled something about the path he'd chosen not being easy and he said nothing was hard when it was what you really wanted.

Our shift changed to days. Days were full of interruptions and Bonamaker and I found little quiet time to talk. Perhaps we didn't want to. Our last conversation had touched some hidden places and we needed time. When the shift changed again, Bonamaker told me he'd been spending evenings with a group from Mannheim and I thought, good, he'd been with others like himself, and then spent agonizing hours castigating myself for such a careless observation. By the time he took a few days off before Thanksgiving, I'd disregarded superficial differences and made several mental lists of the countless ways we were like each other.

With the added responsibility of covering for those on leave between the holidays, our shift was almost through December before I sat across from him in his office, tired, uneasy for no reason, anxious for the shift to end on that last night before the work force changed to days. When I'd arrived at the Barracks, I'd escaped a drenching downpour into the entry of the building, shaking my umbrella, stomping, my shoes soaked, my feet wet to my ankles and a long night ahead. A decorated Christmas tree had been placed in the German worker's lounge. The ubiquitous burst of colored lights gave me no joy of the season. It reminded me of past years' deprivations, of Günther whose letters were increasingly reports of a life in which I had no part, of Anna whom I'd let disappear. Now this.

Bonamaker was leaning toward me across his desk, "Tell me honestly. Did you know?"

We'd had elections. Surely he couldn't believe that when ordinary Germans went to the polls, they'd grit their teeth and thought they'd get Hitler into power and then they'd build those camps. I filled my lungs and exhaled slowly. "Perhaps I can explain some of his appeal."

"Try me."

"He played on our emotions. The uniforms, the bands, the blood red flags …"

"You inheritors of the power of imperial Rome fell for pagan rituals?"

"A chancellor at the university said our need was for another Siegfried and along came Hitler proclaiming 'I am Siegfried'. Read *Mein Kampf*." His pencil was a blur of twisting blue. "Our land, our legends are such a part of what we are. We're at home in our mist-shrouded forests. The Jews are desert people. How could we mix with desert people?"

"You're serious about this."

"I don't expect you to understand. You Americans are so proud to be a stew."

"A melting pot," he said.

"Well we were proud that we are pure. It didn't seem wrong to isolate those who would contaminate us."

"Contaminate you?" Bonamaker wrenched his center drawer against his stomach and stared at a trough of paper clips and pencils before slamming his blue pencil down among a group of yellows. "So whole villages got together and posted signs: Jews Not Wanted Here."

"In the cities there were ghettos."

"Across the tracks. I understand."

I was sure he didn't. I told him first he had to accept the concept of human inequality. The absolute inferiority of some people.

He said, "Three-fifths of a human being."

I didn't question.

His hand closed around a pack of cigarettes. He found his lighter. "Did the Jews grow up like other Germans?"

I said, "Of course. They were integrated into every aspect of every German city."

"So, being German and respectful of authority, they just climbed into the boxcars."

I fought a memory of the times I'd tried to rationalize, defend, explain. The Jews were too docile, too willing to comply. I'd tried to believe they knew they were inferior.

"They were just so damn German," he said.

I said, "Jews weren't German after they reached the camps in Poland. Citizenship was lost by being resident in another country."

Bonamaker crushed the length of his new cigarette into his glass ashtray. "Someone really had you people figured out."

His long and only slightly tapered fingers were not unlike Herr Steynor's as they extinguished his cigarette into a porcelain ashtray on a visit I'd made with Eva and her family to the elegant home of an elegant woman who lived in Frankfurt. Eva's paternal grandmother. With an overwhelming sense of loss I remembered how Eva had cried the day she told me her grandmother refused to leave her home and go with them to England.

Bonamaker said, "You've not convinced me of his appeal."

"You Americans will lose a lesson of history if you consider Hitler less than what he was. We believed him when he promised to lift Germany from the degradation we still suffered fifteen years after the Great War. When he did, he seemed a god. My friends and I, we sang his praises at our parties. We prayed for his blessings to follow us at night. During his first four years in office our standards of health were raised until tuberculosis and other feared diseases were infecting so few, other countries paid attention. Why wouldn't we believe him when he told us the Jews were enemies of our astonishing new state? He and Goebbels created such a system of public enlightenment …"

"Public enlightenment? A fancy name for the way they chained your minds?"

"We didn't consider ourselves unfree. Hitler gave us back our pride. You'd have to be German to realize what that meant."

"I know what pride is and what it is to be without it."

I reminded him of the years America was in deep depression while Germany had full employment. Hitler built roads and concert halls and swimming pools. We had the Wilhelm Gustloff, a cruise ship for government sponsored holidays. Workers and their families who'd never seen an ocean, danced and dined and breathed fresh air all the way to Madeira. "Strength through joy."

"Another Nazi slogan?"

"We had a whole new social order in which private clubs and professional associations were replaced by National Socialists' leagues. It was hard to advance in any career if you weren't a member of a league."

"And the Jews were not admitted."

I said, "Read your history. All Europe had their pogroms."

"That doesn't excuse what happened here. Your pogrom was systematic genocide. Your Jews were not expelled but murdered."

He stood and paced the room. He closed and opened the door. "You, personally, how did Jews treat you?"

"I didn't know one." Bands across my chest were tight until my heart was bursting. My head, too. The Steynors, I wanted to scream. Eva was my friend. I enjoyed cherry tarts for tea at her grandmother's table.

He said, "You must have seen one. Your government made all Jews wear a yellow star. Did you realize what such an obvious mark of segregation must mean?"

I was squirming. "I remember the night of riots and before that when books were burned. My family was more afraid of the ruffians who did that than of Jews we thought could hurt us."

He stopped his pacing. He'd seen newsreels. He knew university students in Berlin were throwing books into the fires. "But maybe your family should have been afraid. Those students were your thinkers. Your future leaders."

I took a firm grip on my evasions. "Not only students thought him charismatic. Members of our intellectual elite fell victim to his charm and became enthusiastic advocates of his programs."

"His programs?"

I hadn't meant quite that.

Bonamaker retreated behind his desk, rocking his chair until the front legs balanced off the floor. "I can try to understand barbarous acts done in a fury of revenge or battle, but by bureaucrats? In an office? How can you even think about it without beating your fists against a wall?"

My breath was gone. It was beyond me to inhale.

"I'm told our generals prepared to launch a post war offensive against an insurgent force you called the Werewolves. It never materialized even though such resistance fighters defied your armies in Holland, Norway, Italy, France. Yours was the first nation I'm aware of in which no Werewolves carried on."

"Humans get driven by errors in judgment and those errors get compounded."

His chair slammed forward. "Where are your words like responsibility? Choice?"

The rain had stopped, the wind was still. Voices in the hall moved on to other places. "We thought Jewish children didn't belong in our clubs. We were glad when they couldn't come to school."

"You thought Jewish children could hurt you by sitting next to you in school?"

Earlier conversations about other children who thought they'd be hurt by sitting next to him in school brought a sliding drop of moisture to my temple. I brushed it with my finger.

"You know Chris Iverson? Upstairs. Fault Control. Chris and I sometimes share a beer in Seckenheim. Last time was just after I'd read about a lynching written up in a newspaper my sister sends from home. I was beyond containing because a couple of veterans had been hanged, with God knows what accusation. Hanged by men who love their wives and children. Who get up Sunday morning and go to church." He lit another cigarette. The tip glowed red as he inhaled. "Chris reminded me it takes an unusual kind of courage to challenge what is publicly accepted. He reminded me no one took to the streets in California to stop the Japanese evacuation."

I glanced at my watch. I had to get back to my duties.

"Chris had Japanese friends, his father's secretary was of Japanese descent, yet one weekend afternoon his family drove south to a place called Tanforan. Tanforan was where barracks had been built to receive the Japanese, a holding area until their forced evacuation. For crying out loud, Frau Schuler, Tanforan is a racetrack. A big fenced area for horses."

I wasn't sure what he expected. I said, "Sergeant Iverson's family couldn't have been afraid if they went to see."

"People weren't afraid in San Francisco. They were just ordinary folk who had other concerns they thought important. They were respectful of authority and believed their government wouldn't relocate these people if they weren't a threat." He stood and I stood with him. He wanted to know if he must accept that it's good and honest people who forbid him seating in their restaurants, who won't sell him a house on their street or rent him an apartment. He said he was sure my family considered themselves good and honest but if a Jewish neighbor had been taken would we have gone inside our comfortable home and closed our door? "Good and honest people don't look away, Frau Schuler. By the time that door latch fastens, you're beyond the point where rational condemnation can take over. I'm not talking riots in the street. I'm talking basic human failure. Evil men will rule the world if ordinary people let them."

I wondered if Christmas in Germany was as bleak for him as when I saw the multi-colored lights in the German worker's lounge and, with my hand already on his office door, I asked if he'd share my family's Christmas. Meet my father. My daughter too. I didn't want to think of him alone. I remember looking back and seeing his fingers close into an igloo over his stacked cigarettes and lighter. He said he wouldn't be alone. He'd be traveling with a woman who was part of the group he'd met in Mannheim. I hesitated. In such groups the women were usually married to the soldiers. He said, "She's not a friend. A female companion."

The doorknob was slippery in my hand.

"I've only been with her a couple of times and then this trip. She seems to think I asked her."

That would be like Anna.

"I'll go along with what she seems to want so badly but I'll make sure when the trip is over, there'll be no more."

I felt my throat constricting but managed to ask if after the holidays he'd visit my home.

He said, "That would mean a lot to me."

I was preparing to leave my station at the end of my shift on Christmas Eve when I was summoned to Sergeant Miller's office. She handed me a small white package. Curious, I carried it to the deserted break room. Inside was a gossamer dress of the palest color. Pink. Like a blush, or a new morning. Cross-stitching edged the collar and the hem. A formal card fell from the folds of fabric and I stooped to retrieve it. 'For Katarina' was written on a card above Johnson Bonamaker's engraved name.

I put the dress away with a brown bag of oranges and toothpaste and soap, a gift for their less fortunate co-workers from the Americans in the building. Both would be under our tree at a small celebration Mother Schuler and I had ready for Kati's first Christmas. The Zieglers would be there. Mother Schuler's sister and her husband. They'd ask about my work with the Americans and I'd tell them about my friend.

Except for an unseasonable fog, persistent along the river but burning off the parade field by the time a cold sun had risen, the day shift had settled into routine again after the holidays. I was at the break room door when I heard the question shouted. "Did you hear about Bonamaker?"

"No, Fred," Sergeant Miller called from her office. "What'd he do?"

Gamboli was heading away from his desk in Radio Repair but stopped before he reached the swinging half-doors of supply. "John didn't make it in this morning after his leave. He didn't call or nothin'."

"That's right," Fred said. "Because he was killed last night."

Soldiers crowded the hall from every office.

"What'd ya say?"

"John? Dead?"

Fred turned to this larger audience. He'd been in the orderly room the night before when the MPs called to report John's car hadn't cleared an underpass on the Autobahn. "The one before the turn-off, right before the sign. You know the one I mean."

"Sure, sure, we know," Gamboli seemed about to burst.

"Well, he must've hit that slab of concrete going flat out. His Kraut girlfriend said …"

"She with him?" Gamboli asked.

"Sure she was with him. I'm trying to tell you."

"She dead too?"

Sergeant Miller put her hand on Gamboli's shoulder. "Go on Fred, what'd she say?"

"She said they were shouting at each other but she remembered the speedometer. Bonamaker must've had that big Buick right down to the floor when he caught that dip before the trestle."

"How come she wasn't killed?" Gamboli asked.

"Gamboli, for God's sake, how do I know?"

"Will she die, Fred?" Sergeant Miller was visibly shaken.

Fred said he didn't think so. She was cut up pretty bad, but the MPs seemed to think she'd be all right. "They have her over at that Kraut hospital across the way."

"The Catholic hospital?"

"That's the one."

A hovering listener from supply asked about the Sergeant and Fred said, "Man, he didn't know what hit him. The MPs say the steering wheel came off and the drive shaft went clean through his body."

Gamboli said, "Damn. What d'ya think of that big black buck?"

Master Sergeant Christopher Iverson sent for me that same day, just before the afternoon shift came on duty. I didn't want to talk to anyone, I was anxious to be with Kati, to see my father, just to be home with those I loved, away from the shadow of John's death. Sergeant Iverson's message was an intrusion but when I was able, I left my switchboard with a pass to meet him in his office.

There was no smile when I entered, no flicker of recognition. "I've called you here for Johnson Bonamaker," he said.

"He's ..." But of course he knew.

Sergeant Iverson lifted a leather suitcase to his desk. The lid flapped open scattering papers that needed his attention. In the suitcase I counted six cartons of cigarettes, a pair of nylon hose, two pounds of cocoa, a box of tea. Sergeant Iverson touched a brown sack of commissary coffee. The suitcase held eight more. He told me he was present while the Military Police went through John's things. John's sister would get his personal effects but the army wouldn't send the contents of the suitcase. As the ranking non-com in the room, he'd been able to say he knew whom it was for. He thought John would want me to have it.

My imagination fled to John's room at the barracks, the MPs digging through each drawer, checking the carefully pressed uniforms hanging in the closet. I was flattered the upright Sergeant Iverson had thought of me in the midst of such formalities. He could easily have let the suitcase go. Anyone could use it in the enduring black market.

As he paced the area his oversized desk permitted, Sergeant Iverson said John had stopped by his room the previous day. "My mind was on my reading when John said he was meeting the girl from Mannheim. I figured he had a pass, or maybe he was still on leave." He took a carton of cigarettes from the suitcase beating a rhythm against his palm. "I should've paid attention," he said.

I didn't want to learn my fears had faces but I wouldn't let myself be foolish. Other women lived in Mannheim. The injured woman could be very needy. I told Sergeant Iverson I'd see she got the suitcase if he'd get it past inspection.

A sharp wind promised snow as I shuffled through the German checkpoint. Sergeant Iverson drove past. I knew he saw me as I saw him though neither of us nodded. Still, it was clear he'd been watching because he stepped out of his car, striding through accumulated slush with almost military precision as I approached. At the back of his car he brought the suitcase from his trunk.

"Do you want …?"

I stumbled backward up the curb. "No."

For a moment I thought he was going to say more, but he only tested the trunk's latch with one gloved finger. Giving me a half-salute, he got back in his car and drove away.

The Catholic Hospital was too close to squander Deutschmark on a taxi, too far to walk on such an evening. Sergeant Iverson had been about to offer me a ride. I knew that. I was furious for letting myself back away. I could easily have accepted, or even asked for one if he hadn't offered. I shifted the weight of the heavy suitcase from one gloved hand to the other and stepped out into tracks other feet had scraped in the old and dirty snow.

My face felt stretched and raw from the cold by the time I pushed into the small square hospital set back from the traffic on Rohrbacherstrasse. I asked a sister in a quietly rustling starched white habit about the accident case brought in the night before and tried to convince myself it was imagination that she frowned when she told me the woman had been taken to an upper floor. I stopped a second sister. At her direction, I opened the indicated door.

"Renate! How did you find me?"

The suitcase slipped from my grasp, its brass clasps snapping open when it hit the floor. "You and Johnson Bonamaker."

"Johnson Bonamaker!" Anna's words were a scream. "Don't say that name to me."

"Sergeant Bonamaker's female companion."

"That bastard. That evil rotten bastard."

"Anna, he's dead."

"I know he's dead. Good. He should be dead a thousand times. He could've killed me too." Anna fell back against the pillows dropping the sheets to expose a swathe of bandages that circled her body.

I grasped backward for the single chair whose thick layer of added paint was new and white, like the bed, but chipped in places to a pale green.

"Look at me!" Anna's pillows slipped unheeded to the floor. "Do you know what he's done? The scars I'll have when these bandages are gone? I could've lost my breast." She thumped the padded whiteness until the effort left her sobbing. "And do you want to know the worst? The very rotten worst? I may not lose the baby. All that horrible crashing around, it didn't kill the baby."

I gripped the painted wood.

"I never should've fixed the condoms. I knew from the beginning he wouldn't stay with me but I thought he'd help a baby."

"You fixed the condoms?"

"I'm ruined. Who'll want me?"

Suddenly John's image was there before me. Straight. And honest. With so much to contribute to a principled future. I could only imagine his rage when he realized the woman he'd been trying to treat with honor had deceived him.

"I couldn't believe it when he said he'd met me one last time to give me money to pay for an abortion." Anna's anger faded. She sank back on the bed. "I wonder what happened to all those greenbacks. He'd brought more than enough."

I struggled from my chair, away from Anna reaching toward me, trying not to touch anything which in turn could touch the other woman.

"Don't leave, Renate. You've just come."

I said, "I won't stay and listen to any more of this. Johnson Bonamaker was my friend. We worked together at the Barracks."

"Renate Weiss was a jigaboo's friend?"

"He was a good man, Anna. He was too good for you."

"That murdering bastard was too good for a German woman? My God, Renate, how you've changed."

"Not enough but I keep trying."

As I let the door fall shut behind me, I saw Anna's feet

stretching unsteadily over the edge of the bed, Anna's hand pulling at John's suitcase, spilling its contents across the floor.

Master Sergeant Iverson was leaning against the MP's desk at the entrance of our building when I arrived for work the following morning. He turned from his conversation when I stepped inside. "Was John's girl happy with what you gave her?"

I didn't remind him Anna wasn't John's girl. "She can use it."

Sergeant Iverson laughed. I wasn't sure that he believed me.

My father failed while the last harsh winds of winter blew unchecked across the land beyond us to the east. A frozen land that in the past had routed armies. For days he lay staring. If he listened, it was only to the wind.

I found him one gray morning as I prepared for work but before I called the Zieglers, before I ran to tell Frau Schuler, I sat beside his bed listening for the wind that had blown beyond us in the night.

The letter I wrote to Günther followed him to three Italian cities before he received it, delaying by more than a month the answer I'd watched for daily. In a long condolence for the man who'd been my father he shared remembrances of his father, telling me of days they'd walked together through the grape fields on the outskirts of their city, how his father had sat lost in concentration while Günther sang. "My father would have loved you," he wrote. "Though he welcomed each son in turn, he longed to have a daughter." I folded the letter away for later reading and sorted my memories into segments. Family. Friends. Duty. Safe and painful too. I tried to think about the one marked future and turned the envelope in my hand. The letter was from Naples with a new, a farther address.

In the comfort of Mother Schuler's kitchen, just the two of us and Kati sleeping, "Naples?" she asked. My fork made soft scraping sounds against my plate as I pushed at the food she'd placed before me. From her quiet control, I knew that she'd been anticipating something that I hadn't. She said since this house had always been my home, it would be easier with Kati if I lived here with her. She had no reason to suggest change when her tenants left. It would have been unthinkable with my father, but now, before she was assigned another family ...

I put my fork across my plate. An emptiness I'd felt since reading Günther's letter was compounded by what we left unsaid. Although, in my grief at my father's death, I hadn't suggested a date when Günther and I could be together, we both knew the Deutschmark had kept its fervent grip on value. Travel documents were easier to obtain. I said, "Paul's room?"

She said, "Kati's father."

I bent to cover Kati who was stirring in her sleep.

A late snow fell on the day Herr Ziegler helped me pack a few memories of my childhood and carry them to Mother Schuler's. I took little. My life in the gabled house would be remembered as a whole with my brother in it, my parents. Gerda. The rest was bits and pieces. In addition to Kati's crib, the things I took were only small reminders to connect my daughter to a family she'd know only by what I told her.

Paul's room had been a place of mystery when I was small, a hiding place for secrets Paul and Hartmut let me share only when I was older. I stood amid the clutter of my possessions, studying bright patches where his pictures had been hung. The brightness surprised me. More, the faded paper on the wall. The whole room must have been bright when we were children, but then time dulled the walls and we grew tall.

Sitting on Paul's bed, I imagined our daughter growing and thought of all the things that I must tell her. I wouldn't flinch when she was old enough to ask. I wouldn't try to moderate her outrage, but I'd be sure she understood that like the walls so much can happen so unseen. When her father and I were young the constant pressure to conform left little inclination to hear lies or criminal evasions, even as the world became aware that we'd put in power men with a flawed arrogance that when combined with public acclamation caused our destruction. It's too late for us to be cautious about our leaders and our hell is that it will be too late forever.

Avoiding the kitchen where Mother Schuler was busy with preparation for our evening meal, I strode restlessly around the confinement of my new home. Upstairs to an attic where, as children, Paul and Hartmut and I sought adventure in hidden corners, played at being pirates, knights of old. In Professor Schuler's library with its scattering of first editions, I touched books we'd read together. Some familiar volumes were missing, and emblems of the old regime.

Every crowded part of the living room was familiar. Above a door was an oil painting brought by Professor Schuler's parents when they moved from their home by the waters of a northern sea. A murky picture of a fishing vessel, all gray and oppressive blue. As a growing child I'd found the image distressing until one day I thought I saw a flash of sun on a seagull's white wings and decided the bird caught above the mast in stationary flight was a promise of hope to the men who seemed so dangerously at sea. I lifted a porcelain dish and turned it over, trying to remember why it was kept from trading in those first years after the war. The decorative border of violet flowers was beautifully hand-painted but, not traded, it had no value. Perhaps its value was in a memory for Mother Schuler.

The formal dining room had been closed for many weeks against the winter's chill but I remembered it bright with festive dinners, both families present, everyone talking with such animation. All the tall men who gathered here before the world gave in to war were dead and my mother with them.

Hartmut, gone so long it was hard now to remember.
Professor Schuler.
Paul.
My father.
I added my black friend.
And Günther?
I sat at the thick carved table and wept for each in turn.

*Zurich, 6. March 1949*

*My dear Renate,*

*I'm comforted to know you're living with Frau Schuler. Please give my thanks and good wishes to her and to the Zieglers for helping you through this difficult time.*

*I've decided not to go to America. The future of opera lies in Europe where I work hard with a variety of teachers. I've even found an agent, a company in Munich. They keep track of my travels and see that I'm increasingly successful. To that point, I've enclosed another program. Colline.*

*Renate, I know this letter should be longer. It's a matter of exhaustion.*

*G.*

# Spring
*through Summer, Autumn and into Winter*

*1949*

My late shift was just nights away from another change and I wasn't looking forward to spending days in the basement of the Signal Office. My gaze kept drifting away from the apron I was mending to the promise of blue skies beyond thick drapes pulled back from Mother Schuler's window. A newspaper was neatly folded by my chair. I didn't need to see the pages. The same determination that accomplished a successful currency conversion had gripped the West when our constitution was written and federal power was established even though legislation was still subject to an Allied veto. An editor on an inside page urged the American Congress to release Marshall Plan funds so ships waiting, filled, in eastern harbors could be at sea. I knotted my thread and cut it with my teeth.

With my daughter in my arms I crossed the castle courtyard ignoring still desolate buildings because among sprawling potato plants and curly cabbage, someone had planted blue hyacinth and yellow crocus. Where great stone dogs brought down a carved stone stag whose open mouth once spilled water into an oblong basin, I put Kati to the ground and flattened my hand across a remembered pool. Kati tottered off, lured by a solitary pathway shaded by tall trees. Loose gravel tripped her and I swept her up, laughing, whispering, whirling into a dance step until she squealed in glee. The dance stopped abruptly when I saw a soldier watching.

Master Sergeant Christopher Iverson was sitting on a bench of rose-tinged stone, a slick paper booklet and a heavy black camera open in his lap. He looked surprisingly severe sitting there on such a relaxed and sun-drenched morning but that wasn't entirely his fault. The American military still required full uniform for all soldiers, even when off duty. I smiled tentatively, as if the occasional nod of recognition we'd exchanged since the business with the suitcase had been a friendly greeting. In that moment Kati wiggled to the ground and tottered toward him, but the joy on her face collapsed when he reached forward. She fell back, screaming at his sudden movement.

"I didn't mean to cause that," the sergeant said, his even features less unyielding than they seemed in an official setting. "I rarely make a baby cry."

Scooping her up, cradling her tears against my shoulder, my words were a torrent of incoherence as I tried to explain it was our fault. We were the intruders.

He said, "No harm," and snapped his camera shut.

From a breeze-filled branch above our heads a small bird drifted to a patch of grass, its pale beak digging at the ground, its splayed tail tipping up as its head went down. Her fall forgotten, Kati twisted from my arms but the bird flew to a farther spot and she turned to catch a patch of sun. Sergeant Iverson was already reaching for his camera. A wide, incongruously colorful strap caught behind his collar as he brought it forward. "Do you mind?" he asked as he focused on Kati, taking several pictures in a row. "The camera's new and I've needed some action to test the way I set the speed."

To my surprise, after he'd folded his camera back into its case, he asked if he could tag along wherever we were walking. I wasn't sure if I minded or not but the air was fragrant beneath the trees, speckled with shadows from the sun. Somehow he didn't seem much of an intrusion striding there beside us, even lifting a complacent Kati when our path curved by deeper pools. On a gentle slope crowned by a temple of Mercury, I removed Kati's high-topped shoes and then her stockings, laughing with her as blades of grass tickled between her toes. I confided to the sergeant that I lived nearby. This had been my favorite playground when I was Kati's age.

I had to suppress a giggle as I watched him struggle with the normalcy of that confession and nearly made a comment but thought better of it when he pointed toward the Moorish Pavilion and said that earlier he'd taken several pictures, imagining all kinds of things that could capture a child's fancy. I wondered if he knew of the pavilion's use in those first months after surrender, when it was an illegal club where American officers brought hungry German women. But as I watched him pull a flowering branch toward Kati, using his light meter one more time to adjust the camera's setting for the sudden shade of one white cloud, I decided he didn't know, or if he did, he hadn't made much of it and perhaps all the women weren't brought here out of hunger. Perhaps some were like Anna when she relished life for all it offered. Perhaps some were couples who truly loved each other but had no other place to be together. I found myself wondering what this very proper sergeant would be like away from the formality of his uniform, the double row of ribbons on his chest.

Pictures came in rapid succession until he stopped to adjust his camera one more time and Kati stumbled against his leg, clutching at his trousers. I can laugh now at how quickly I leaped forward, blurting out, that Kati's father loved this garden, too.

He said, "The child's father is a German?"

And there was that distracting ordinary in our lives, the trivial concern that at some moment seems important. I didn't want to discuss my country's continuing crisis with the East or try to explain why we had believed our genocidal leaders. At that moment I just wanted him not to have heard what I feared was common knowledge in our gossip-laden office.

"I'm sorry," he said. "The child's father is none of my business."

"No, he isn't," I answered.

Sergeant Iverson closed his camera and straightened the colorful band around his collar. He seemed undecided but I was hesitating, too. The patterns in the sky were changing. I sat on the ground to tighten laces and he took one more setting in the direction of the sun, asking if he could take another picture, of the two of us together. I paid no attention when he stopped closing his camera, focusing intently before taking still one more. I was remembering the child I'd been, running after Hartmut as he chased Paul, feeding swans when they still swam beside our quiet trails. We'd heard peacocks crying, watched them spread their grandeur for a peahen's notice. I tried to bring my walks with Günther into focus, but saw him sitting in a sun-warmed southern courtyard with a young Italian soprano by his side. He was smiling quizzically at her in the way this American sergeant from the Signal Office now smiled at me. My fingers tightened on Kati's laces.

The brightness of spring in Mother Schuler's garden changed to the stable blooms of summer before I saw Sergeant Iverson again. For absolutely no reason I'd allow myself to consider, I secluded myself at my switchboard or in the German workers' lounge while our shift worked days. Then, through the weeks of afternoon and late night hours, I put our meeting from my mind. I was working days on a second rotation when I saw him from a distance. I assumed he hadn't seen me because there was no sign, no nod of recognition, but the next afternoon my relief operator brought a forwarding envelope with my name, Renate Schuler, scrawled in the next clear space across the front. Twisting the string closing, I made my way behind the other operators, but after I'd passed Johanna's desk, a shriek of laughter from Bonamaker's old office sent me rushing toward the lounge. In a quiet corner I opened the envelope and leafed through many pictures. The softness of the air was in each photo, the fragrance of the gardens and the gentle breeze. With them was a single typewritten sheet. "I'm sorry I didn't get these to you sooner. Let me make it up with dinner after work tomorrow." It was signed Chris Iverson with the same broad scrawl that had addressed the envelope. I was surprised my fingers trembled.

The next day I wore a dress I'd made from new material for Katarina's christening, and a touch of pale lipstick. Every hour seemed interminable but when the shift was finally over, I found reasons to remain at my switchboard until the halls had emptied. Master Sergeant Iverson was talking with the military policeman checking passes at the entrance of our building. He finished some point before he turned and took my hand, drawing it under his arm in an American way. But as we left the building, he released it again. He'd have to drive his car, alone, to the street in front of the Barracks. Being forbidden a ride through the gate became embarrassing and hostile. I closed my purse beyond inspection. When I reached his car, "I had nothing," I said. He said he hadn't suspected that I did and followed me around to close my door behind me.

In Heidelberg he chose a narrow parking lot across from the city theater, near the printing shop where I'd folded papers and the library where I'd met my students. We'd walked a block before we turned into Sandgasse. On that street, in that direction, were two clubs. The Harmony Club for American first-three-graders, the ranking enlisted men in the army, and the Rodensteiner a short way closer. The Rodensteiner was a club where both Germans and Americans crowded through a darkened entrance and up a narrow flight of stairs. I'd been to both. I remembered the white tablecloths and black-suited waiters in the Harmony Club, the shrieks, the odor of stale urine in the other. Anna had laughed when she told me she'd seen a drunken soldier at the Rodensteiner take a woman right on an oblong table between the steins of beer. We passed that entrance without comment. At the steps of the Harmony Club Sergeant Iverson held the door. "Hungry?" he asked.

"Yes." I wasn't.

"Did you like the pictures?"

"Of course."

"Your daughter is a little charmer."

At a linen-covered table in the dining room, he ordered for both of us from a hovering waiter and while we waited for our meal told me about his home near a park in San Francisco where fog rolled in across low hills and Ernie Andrews sang in clubs. He said I must stop calling him Sergeant Iverson, his name was Chris, but I couldn't call him that. I sensed he had trouble saying my name as well, the strangeness of it, the Germanness. While we ate, a small band began playing. He asked if I'd like to dance when we were finished and I said, "For a while."

The wide ballroom was almost empty this early in the evening, the music wistfully cadenced. A magical light sent sparkles around the room and across our faces from a mirrored globe above our heads. He wasn't the best dancer who'd brought me here but it was easy to relax against the gentle movements of his body, and comfortable just to listen to the music while we sat at low round tables during some sets.

A performance at the city theater finished as we left the club. A crowd, laughing and lighthearted, surged through a row of doors and down broad steps to join us on Hauptstrasse. Chris took my arm against the jostling. "Whatever they saw, it must've been funny," he said.

"*Gitta*," I said as I leaned toward him. "A play. It's very popular."

His fingers slipped through mine. "Want to walk a while before we get the car?"

I must have nodded.

Near the Perkeo, newly reopened as a German restaurant, Chris dropped my arm and straightened for a quick salute toward an officer making slow progress toward us.

"Good evening, sergeant," the officer said.

"Good evening, sir," Chris answered, and then to me, "Poor man. He looked unhappy."

I glanced across my shoulder, toward the officer disappearing in the crowd, and realized I was far from that condition.

At a corner near the American Post Exchange Chris turned down the curve of an empty alley to a street that ended where the Stardust Club had been. It had another name now, another purpose. The interior had been rebuilt after fire gutted the stage where dance bands played and it was a Special Service Center with arts and crafts displays and a nickelodeon. Around a corner past the Father Rhine, a bar off-limits to American soldiers, Chris took my arm. "Are you cold?" he asked. I was sure he'd felt me tremble.

We passed Saint Vincent's Hospital and a high stone wall that hid a garden, to a concrete bridge that had replaced a smaller temporary structure. Moving quickly between two streetcars on their way to Handschuhsheim, we passed Bismarck Platz and another high wall secluding a university clinic before crossing to walk above the river. Here the riverbank plunged to the water. Lights from homes across the way were bright arrows in the dark.

On Vangerowstrasse, by the American swimming pool, Chris asked if I was tired. When I admitted I was, a little, he said, "Let's sit awhile. No one cares after the place closes." We sat on wide steps in front of offices and dressing rooms abandoned to the night. The splashing of a fountain in the enclosure beyond the building was the only sound until the repeated clicking of his lighter.

When his cigarette was finished, Chris split the fragile paper and scattered the last of the tobacco. "Ready?" he asked as he rolled the remaining scrap of paper into an invisible ball.

Walking more slowly on streets away from the river, we passed a field where brightly striped tents had been erected when circuses roamed across our borders. Trapeze artists flew across my memory as I told Chris how I'd come here with my brother to see lions and clowns and delight in the music from the calliope. I hadn't realized he'd stopped walking. He pushed his hat back from his forehead before he took it off and gripped it with his elbow. "I don't know about this," he said.

"About what?"

"This."

Ours was a friendly kiss between two people who'd enjoyed each other's company. "I don't know about that either," I said.

At the end of the street we turned toward Bergheimerstrasse. Tall vines cloaked the *Augenheilklinik*, where, just before surrender, American artillery killed four patients and darkened lights throughout the city. Its wood doors were highly polished now. From the railway station a taxi took us to Chris's car.

We were enveloped by a haze of summer sweetness in Mother Schuler's garden when Chris kissed me again. This time the kiss left us studying each other as he backed down the drive. He was almost to the street before he waved and walked quickly to his car. Upstairs, before I changed into my nightgown, I stood before a small mirror on my dresser. The reflected image was deep in shadow, barely clear enough for recognition as I silently questioned the smiling person who was staring back.

I still find it startling to think how quickly Chris and I became a couple. The ease I felt with this quiet man pushing aside a half-drunk mug of coffee, crushing another half-smoked cigarette, was not unlike remembered ease I'd shared with Günther when our lives were measured out in other cigarettes and coffee. I'd stopped counting the weeks without an Italian letter, the months since I'd thought of Mannheim. Günther and Anna were a part of a life that couldn't be discounted but no longer on the surface. The surface was Chris accommodating himself to my shift by staying late after his day shift ended, sorting files in his office, filling time, waiting to sit with me in a quiet corner cradling mugs of steaming coffee he'd brought to the Barracks in a silver thermos. The surface was his always ready transportation. When my workday changed to begin when others were in bed, he wouldn't listen to my protest that a bus ran with some regularity even at that hour. He came to Mother Schuler's after night obscured the highway and drove me to the Barracks. The surface was evenings at the Harmony Club with an increasing circle of good friends. Most were American men from Seckenheim who brought a rotation of German girlfriends, but occasionally a young woman from one of the Allied nations who worked somewhere in the Barracks joined us. Tourists had not yet flooded back to Europe.

At work, a lieutenant had replaced Sergeant Miller. One stifling day I barged into him while hurrying from the lounge. It was so like the day I first met John, I felt haunted. Like Günther and Anna, John had slipped into another time. I recognized part of the reason the day Chris told me about his father. A gentle man who never meant harm to anyone, but he'd grown up in Georgia. Chris said he was amazed at the depth of racist indoctrination he'd received as a child. "When Truman called for desegregation," Chris said, "I thought, that's fine, I'm a soldier. My Commander in Chief says desegregate, I desegregate." And he did so as his duty. But I knew exactly what he meant when he confessed traces of prejudice remained in his blood even after it was banished from his brain. He said John and he would drink beer at a small club within the Seckenheim compound but it would have been an anomaly for them to go to Mannheim or Heidelberg together.

A threatened summer storm broke as I shuffled through the checkpoint behind a woman with pale hair. She was so like Anna in the way she shrugged her shoulders and laughed with her companion, I was still fighting memories when I slid into the protection of Chris's car and shivered up against him. The noisy sweep of his windshield wipers against a heavy rain did little to quiet my agitation as he maneuvered into the changing traffic. "I wonder what she did with it," I said.

"She? It?"

"John's companion. The suitcase. You remember."

A lumbering ox-drawn wagon blocked the road ahead. When he was finally able to pass and let the car gain speed, Chris said, "Didn't you hear?"

I'd heard nothing since I'd rushed out of her hospital room, but I'd sometimes wondered if the suitcase helped her.

"I don't know how you missed it."

In a burst of frustration I shook his arm, sending the car into unexpected swerving.

"Hey." He quickly gained control.

I was beyond accepting any rational reason for being so upset but I couldn't let my memories go. I cautioned Chris to stop teasing.

"I have, I'm not." He said nothing more until we were on the Autobahn. Then in his gentle way I'd come to love because it was so like what I remembered of my brother, he said he'd heard Anna had gone to work in the travel department at American Express. A major came in and they worked out a tour of Italy for him. He went back to thank her and she fixed him up for France. When she planned his trip to Austria, he invited her along. Next thing Chris heard, they were married. She'd gone home with him to the Pentagon.

"Anna?"

"If she was the woman in John's car. You were working nights. I suppose I never mentioned it because it didn't seem important."

As if it were some colossal failure on my part that I'd never explained to Chris how I was involved with the woman who took John's suitcase, I moved away from him, staring out the window at dark fields lost in the downpour, remembering Anna as I'd seen her last, bitter, defiant, screaming out her rage and disappointment. I'd come to understand it was as much at Charlie as at John and I should have been happy for her now, but as I looked out I was hurt and disappointed. I wanted Anna to have contacted me about the wedding. I wanted to have known. I asked Chris if he knew anything about the major.

"Only that he worked at Patton Barracks."

A lone car sped past going too fast on the rain-slicked highway. I did a quick counting on my fingers. "And the baby. Did the major take the baby?"

"You know, there was a rumor about a baby. I guess I didn't quite believe it. No baby was mentioned in the talk about the wedding."

The even rhythm of the engine faded as Chris slowed to the curb in front of Mother Schuler's. I slid wordlessly across the seat and let my head find a familiar place against his shoulder. I hoped the major from Patton Barracks recognized the Anna I wanted to remember. The one who laughed so easily, who'd been my friend.

Chris's arm settled around my shoulder. "You know, more than once John tried to convince me Germans weren't so bad. I guess he was right. You're not so bad. You're even kinda pretty. I think I may be falling in love."

I brought his hand to my face, cool against a burning. It wasn't the first time he'd mentioned love but he was always casual about it, always hastening on to other matters: work, a change in the weather, our plans for a coming weekend. I let this declaration pass as I had the others. I wasn't ready for an answer. Chris loved me, for some time there'd been no question. The question that kept me silent, that wouldn't let me rest when I was alone and thinking about a future, was did I love him and what did I want to do about it?

Chris brought a tan commissary bag from the back seat of the car, shielding it with his coat as we plunged through the rain. Inside, he abandoned it on the stand for umbrellas and coats and closed his arms around me. "Umm, that was nice," he said.

It was nice. I did respond to his kisses and to prove it to myself I stood tall and kissed him one more time before I reached around him for the bag, asking what he'd brought us.

"English chocolate for you and coffee for Mother Schuler."

From previous presents I knew who wanted the English chocolate and handed a black tin box to him.

Accepting the coffee from me and a quick kiss on her cheek from Chris, Mother Schuler stopped me as I reached for Kati. She said she was making something special for our dinner and it would take more time. Kati was all right, sleeping. Chris was studying the black tin box and I couldn't help but smile. We'd grown so familiar with each other, I even knew which square of chocolate he preferred. I found comfort in that knowing and in the straight lines of his profile, the way his jaw set in concentration. I put my arm around him, guiding him across the hall. "I was thinking of Kati's father," I said. "And the time he'd brought me chocolate. Part of an early program the Marshall Plan included for German students."

Chris replaced the black tin lid and put the box on a table before we sat together on the sofa. His long legs stretched out into the room. My hand found his. "Isn't it time you told me more about him," he said and my hand snapped back. "We only talk about him as a student. He was a young man, Renate. He must have been in the German army."

Our relief must seem bizarre now, but in the spring of 1942 when Paul accepted his commission, we were more proud than anxious. Germany was caught up in what everyone considered our unstoppable advances. Paul's battalion was stationed north of Stalingrad. He would be fighting untrained men in civilian clothing. Russian peasants without guns against our Panzers. My gaze drifted to the familiar picture above Mother Schuler's door. The gray ship, the gray water, the gray bird hovering above the huddled figures who seemed in such danger fighting the cruel North Sea. By the second winter we were hovering over Mother Schuler as she scanned lists of casualties filling newspaper pages lined in black. Goebbels informed the nation that not a single man survived. Göring broadcast a funeral oration for an entire army.

I started by telling Chris about a boy I'd seen wearing a Wehrmacht uniform. A large bright swastika band was around the arm he pressed against a window. I asked Chris to remember that symbol is absolutely forbidden. I hadn't seen one in years. Someone had dressed the child as a German soldier and put him on an American bus.

Chris said he didn't get it and I reminded him of the sweeper we'd seen on a street near the Ploeck. The one who wore army fatigues, even the boots and hat. "Remember? He made you angry."

"Well, it's illegal to wear any part of our uniform. If I didn't know an American wouldn't be cleaning gutters …"

"Exactly. But you didn't stop him."

"If I remember correctly we were in a hurry and he wasn't doing any harm."

"Harm? Chris, didn't you see what the Germans were doing?"

"I suppose they were laughing."

"Of course they were laughing. At you Chris. At the occupation."

"They can't mock American power."

"They did. They are. And what do you suppose was the purpose of that boy with all those Nazi symbols riding all over town in one of your buses? Germans can't ride your buses."

"But those are just pranks."

My gaze fled to the dark picture, to the grays and the depth of blues. "If people laugh and nothing happens even pranks undermine the occupation."

"What are you trying to tell me, Renate?"

"That his group was capable of less prank like planning."

"And?"

"Paul was killed. Murdered."

Chris pushed away from the couch.

"He looked so young at his funeral. So like the student who came home from Tübingen for his holidays."

Chris stood for a long time at a window overlooking the garden before he asked how many people knew, but before I could answer he wanted to know if any of it was in my records.

"Only that we married and that he died. The police never learned who did it."

Long strides brought him back across the room. "Renate, I'm due to leave Germany after the first of the year. I want you and Kati to come with me. Leave all this behind. Marry me, Renate."

Not now, not yet. The chocolate started this. The English chocolate in the black tin box and the malt-like chocolate that had been given to German students. But I was remembering other chocolate I'd shared with Anna and Günther in the forest. The chocolate in white wrappers that had been thrown to a defeated enemy by soldiers quite like Chris. I tried to remember how that chocolate tasted when I was hungry, how it melted on my tongue. I couldn't even sense its texture. I smiled at Chris, wanting to laugh and be happy with him and for the future. Then I wanted to cry. I still hadn't told him about Günther.

Thanksgiving Day was cold and bright.

"Football weather," Chris told us, grinning. Like most of the American army, he was on holiday but because I was due at the Barracks in the afternoon, he'd come to Schwetzingen early, bringing two tall bags which he lowered onto Mother Schuler's kitchen table. One bag contained a turkey bought for him in the commissary by a married friend, the other, green cans of jellied cranberries, celery, onions, a long loaf of soft white bread. From this second bag he took a square carton and opened it to an American-style pie. "It's pumpkin," he said. "Like the one I carved for Kati on Halloween."

Kati had squealed with delight when he lit the candle inside his carving but that toothless, grinning face had reminded me that at Halloween, a year had passed since Günther left me.

Chris slit the waxed cover on the loaf of bread and spread it near the stove for drying. "My mother always boiled giblets for the dressing," he said to Mother Schuler. "Here, these." He pulled from the thawed hollow of the bird an oozing neck and organs.

"Ach! Go!" Mother Schuler seized the dripping pieces. "Wash your hands. Leave this to me. A turkey can't be so different from a goose."

Laughing, Chris washed his hands and brought Kati to his shoulders, her face alight, her tiny hands clasped across his forehead. In the living room he brought out a basket of polished blocks he'd bought for her at the army's new exchange for toys and built a small tower which she gleefully knocked down. I hadn't noticed he was growing quiet, I was actually cherishing his presence as I watched the way the curve of his neck disappeared into his collar, the strength beneath the roundness of his shoulder. With his head and Kati's bent away, I was remembering the first time he'd joined us around a table. Mother Schuler, her strong hands folded prayer-like, Kati in her highchair. "*Guten Appetit*," Mother Schuler had said. I'd explained that even in those first winters after the war, when there was just a boiled potato for a meal, we always said it and Chris had struggled with the German words.

"I've needed to be alone before I told you," he said from the floor.

I reached for a soft rag doll I'd made for Kati. "Told me what, Chris?"

He stood and took the doll from my hands. "My rotation date has been moved forward. I'll leave Germany before Christmas as things look now." He dropped the doll toward Kati.

My gaze fled to the familiar picture above the door. His ship would sail from Bremerhaven. For a moment I smelled salt brine. "Before Christmas?" I said. "Why would they do that?"

"Jesus, Renate, I don't know. They tell me it's for my morale. The military believes the troops are happier being home for Christmas with their families. I tried to tell them you're my family now but I've already been granted two extensions. It looks like I'll leave Germany in just three weeks."

Chris had been patient, not urging for an answer to the question that filled my waking because we had time. But now. Next month. I moved to a tall piano in the corner, touching the middle C before my fingers stretched into an octave. He came to stand behind me, lifting my hand from the ivory casing, surrounding it with one of his. The other closed a book of music. "That was Schubert," I said as the tiny dots and wings of melody disappeared. "My mother's favorite."

"Let's go for a walk over to the castle with Kati," he said. "We've a lot to talk over."

Air pulled through my nostrils until my lungs were full and my next words were a gasp as I struggled to both hold and release my emotions "I wouldn't make a good American, Chris."

Everything I loved about him was in the tender way he turned me to him, touching my forehead, lifting my chin so my gaze met his. "Don't say that, Renate. You are American. The way you look. The way you act."

I couldn't help myself. I laughed out loud.

Chris drew me to a gold etched mirror above a polished table. "Look at yourself. Look at the way you dress, your shoes. Look at the way you've cut your hair. Main Street, USA."

"Chris, it's only what you want to see." With the back of my hand to each cheek in turn, I felt flushes growing. I didn't want to hurt him. I couldn't hurt him. I loved him, too. But it wasn't a love that answered need, a deep primeval yearning.

Chris eased us away from the mirror, studying my palms. "Sometimes in the barracks when I couldn't sleep for thinking about our future, my mind would go blank and my hands would sweat and some joker going to the latrine would sound like an elephant in the empty hallway. I'd yell at him to keep the hell quiet, and my shout would anger others, who'd yell at me …"

"Chris, I do love you."

"But not enough."

"I guess that's it. Just not enough."

My love for Günther surmounted distance, time, pain, misunderstanding. My desire to feel his flesh on mine, to share the completeness of his efforts, was as urgent as it had been on that long ago night looking down into wind-roughened waters from the Alte Brücke in Heidelberg. I reached for Kati who was trying to steady one block on another as Chris had done, squealing when her tiny tower toppled. She gave one final swipe as I reached for her, scattering blocks across the floor. "Come," I said to Chris. "We'll tell Mother Schuler of my decision together."

We came by taxi that last time to the city, Kati sitting small and bundled between us. Up the long ramp from the Autobahn, past the first isolated houses with frost-crisped winter vegetation in the gardens. I shouldn't have come, I thought. This only makes it harder for all of us. I didn't look at Chris or at Kati who sat so still in her patient child's way seeming to understand that something of import was happening.

The driver snaked his way through cobbled streets where soldiers came from their barracks in long military buses. He stopped in the paved oval before the railway station.

"I shouldn't have come," I said.

"I wanted you here." Chris reached into his pocket for crisp new dollars to pay the driver, then held his arms toward Kati who scampered over the seat and into them.

I slid across, slipping out to the assistance of his hand, and followed him through an almost empty waiting room where only a few families escaped the cold. On the swarming station platform we confronted a train of shining coaches. Kati burrowed her face on Chris's shoulder, hiding from the noise and disorder. He spread his hand across her small capped head.

In the Railway Transportation Office streamers of silver Christmas decorations looped against the walls. A colored Christmas tree glowed in the corner. My mind closed against the celebration, against confusion, against decisions made and argued and reconfirmed with patience and with love.

A duty officer from Transportation strode through the crowds, urging the men to be on board, putting his hand firmly on one soldier's shoulder, tapping his clipboard against another soldier's arm. A large dog barked, digging at the cage where it was confined for transport.

By the coach where he'd been assigned, Chris put Kati down between us. She clung against his knee. "I know it's hard," he said, "but I really wanted you here." Only a touch along my arms still questioned whether what might have been was over. Far down the train, dark-uniformed attendants were already closing heavy doors.

I felt a final pressure on my wrists before he leaped away, up steep steps, and was inside when the carriage door slammed shut behind him. The train crashed back into its couplings, then forward. The engine whistle wailed. From the crowded vestibule his hand pushed out. "Renate! Here!" he shouted and I left Kati to grasp for his reaching hand but only scratched the metal handle as the door lurched on beyond my reach. My fingers trailed below a line of open windows as the train gained speed.

At Kati's frightened cry I turned back to clutch my daughter, even then aware of a growing exhilaration, a swelling of anticipation, a coming back to life. The crowd surged on around us, shouting one final consummate farewell, but was already clearing the station platform before the last coach disappeared around a curve toward Weinheim.

The transportation officer heaved an audible sigh and clasped his clipboard under his arm, a porter struggled with the wagon that had held the dog. A photographer dropped used flash bulbs into a metal receptacle, striding away as they bounced and clattered in the sudden silence. Inside the Transportation Office with its glittering tree I could almost see a suggestion of Anna clinging to the arm of her major, waiting in the seclusion of that decorated room for a train not unlike the one that had taken Chris away. "We'll take a train, too," I said to Kati. "Maybe more than one. It depends on what we learn from an agency in Munich."

Through the waiting room and out beyond the arches, I raised my hand in signal to a taxi, then quickly waved it in rejection. "Let's walk first," I said.

Slowly, with Kati by my side, I passed the Anlage, the Ploeck, the gentle winding of the main street. Carrying Kati again, I strolled the length of Bismarck Platz and crossed onto a wide white bridge that had just been opened, the last in a series of bridges from the first pontoons along the water. A sharp breeze lifted my hair. I shook it back as I leaned out to follow the shimmer of a winter sun on the ripples in the water while my thoughts skipped backward through the years to that April day in Aland Nord when I thought my life had ended though I lived on and I took my first frightened steps in a journey that brought me to today.

The river disappeared into a curve toward Mannheim but I followed in my mind, to its meeting with the Rhine, the plain beyond, and the low hills lost in the distance.

# Glossary

*Abitur*—Examination for admission to University, taken after secondary school
*Augenheilklinik*—Eye Clinic
*Alte Brücke*—Old Bridge
*Ami*—German slang for American
*Arbeitsamt*—Employment Office
*Autobahn*—Super highway
*Benzin*—Gasoline
*Bowle*—A wine drink
*Bueno, Gut*—Good in Spanish and German
*Bürgermeister*—Mayor
*Bund Deutscher Mädel, Hitler Jugend*—Youth groups during Hitler's era
*Einsatzgruppen*—Mobile terror squads under the direction of the SS
*Eiderdown*—Goose down comforter
*Eintopf*—One dish meal
*Ersatz*—Substitue
*Fragebogen*—Questionnaire required in the American Zone
*Gauleiter*—Chief of a Nazi Party district
*Golden Party Badge*—Sign of a long term Party member, or one who performed unusual service
*Great War*—World War I
*Gruppenleiterin*—Group Leader
*Guten Appetit*—Good Appetite
*Gymnasium*—German secondary school, admission usually based on merit
*Heide*—Natural area with certain typical plants: ie juniper and heather

*Herr, Frau, Fräulein*—Mr. Mrs. Miss
*Heiligenberg*—Holy Mountain
*Kaserne*—Military barracks
*Ilse Koch*—Notorious female Concentration Camp commander
*Krauts*—American slang for Germans
*Jawohl*—Yes
*Lederhosen*—Leather pants
*Liebchen*—Term of endearment
*Liebfrauenmilch*—A type of wine
*Luftwaffe*—German Air Force
*Mädchen*—Girl
*Mein Gott*—Exclamation
*Platz*—Place, often attached to another word as in Kornmarktplatz
*Rathaus*—City Hall
*Reichsmark, Deutschmark, Pfennig*—money
*Schatzie*—Slang expression used by soldiers to young German women
*Schloss*— Castle
*Schwartze*—Black Soldier
*SS*—Elite units in German army
*Strasse, Gasse*—Street, Lane often attached to another word as in Hauptstrasse (Main Street)
*Tor*—Gate
*Walpurgisnacht*—Celebration in the Harz Mountains
*Wehrmacht*—Germany army

Venetian Glass - ~~Greek~~ Clock.